Forever Kate

Forever Kate

a novel

Cheri J. Crane

Covenant Communications, Inc.

Published by Covenant Communications, Inc.
American Fork, Utah

Printed in the United States of America
First Printing: August 1997

04 03 02 01 00 99 98 97   10 9 8 7 6 5 4 3 2 1

Crane, Cheri J. (Cheri Jackson), 1961-
    Forever Kate / Cheri J. Crane.
        P.   cm.
    "Sequel to Kate's turn and Kate's return."
    Summary: As she faces decisions about college, marriage, and
whether or not to serve a mission for the Mormon Church, Kate
recognizes the need to get on with her life.
    ISBN 1-57734-127-9
    [1. Interpersonal relations--Fiction. 2. Mormons--Fiction.
3. Christian life--Fiction.] I. Title.
PZ7.C8477Fo   1997
[Fic]--dc21   97-26015
                                                      CIP

Dedicated to the memory of Julie, Toya, Brittany, Dave, Andy, and Jenny. *Adieu pour le moment, mes amies.*

Acknowledgments

As always, I find myself indebted to several people. I'll start by offering gratitude to Trisha Donaghy Crane, and her mother, Betty Donaghy of Dumbarton, Scotland, for the materials and information they provided. With their guidance, I've tried to accurately portray a land of beauty, grace, and tradition.

Thanks also to Susan Skinner Crane and her husband, Colton Crane, two wonderful people whose experiences added colorful flavor to this novel.

Again, I wish to thank the "Burdick Bunch of Bennington" for always being so willing to proofread and for having the courage to point out glaring mistakes. *Merci beaucoup, mes amies! Je t'aime,* Shelley!

I would also like to express appreciation to the wonderful people at Covenant Communications. Thanks for all you do! Kudos to editors Valerie Holladay and JoAnn Jolley.

This list would be incomplete without adding thanks to my husband, Kennon, and our three boys, Kris, Derek, and Devin. Without their support, encouragement, and cooperation, writing would still be a hobby.

CHAPTER 1

Sandi Kearns Campbell stepped out of her small Geo Metro and scowled at the smog-filled sky of Salt Lake City. The air was hot and humid; its slightly brown cast added to the stifling feeling she'd endured all day. Relieved to finally be home, she walked up the sloped ramp toward the condominium she shared with her husband.

As she thought of Ian, she smiled. He was funny, intelligent, sensitive, good-looking—in her opinion, the perfect man. There were days when she couldn't believe how lucky she was. Quickly unlocking the front door, she stepped inside the spacious condominium. The air-conditioning felt wonderful compared to the temperature outside. "Ian?"

"In here," Ian called out.

Grinning, Sandi set her backpack near the door and headed down the hall to the study. Her long brown hair bounced as she eagerly sought out her husband of just two months.

"How was your day?" Ian asked, easing his wheelchair out from behind the computer desk. When his knee bumped into the desk, Sandi winced, a familiar pain tugging at her heart.

"No worries, it's just a flesh wound," Ian quipped, laughing it off. Extremely independent, Ian used humor and stubbornness to make it through each day. Sandi was still adjusting to the challenges Ian faced. It hurt her to imagine what he had suffered in the car accident that had left him paralyzed from the waist down. After surviving a crash triggered by a man suffering a heart attack, Ian refused to allow self-pity or physical challenges to stand in his way. He had earned a degree in accounting and now worked for a large law firm with plans to someday start his own business.

As Sandi approached, Ian's eyes gazed warmly at his attractive wife. Her small, upturned nose and warm smile had appealed to him from the day they had met. Her soft brown eyes revealed her compassionate and loving nature.

"How was your day?" he asked, smiling.

Sandi grimaced. "Hot, uncomfortable, and I didn't get the grade I wanted on that microbiology test I took two days ago," she said glumly.

"Come tell me all about it," Ian invited sympathetically. Sandi responded by sitting on his lap. "Now, isn't that better?" he asked, leaning toward her for a kiss.

"Much," Sandi sighed, resting her head against his broad chest.

"What did you get, an A instead of an A+?" Ian teased.

"I wish. I pulled a B-," she complained.

"That's still passing."

Sandi shook her head. "I have to do better than that. Getting into this nursing program will be tough. It's so competitive. The "U" only takes so many nursing students."

"You'll make it," Ian soothed, rubbing her back, "and be the best RN this world has ever seen." He grinned. "I've been telling the guys at work that I'll soon have my own private nurse. They're very jealous." He waited for a response, but Sandi remained silent. She had been thrilled at her acceptance to the University of Utah, but she had found the classes more difficult than she had expected. "Okay," he said, "let's try a different approach. Want some good news?"

Sandi nodded.

"I took care of dinner." Ian's blue eyes twinkled.

"When did you have time to do that? Didn't you have to work today?"

"Absolutely, and I barely beat you home tonight."

"Then how—" The doorbell cut her off.

"Good timing," Ian said as Sandi quickly jumped up to answer.

A few seconds later Sandi opened the front door to see a pizza delivery boy holding a large box, then glanced back at Ian. "You must've slaved all day."

"I even ordered pepperoni," Ian said, wiggling his eyebrows.

Sandi returned his smile, then reached for the backpack to retrieve her wallet.

"I've got it covered," Ian insisted, wheeling closer to the door. Pulling out his wallet, he spoke to the delivery boy. "I'll take that off your hands."

"Are ya sure ya can handle it?" the teenage boy asked, glancing at Sandi for approval. Sandi nodded, irritated by the assumption that her wheelchair-bound husband was helpless. Ian calmly took the box from the delivery boy and handed it to Sandi, then paid the delivery boy as Sandi carried the box into the kitchen and set it on the table. Staring out the window at the departing teenager, she was tempted to go after him. Instead of a tip, she wanted to give him a piece of her mind.

"Smile," Ian insisted. "It was worth it—the pizza smells wonderful." He sniffed the air appreciatively.

"It does," Sandi agreed, deciding not to let the delivery boy's ignorance ruin her meal. "I didn't have time for lunch today."

Ian frowned at his wife. "Young lady, we won't have you starving yourself."

"You sound like my mother," Sandi teased, setting two plates on the table.

"Now I'm really insulted," Ian exclaimed, turning his wheelchair around until his back was facing her. "I'm not even going to tell you what came in the mail today."

Sandi giggled. Ian was learning to appreciate her domineering mother, but there were still times when Harriet Kearns overstepped boundaries. "I take it back," she said.

"Not good enough."

Walking around to confront Ian, Sandi offered a lengthy kiss.

"Now you're talkin'," Ian sighed with contentment. "How about a second helping?"

"What came in the mail?" Sandi asked, refocusing the conversation.

"Killjoy," Ian replied, pointing to the nearby counter.

Sandi ran a playful hand through his thick blonde hair, then turned to search the counter top. "Ow!" she exclaimed as Ian pinched her. "Behave yourself." Picking up a small pile of envelopes, she sifted through them. "Bill, advertisement, bill, junk." Then she smiled brightly, holding up a thick envelope. "A letter from Kate."

"I knew that would get a smile out of you," Ian said. Wheeling himself to the table, Ian opened the pizza box and dished up a large slice for himself. "How's she doing?" he asked a few minutes later after Sandi had had a chance to scan the letter.

"Good. She loves working for her father's computer company."

"Doing what?"

"Secretarial work. The same thing she was doing here in Salt Lake last year for her uncle Stan." Sandi smiled, picturing her former best friend. Ian now filled that role. Ironically, Kate had introduced Sandi to Ian and served as the maid of honor at their reception two months ago.

"Is she staying out of trouble?"

Sandi didn't answer right away. In the past, Kate had suffered through several misadventures. After reading today's letter, Sandi wondered if her friend was headed toward another crisis.

"What's up?" Ian asked.

"She's been seeing a lot of Keith this summer."

"Keith Taylor? Your old boyfriend?"

"*Friend*," Sandi countered. "Someone I dated a few times in high school. We were never that serious."

Ian gave his wife an incredulous look. "I was afraid your *friend* was going to bend me into a pretzel at our reception." He offered a mock shudder, remembering the dark look on the football player's face as Keith came through the line. "Keith and Kate," he said thoughtfully. "Their names sound good together. Works for me." Leaning forward, he selected another large slice of pizza.

"The timing is lousy. Keith is supposed to leave on his mission next month. And Kate is already registered at BYU, something she's dreamed about for two years. Besides, Kate has enough men in her life right now. Mike barely left on a mission and Randy gets back this fall."

"Ooooh, the plot thickens," Ian commented. He glanced at what was left in the pizza box. "You'd better come eat some of this. It's going fast."

Nodding, Sandi moved to the table and slid down into a chair. "I hope Kate knows what she's doing."

"She's a big girl now," Ian responded. "I'm sure she'll be fine. She was blessed with a talent for attracting men."

Sandi's eyes twinkled. "She certainly caught your eye last year."

"This again?" Ian avoided the mischievous look on his wife's face. It was true. He had dated Kate last year and had been convinced he was in love with her—until he met Sandi.

"Men don't seem to be able to think straight when they're around her," Sandi teased. "You of all people should know that."

Ian gave his wife a patient look. "And your point is?"

"I don't want to see Kate or Keith get hurt. It would never work out between them. I know them too well to ever believe it could. They're too different."

"People said the same thing about us, especially your mother."

"I know," Sandi muttered. "But it's not the same thing."

"Eat. Later, if it'll make you feel better, write Kate a letter, or give her a call."

But when Sandi attempted a call a short time later, she was informed that Keith had taken Kate to a movie. With a heavy sigh, Sandi began a letter to Kate. Later she would tackle the books she had brought home to study.

CHAPTER 2

Sandi wasn't alone in her concern about the blossoming friendship between Keith Taylor and Kate Erickson. Several people in their hometown of Bozeman, Montana, felt they had a personal stake in this relationship. Misguided in their assumptions, it was as Sandi feared, the beginning of a crisis.

"I can't believe Kate—first she sends my brother off on a mission—now she's dating his best friend!" Mike Jeffries' younger sister, Jennifer, complained to anyone who would listen. Jennifer had never liked Kate and had caused Mike and Kate untold misery from the vicious rumors she had spread in the past.

The new rumors amused Kate and Keith. They even made it a point to sit together during Sunday School and sacrament meeting, adding fuel to the fire that was spreading in their small branch.

In the beginning, Sue Erickson silently watched, hesitant to question Kate about the situation. But, after several weeks, she had decided it was time for a mother-daughter chat.

She waited until she could be alone with Kate, then cornered her lively daughter downstairs in the family room one afternoon. Sue smiled, inviting Kate to sit beside her on the couch. Stalling as she pondered a way to tactfully approach the subject, she helped Kate finish braiding her long auburn hair.

After exchanging a few pleasantries, Sue bravely plunged to the heart of the matter. "Kate, where is it you and Keith are headed with this thing?"

Mildly surprised, Kate gazed at her mother. "What thing?"

Sue gave her nearly nineteen-year-old daughter a stern look.

"You know what I'm talking about—the time you're spending with Keith. I wouldn't worry, but your attempts to provide our branch with juicy tidbits are getting out of hand. I thought Jennifer Jeffries was going to have a stroke yesterday when Keith put his arm around your shoulders during sacrament meeting."

"Mom, it's nothing serious. We figure if people want to talk, we'll give them something to discuss," Kate said impishly.

Sue gave Kate a concerned look.

"Tell me you're not falling for those rumors going around," Kate begged.

"No, but Keith *is* only human, and I may be a bit prejudiced on this one, but you are a very attractive young woman."

Kate met her mother's worried gaze with a smile. "Thanks, people say I take after my mother," she blithely replied.

Sue ran a hand through her short red hair and sighed. It was true, there was a strong resemblance between the two, but Kate's attempt at flattery did nothing to dispel her concern.

"Quit worrying, Mom," Kate said. "It'll give you wrinkles. Despite what the gossipmongers are spreading, it's not serious between us at all. We haven't even kissed." She paused, amused by the relieved expression on her mother's face. "Keith has just been so lost since Sandi got married. He had some pretty intense feelings for her. I'm trying to cheer him up. And it's working. He's finally smiling again."

"That's what has me worried."

Kate rolled her eyes. "Mom, think about it—the last thing I need right now is a serious relationship."

"Isn't that the same thing you said last year when you met Ian?"

Kate gave her mother a dirty look. "It all turned out fine."

"Why tempt fate again?" Sue asked, gazing intently at her daughter. A phone call from Keith interrupted the conversation.

* * *

Kate slipped out of her shorts and T-shirt to reveal a bright green, one-piece swimming suit. She rubbed a generous amount of sunscreen on, then flopped onto her stomach, stretching out on the large beach towel she had brought. Readjusting her sunglasses, she looked out across Glen Lake. The 300-foot beach front made for perfect sunbathing. She smiled, convinced this summer was perfect. Good weather, good times, and a good friend to share it with. The only problem was that the weeks were passing too quickly. She cherished this time spent with her family and Keith; it wouldn't be long before she returned to the hectic momentum of college life.

Living nearly a year in Salt Lake City had given Kate an appreciation for the slower pace of Bozeman. She loved the fresh, clean air and the openness of Gallatin Valley. Her part-time job allowed her to work in as much hiking, fishing, and swimming as she desired. Keith was killing time until he left for the MTC and he often accompanied her.

"You should have heard the lecture my mom got from Edith Rhoads last night at the grocery store," Keith said, stretching out on his own beach towel. He reached for Kate's sunscreen and applied it where his T-shirt and purple swimming trunks didn't cover. In his quest for a tan, he had ended up with a nasty sunburn that was still healing. It wasn't an experience he wanted to repeat.

Kate pictured the ill-tempered older woman from their church branch and shuddered. Edith had stirred up a lot of trouble for her in the past. The woman didn't seem happy unless she was basking in someone else's misery. Turning onto her side, Kate looked at Keith and waited for him to continue.

"Edith thinks I'll never make it into the mission field because of you." Keith glanced at Kate for a reaction, but her sunglasses didn't reveal anything. He smiled. Pursuing a serious relationship with Kate was a tempting thought. Kate was a delightful young woman. Someone who wouldn't be waiting around in two years, he was sure. Some lucky guy would end up with her. His smile drooped into a frown as he thought of Sandi.

"Don't worry about it, Keith," Kate said, noticing the look on his face. "Rumors don't bother me anymore."

"You'd think the people in this town would find more to talk about than you and me," Keith replied, shifting his gaze to the lake.

"Past experience tells me these people are really bored," Kate said, rolling onto her back. She stretched, her hand reaching above the large beach towel she was laying on. Digging her hand into the soft, warm sand, she smiled. "I don't know why, but they've always been interested in what I'm doing."

"They're not alone," Keith said softly, lifting up his sunglasses to gaze appreciatively at the young woman lying beside him. He was continuously learning why Mike had fallen so hard for Kate during their senior year in high school. Unlike some girls, Kate didn't seem aware of her beauty. Her warm nature and love for fun heightened the attraction.

Keith had enjoyed this summer with Kate. He'd loved how she had insisted on baiting her own hook on their fishing adventures, and he had laughed at her excitement each time she managed to reel one in. She had drawn the line at cleaning her catch, however, leaving that unpleasant task to him. On the long hikes and bicycle rides, she never complained and even managed to keep up with him most of the time.

Now, as Keith admired Kate's long auburn hair, his gaze shifted to her face, to the sunglasses that hid her emerald green eyes. Eyes that could flash dangerously if given just cause. Lying back down on his towel, he silently cautioned himself, *Easy, big guy. Danger zone.*

As he turned onto his back to avoid looking at Kate, she sat up, hugging her knees. "I got a letter from Sandi today."

"Oh?" Keith replied, trying to sound indifferent.

"She and Ian are so happy!"

Keith remained silent.

"How long are you going to hold a grudge?" When Keith refused to answer, Kate prodded his side with her big toe. "Anyone home? Are you still breathing? Do we need a lifeguard to offer mouth-to-mouth resuscitation?"

Giving in to an urge he had tried to ignore for weeks, Keith quickly sat up. As he reached for Kate, she giggled, pulling away to run down into the water. Misinterpreting Kate's teasing, Keith chased her. After dunking her a couple of times, Keith embraced her, kissing her with an intensity that surprised both of them. Kate tried to pull away, but Keith, a former defensive back for Ricks College, was not easily daunted. When he finally released her, Kate stared at him.

"What?" he asked.

"What was that?!" she angrily demanded.

Keith smiled sheepishly. "A little something for you to remember me by."

"Keith—"

"Shhh. Don't ruin this moment. It'll give me a fantasy to reflect on while I'm serving my mission."

Kate gave him a dirty look. "Fantasy is right!"

"Sorry!" Keith said, stalking out of the lake. "I guess I picked up the wrong signals this afternoon!"

"What signals?"

"That bit about mouth-to-mouth resuscitation!"

Kate closed her eyes. Her mother's warnings surfaced. She saw again the subtle hints in Sandi's letter. Groaning, she realized she was as much to blame for what had happened as Keith was. "I'm sorry," she said, walking back to the towels. "I wasn't thinking—"

"Neither was I," Keith admitted, reaching for his towel. Shaking it out, he avoided Kate's probing gaze.

"I didn't mean . . . we've had a lot of fun together," Kate stammered, self-consciously wrapping her towel around her hips. Reaching for her T-shirt, she quickly wiggled into it. "Let's not spoil it. You're a good friend, Keith," she added softly, pulling her braided hair out of the back of the shirt.

Keith finally returned her gaze. "And that's it?"

Kate slowly nodded.

"Okay. No harm done." He forced a laugh. "Mike would probably kill us both anyway."

"Keith—" she began.

He cut her off. "Well, I don't know about you, but I've soaked up enough rays for one day. Let's head home."

Keith tried to keep things light on the drive home, but Kate sensed the tension that now existed. The easy, comfortable relationship had become awkward and stiff.

As the days passed, Kate and Keith avoided each other, which only caused more rumors to fly. Edith Rhoads and Jennifer Jeffries enjoyed themselves immensely.

"I'm so glad Keith finally came to his senses," Edith was overheard crowing to Keith's mother.

"Kate isn't happy until everyone is as miserable as she is," Jennifer sniffed to her friends.

Doing their best to ignore the gossip going around, Keith poured himself into preparing for his mission as Kate tried to come to terms with her conflicting emotions. Daily, she relived the time spent with Keith, wondering what had been misinterpreted, what had led to the day at Glen Lake. Apprehensive about Mike's reaction to what had taken place, Kate agonized over the version she knew Jennifer would send her brother. Sue advised her not to worry about it, reminding Kate that Mike was well aware of Jennifer's past hostility.

* * *

Slowly the weeks passed until it was time for Keith to leave.

"Friends?" Kate pleaded after Keith's farewell meeting the second Sunday in August. Reaching for a hug, she was stung as Keith settled for a handshake instead.

"Yeah, sure," he stiffly replied. He hadn't meant to sound angry, but being around Kate was confusing; it was the last thing he needed today. "Send me a postcard some time," he added in a softer tone, offering a smile that Kate missed as she turned away. He started to go after her, but was cut off by the crowd that moved in to wish him well.

Keith's unspoken anger, his mother's glare, and Jennifer's quick tongue had taken its toll. Fighting tears, Kate quickly moved out of the building.

Sue saw the devastated look on her daughter's face and tried to follow. It took several minutes, but she finally managed to catch up as Kate slowed down to walk home.

"Why do things always turn out this way?" Kate tearfully asked. "I try so hard to do the right thing and nothing ever seems to work out! People will never let go of who I was! And they're only too happy to rub it in my face every time I mess up!"

Still trying to catch her breath, Sue slid her purse up on her shoulder before meeting her daughter's troubled gaze. Kate had come so far in two years. Turning from a rebellious past to embrace the gospel, she had fought an uphill battle to convince others that she had changed. Sue would be forever grateful that there had always been wonderful people in Kate's life. Leaders, friends, and family members who buoyed her up when life knocked her down. Sue sensed it was her turn today.

"Kate, you're letting a handful of people speak for the rest of us. You know most of the people in this town love you. Don't let today get you down." She brushed a stray tear from Kate's cheek. "No matter how hard you try to do the right thing, there will always be challenges. It's part of life. Part of the test. There will always be days that don't go the way you've planned."

"I really messed up with Keith," Kate mumbled.

Sue sighed. It would be cruel to make this into an "I-told-you-so" moment. She drew Kate into a hug instead and listened quietly as Kate unloaded what she had been keeping inside for weeks.

". . . I thought Keith understood. Mike and I are still writing to each other—I get a letter from him almost every other week." Kate pulled a face. "His last one was a disguised lecture. I don't know what Jennifer wrote to him, but he hinted big time that Keith really needed to get into the mission field. Like I'm sure I would stop Keith from serving a mission!" She sniffed, gratefully taking the handful of tissue Sue pulled from her purse. "Then there's Randy. He comes home in a couple of months. The short notes he calls letters don't really give me much to go on. I don't know what to expect from him."

Sue pictured the tall missionary in her mind, remembering the mischievous smile that had caught her daughter's attention in Jackson, Wyoming, during a family vacation. Randy, the young man who had sent flowers after Kate's accident in Salt Lake and who had come to visit while Kate had been in a coma. The young man who had stolen Kate's heart before leaving to serve a mission in Ireland. "Have you heard anything from Randy, lately?" Sue asked.

"He sent me another *note* last week. He's busy, he says he's not sure how he'll ever leave Ireland—my interpretation, I don't think he's too eager to come home to me."

"Oh, Kate, I doubt—"

"Men are nothing but trouble!" Kate exploded.

Sue tried to suppress a smile.

"I never know where I stand with any of them! I think I'm being clear, up front, and then it turns out we're not even having the same conversation!"

Sue smiled. "What's that best-selling book about men and women being from different planets?"

"I don't know but I believe it!" Kate exclaimed.

"But still, men are nice to have around," Sue countered, thinking of her husband, Greg. She frowned, remembering the pile of dirty clothes he had left on the floor in their bedroom this morning. "Most of the time," she added.

From Kate's look of disbelief, Sue saw that her daughter wasn't buying any of this. She slipped an arm around Kate's waist, and they walked in silence for several minutes. "Honey, I don't envy you at all right now," Sue finally said. "You're facing a lot of decisions. And I don't think the dating scene has gotten any easier since I was there. It's tough to weed out what you're feeling, what someone else is feeling. And in the middle of that, those hormones start kicking in. Physical attraction can lead to difficult situations."

"Like with me and Keith," Kate muttered.

"Like with you and Keith. One-sided relationships can happen. It's a rare and wonderful thing when two people discover they feel the same way about each other."

Kate gave a little smile. "Like you and Dad?"

"Yes. Even then, it takes time, patience, prayer . . . a lot of prayer—did I mention prayer?"

Despite her current frame of mind, Kate laughed. "How do you sort it all out . . . if you pray and there's no solid answer. How do you know which guy, when it's right, stuff like that?"

"Stuff like Mike and Randy?" she asked.

Kate nodded.

Sue thought for a moment, then, taking her own advice, she silently prayed for guidance. This would be difficult. Sue could understand her daughter's dilemma. She liked both young men. Randy, with that thick head of black hair and those twinkling blue eyes, the young man who had helped Kate begin the transition from her rebellious past. Mike, who had dated Kate their senior year, helping her to rediscover the self-confidence that judgmental people had destroyed. Mike, whose tender brown eyes had seen past Kate's stony facade after a close friend's tragic death.

Both young men were attractive, good natured, sensitive, active in the Church, everything Sue could ever hope for in a future son-in-law. Again, she didn't envy Kate. Reflecting on her own experience, she realized she had only been involved with one man at a time. She had broken up with a former boyfriend just a few weeks before meeting Greg, who had practically swept her off her feet in a whirlwind romance. Still, it had been frightening when Greg had become serious early in their relationship. It had taken a combination of time, prayer, and several long talks with her own mother to sort through her confused feelings.

". . . I don't know what I'm going to do!" Kate was saying.

Sue snapped out of her mental wandering to glance at Kate. *And I don't know what to tell you,* she thought silently. Out loud she tried to sound more confident. "Take it one day at a time," she suggested. "Focus on college. Get on your knees when you feel confused or scared. I think you'll find that all of the pieces will eventually fall into place. I know they did for me."

"You didn't have to pick between two really neat guys."

"You might not have to either," Sue countered, surprised by her own words. Still, it was good advice. Maybe even inspired. She glanced at her scowling daughter. "A lot of things can change in two years—for you, for Randy, and for Mike. All three of you might end up with someone else—"

"Or no one at all."

Amused, Sue smiled. She doubted Kate would remain single, but on the other hand, it did happen, and to wonderful women. She thought of two close friends who had never married. One was now a college professor. The other worked as an RN. Both lived very full lives, touching people in positive ways, accomplishing things they probably wouldn't have been able to do if they had married and had a family.

"Kate," she said, "my personal theory is, if you're living the way you're supposed to, you'll be guided toward whatever or whoever is right for you."

Kate looked happier as she smiled at her mother. Sue hadn't offered any direct answers, but she had given them both something to think about. In companionable silence, they finished walking home.

* * *

Later that evening, Keith came by to visit. Surprised, Kate led him into the backyard for some privacy.

"Are you still speaking to me?" he asked humbly.

Kate looked at him steadily, taking in again how much older he seemed with his curly blond hair closely cropped. She slowly nodded.

"I couldn't leave without straightening things out between us." He sighed. "The past few weeks haven't been easy for me, but I know it's been just as hard on you." He sighed again then smiled at her. "I finally figured out the problem. You're too lovable for your own good."

"Yeah, right," Kate sarcastically replied, heading for the large wooden swing. Keith followed, sitting beside her.

"I mean it, Kate. You didn't do anything wrong. That's why I'm here. Can you forgive me for being such a jerk?"

Closing her eyes, Kate wondered why she felt a sudden urge to cry.

"Truce?" Keith's voice pleaded.

Nodding, Kate willed herself to remain in control. When Keith reached for a hug, she mischievously offered her hand, a subtle reminder of how he had treated her earlier that day. Puzzled at first, Mike finally caught on and nearly suffocated her in a bear hug.

CHAPTER 3

At home in Bozeman for the summer, Heidi Kearns sat on her bed and stared at the journal in front of her as she slowly turned another page. She should shred this book, she thought. Shred it and then burn what was left! She wished she hadn't written in pen, although to rewrite this painful portion of her life would be nearly impossible. She could add interesting side notes, but that would only confuse future generations. Personally, she doubted she would ever have any descendants to worry about. Passing on the family name and legends would have to be entrusted to her sisters and brothers, all of whom were married—Stephanie, Lacey, Brian, William, even Sandi, the baby of the family.

Heidi flinched at the thought. When Sandi had announced her engagement last February, Heidi hadn't minded, mostly because she too had succumbed to love. *Correction,* she told herself, to what she had *thought* was love. When she had fallen hard and fast for a new member of her college ward in January, she had felt like she was on top of the world.

She had met Terry Quinn at BYU when he had remained behind after her gospel doctrine class one Sunday. He wanted to meet her and to compliment her on the way she had handled class that morning. Flattered by his attention, Heidi had later learned that he had already caught the interest of most of the girls in their singles ward. She had overheard several whispered comments about his dark good looks and his fun sense of humor.

After their first meeting, Terry had asked Heidi out, not once, but several times. Then, just as Heidi was starting to believe that their feelings were mutual, she realized that Terry had been using her to get better acquainted with her slender, dark-haired roommate, Elena. Serious-minded, studious Elena, who didn't appreciate interruptions while studying. Obviously unimpressed with Terry, Elena had presented a challenge he couldn't resist. Terry had dropped by several times on the pretext of seeing Heidi, only to stir up a conversation with Elena. Misinterpreting their heated exchanges and assuming that Elena disliked Terry, Heidi had even argued on Terry's behalf, trying to convince her friend that he was a wonderful human being. Sadly, Heidi had finally triumphed.

As a law student, Heidi could take pride in the way she had successfully argued Terry's case, but there was little cause to celebrate when the dust finally settled. One night Heidi had come home to find Terry kissing Elena in the living room of their small apartment. Elena had tearfully begged for her forgiveness, but Heidi discovered that forgiveness didn't come easily. Everyone tried to tell her that Terry and Elena hadn't meant to hurt her, but Heidi didn't want to listen. She refused to speak to Terry and answered Elena in monosyllables for the rest of the semester until Heidi went home for the semester break. Although she had been invited to the wedding and reception, she didn't attend either one.

Now, as she gazed at the record she had kept, she groaned. "Okay, future lawyer, let's figure this thing out. Who is the guilty party in this crime of passion?" Terry's face came to mind. "He took advantage of me, but I was just as guilty. I let him." Rising from the bed, Heidi took a long, hard look at herself in the mirror above her dresser.

Although Heidi exercised religiously and tried to avoid fatty foods, her weight was a constant battle, one that she fought silently and alone. While her slender sisters took after their father, Heidi shared her mother's tendency to gain weight. The unfairness of her family's gene distribution often bothered her as she watched her sisters eat indiscriminately. Her brother, William, was her only solace since he, too, had inherited Harriet's tendency for roundness.

"But it's different for boys," Heidi had once told him. "A husky guy is considered *macho*. Girls like me are simply called *fat*."

Heidi's self-confidence had grown when she served a mission and found that people were drawn to her cheery disposition and impressed by her intelligence. Near the end of her mission, she experienced a slight weight loss, which had helped her to feel even better about herself. After her mission she worked to keep her weight down and tried not to be offended when well-meaning family members and friends commented on the change in her appearance. Since she didn't want to risk the possible side-effects of weight-loss pills, she stuck with the old-fashioned approach, diet and exercise.

Still heavier than she'd like, but slimmer than she used to be, Heidi had basked in Terry's supposed attention. Later he claimed that his admiration for her had been sincere, that he had truly enjoyed her sense of humor and her ability to explain complicated things with ease.

"I value your friendship. I always have and I always will," Terry had tried to explain the night she had finally seen the truth. "If I gave you the wrong impression about us, I'm sorry."

"He can be sorry all he wants, he still used me," Heidi said defiantly, glaring at her reflection. "When he developed feelings for Elena, he didn't have the decency to be honest with me." Heidi was still haunted by the look of sadness on Elena's face when they last spoke, but there was no turning back. After being close friends and roommates for two years, Heidi still missed Elena at times. She had almost been tempted to call, to somehow make things right, but had resisted the feeling.

"It'll never happen," she groaned, knocking her journal aside so that it fell to the floor, "thanks to Terry!" Ignoring the journal, she moved to her bedroom window and stared at a beautiful sunset she would never see or remember as scenes from the past year continued to haunt her.

CHAPTER 4

"From that grin on your face I'd say married life agrees with you," Kate commented, smiling at Sandi. Ian and Sandi had come to spend a few days in Bozeman before Sandi started the fall semester at the University of Utah. When Sandi's father offered to take Ian fishing, Sandi had jumped at the chance to surprise Kate with a visit. The two friends were now sitting in Kate's backyard in the large wooden swing.

"Thanks. You look pretty great yourself. I'm glad to see you're still smiling."

Kate gave Sandi a puzzled look.

"Mom filled me in on what's been going on thanks to the rumormongers of our branch."

Laughing, Kate shook her head. "It wasn't that bad. I survived and the best part is, Keith and I are still friends."

"Oh good," Sandi said with a sigh of relief. "The last Mom had heard, things weren't too friendly between you two."

Kate nodded, sharing everything that had happened between herself and Keith during the summer. She ended with Keith's final visit before he left for the Missionary Training Center.

"So now it's on to BYU," Sandi mused.

"Yeah, about that," Kate said, sounding a trifle miffed.

Sandi stared at her. "What?"

"Those roommates of yours—"

"Jill, Camilla, and Dee Dee?"

Kate nodded.

"What did they do?"

"Come inside and I'll let you read the letter for yourself," Kate said, leading Sandi back inside the house. Several minutes later, the two friends sat on Kate's bed, examining a letter. Sandi quickly scanned the contents and pulled a face as she handed it back to Kate.

"Kate, I'm sorry—" she began.

Kate shrugged. "It's not your fault."

"I'm the one who talked you into rooming with them this year. I had no idea they would pull this kind of stunt," Sandi said apologetically. "They really are good girls."

"Which explains why they waited until the last possible moment to let me know they no longer want me as a roommate," Kate said dryly.

Sandi reached for the letter and reread it. "I'll bet Jill's mother put them up to this. Jill told me last year that her younger sister, Cosette, would be staying in the dorms this year. It's a tradition in that family. All first-year college students live in the dorms. Jill's mother figures that way, her girls are protected."

"From what?"

Sandi shook her head. "Who knows? I can't believe she's bending that rule for Cosette. Jill used to complain that Cosette, who is the youngest, always gets away with a lot more than she ever did. Their mother must've given in on this one, and said that Cosette could stay with her sister if she didn't want to live in the dorms."

Kate's frown deepened. "So, what do I do? They're asking me to find another place to live—"

"I know Jill was forced into it, Kate. She would never purposely hurt anyone."

"Maybe, but if I give in, I don't have anywhere to live. If I don't give in, they'll all hate me."

"Not necessarily. Maybe then Cosette would have to live in the dorms. Jill would probably appreciate that."

"I can't handle any more contention right now. I've had my fill of it this summer. I'd rather find another place to live." Kate moved to the window in her bedroom and gazed into the backyard.

"Maybe there's room in another apartment in that same complex," Sandi suggested hopefully.

Kate shook her head. "I already called. There are no vacancies left this semester. At least I'll get my deposit back. If I can find another apartment, I'm sure it'll come in handy."

Sandi stood, pacing the floor for several minutes. Suddenly, she stopped. "Why didn't I think of this before?" she said. "It's the perfect solution! Heidi's roommate got married this summer."

"So?"

"To Heidi's boyfriend."

Kate ran a hand through the front of her hair. "Oh, yeah, I think I heard something about that."

"Probably from me. I send letters on a regular basis, unlike other people I could mention," Sandi said, giving Kate an accusing look. "Anyway, Heidi hasn't replaced Elena yet—"

"And you think she would agree to let me room with her?" Kate asked, picking up on Sandi's excitement.

Sandi nodded. "She'll do it for me. I've always been her favorite sister."

Kate's face showed her skepticism.

"I'm serious. She does stuff for me all the time. I'll hit her up about it tonight."

"You're sure she'll agree?"

"Positive. Now, let's talk about something more interesting— like how you're going to cope with Randy coming home."

* * *

"NO! Absolutely not!"

Sandi gaped at her older sister. "Heidi!"

Heidi turned away. "I've already given you my answer. Now, if you'll excuse me, I've got other things to think about right now."

Sandi continued to stare. This wasn't like her older sister. Their mother had mentioned that Heidi had been moody all summer, but seeing it for herself was still a shock. Heidi had always been easygoing, a big tease, and a lot of fun. "But Kate needs—" Sandi stammered.

"Did you hear me? I said NO!"

"Without good reason," Sandi argued. "Kate would make the perfect roommate."

Heidi turned back to glare at Sandi. This was her final year at

BYU and she was going to try her best to enjoy it. That meant no roommates, no boyfriends, no complications. The tiny one-bedroom apartment was barely big enough for two girls. By herself, it would be almost roomy. The word, *roomie,* popped into mind. Shuddering, she renewed her conviction to refuse Sandi's offer.

". . . she's neat, and I mean that both ways—her personality and she's tidy."

In the past, Heidi had enjoyed Sandi's playful bantering. Coming up with ridiculous debates, they had kept each other entertained for hours. This was different. This was an annoying conversation that never should've happened. "You'd better become a nurse."

"Why?"

"Because you're a rotten salesperson."

Sandi gave Heidi a dirty look. "You're not listening—"

"Neither are you. I said no and I meant no!" Heidi started out the door.

"It'll save you money," Sandi frantically offered.

Heidi paused.

Encouraged, Sandi continued. "Yesterday you said things would be tight this year. If Kate shared the cost of the apartment . . ." She waited for a response. There wasn't one, but at least Heidi was listening. "You know what Kate's been through the past couple of years. The coma, Linda's death. She had to wait an entire year to get into BYU. Give her a break, please—for me? It's my fault she's in this mess. I'm the one who talked her into living with my former roommates."

Heidi shook her head, keeping her back to Sandi, to avoid the pleading look in her youngest sister's eyes. "I don't want another roommate and anyone close to me should understand why."

"Elena feels terrible about what happened, and if you'd talk to her—"

"This has nothing to do with Elena," Heidi exclaimed, whirling around to glower at Sandi.

"It has everything to do with her," Sandi countered. Then, her expression softening, she tried a different tactic. "Kate would never hurt you the way Elena did."

Remaining silent, Heidi moved to the large picture window of the living room and stared out into the street. Sandi closed her eyes.

This was just like trying to reason with their mother, she thought. Despairing, Sandi sent up a silent prayer. Several minutes passed.

"She'd be paying half the rent," Heidi finally said.

"Of course," Sandi said meekly. Inwardly she sent a heartfelt "thank you" heavenward.

Heidi sighed in defeat. "She'll have to pick up after herself—and she'll be on her own most of the time. I'm not catering to a college freshman."

"This is actually her second year of college," Sandi offered eagerly. "She went to LDS Business College in Salt Lake last year."

"Whatever," Heidi snapped. It wasn't in her to be gracious about this, but surprisingly, the decision to accept Kate as a roommate felt right. She knew if she didn't agree, guilt would haunt her continuously, and she was currently enduring enough of that emotion—thanks to Elena. Slowly, Heidi turned to face Sandi. She expected to see a gloating expression and was touched when Sandi rushed forward to give her a hug.

"You don't know how much this means to me, how much it'll mean to Kate!"

Heidi slowly returned the hug, realizing that Sandi would never understand what she had asked of her.

CHAPTER 5

"Well, there goes my appetite," Tyler said, staring with mock horror at his sister. Lack of sleep due to worry over the approaching college semester had drained Kate's face of color. Her eyes were red and slightly puffy. "A person shouldn't be exposed to anything that ugly first thing in the morning."

Kate glared at the fourteen-year-old as she reached for the glass of orange juice Sue had set on the counter.

"Tyler, sit down and eat. Don't you have to be over at Brother Watson's at eight?" Sue asked, hoping to defuse the situation.

"Yeah." Tyler shrugged. "I can't believe he wants to work in one more overnight camp. 'Sleeping on the ground is good for the soul,'" he said, mimicking the scout leader.

"Ty!"

Tyler grinned. "Can't wait to get rid of me, eh?"

"Something like that," Sue said, throwing a soggy dishrag at her son.

Tyler caught it with ease and threw it at Kate, hitting her in the face.

"You are so dead!" Kate promised, chasing Tyler out of the room.

"MOM!" Tyler yelped as Kate tried to make good her threat.

"I'm staying out of this one," Sue retorted as Kate poured the rest of her orange juice on Tyler's head and down his back.

"Oh, man," Tyler complained, "now I'll have to take a shower!"

"Good idea," Kate smirked, "considering you'll be out in the forest. You'd hate to attract too many fellow animals."

"Mom!"

"Hit the shower," Sue said, pointing down the hall.

"But—"

"You started it," Sue reminded her son. "And I'm ending it. You're even. A truce is being declared, or you'll both deal with me," she said, giving each of them a stern look. "Now, clean up this mess and then it's a quick shower for you," she said to Tyler, "and breakfast for you," she added, pulling Kate back into the kitchen.

Kate obediently grabbed a handful of paper towels, moistened a couple of them, and handed the rest to Tyler. Wiping up what she could, she motioned for Tyler to take over. Groaning loudly, he grudgingly cleaned the rest of the floor, then threw the soggy towels at the kitchen garbage before marching down the hall to the bathroom.

"The things I put up with," Sue muttered, picking up one of the sticky paper towels that hadn't made it into the plastic garbage container.

"Yeah, like Tyler," Kate commented, slipping up onto a stool.

"And Kate," Sue said, with a pointed look at her daughter.

"Mom," Kate complained.

"You're both giving me grey hair."

"You have grey hair?" seven-year-old Sabrina asked, wandering into the kitchen.

"Nope, thanks to L'Oreal," Greg teased, walking into the kitchen to kiss his wife good morning.

"Thanks," Sue responded, giving her husband a pinch.

"So, Kate, when have you decided to head down to BYU?" Greg asked, quickly changing the subject.

"Monday," Kate replied as she moved to the kitchen table.

"You're riding down with Heidi?" Sue asked.

Kate nodded, pouring herself another glass of orange juice.

"You need more than orange juice," Sue chided.

"I'm not hungry, Mom," Kate replied. "The juice will be enough."

"Isn't Heidi through with college yet?" Greg asked, reaching for a slice of bacon.

"Almost," Kate explained. "She's going into law. That takes a few years."

"I see," Greg said, enjoying the crispy piece of bacon. Sue didn't fry it much anymore and he assumed it had something to do with his blood pressure. The doctor had warned that if it went up much higher, he'd need medication, and Sue had taken that warning to heart. She was constantly fixing tasteless, salt-free dishes on his behalf.

Sighing, Greg slipped into a chair and when his wife wasn't looking, reached for more bacon. Putting four strips of bacon on his plate, he picked one up and chewed it thoughtfully. As Sue set a plate of eggs on the table, she glanced at the bacon on Greg's plate and gave him a pained look. Putting the other two pieces of bacon back on the original plate, he quickly stuck the third piece in his mouth then reached for the piece of toast Sue handed him. He pulled a face when he saw that she had carefully buttered it with the fat-free margarine he was growing to hate.

"When do you start your new job, Kate?" Sue asked.

"Wednesday," Kate said, grinning as her father bit into the toast and wrinkled his nose.

"So you're going to BYU at last," he said proudly a few minutes later. Kate nodded, remembering how excited she had been to finally receive a positive reply from BYU. After registering, she had been fortunate enough to land a part-time job on campus as a secretary in the administration building, no doubt due to the courses she had taken at LDS Business College and the skills she had gained working for her Uncle Stan.

"And school starts the week after that, right?" Greg asked, ignoring the eggs his wife had set on the table and cramming another strip of bacon into his mouth while Sue had her back turned to them. When she glanced his direction, he innocently focused on his glass of orange juice, chewing the bacon only when she looked away.

Amused, Kate nodded.

Greg wiped the bacon grease from his hands onto a napkin. "That darn toast," he mumbled for Sue's benefit. "It might be taste-free—"

"Fat-free," Sue supplied.

"Same difference—it's still greasy."

"Maybe I'll fix it differently next time," Sue offered.

"Good."

"Next time, you can have it plain," Sue said as she set a poached egg on her husband's plate. She turned to Kate. "I'm glad you'll be living with Heidi."

"Me, too," Kate replied. "I'm a bit nervous about it, but at least I have a place to stay."

"Why are you nervous?" her father asked. "Won't it be just the two of you?"

"Our apartment only has one bedroom, Dad," Kate reminded him. "So, yes, it's just the two of us, but Heidi's older. I really don't know her very well."

"That'll change," Greg assured her. "By the time you two move in, spend some time together, walk to campus everyday—"

"The exercise will be good for you," Tyler teased, stepping into the kitchen. "You can lose those extra pounds you've been moaning about all summer," he added, rubbing a towel over his wet hair. Kate reached for the orange juice and refilled her glass, giving her brother a threatening look.

"Not this again," Sue warned, giving her son a stern, no-nonsense glare. "Kate, put the glass down," she said firmly, shifting her gaze to her daughter. Although Kate had complained about gaining a few pounds, Sue could see that Kate had developed curves in all the right places. Her daughter was growing into a beautiful young woman.

Sue held out her hand for the glass of juice, which Kate reluctantly surrendered. As she left the room, Kate made it a point to step on Tyler's foot.

"She crushed my foot!" Tyler howled, dancing around the kitchen, holding one foot in the air.

"Tyler, my boy, it's time we had a little talk," Greg said, jumping at the opportunity to abandon his fat-free breakfast. "I can see I've neglected to teach you how to behave around ladies."

"Dad," Tyler complained. "I have to leave in a few minutes."

"And he still needs to eat," Sue commented, glancing at the plates of bacon and eggs. She had decided to fix these normally taboo items to give Tyler a hearty breakfast before he left for camp.

"We have plenty of time," Greg assured his wife as he led Tyler from the room. With a bit of luck, he might manage to make it out the door without finishing what was left on his plate. Once he had escaped, he would complete breakfast by stopping at the doughnut shop on his way to work.

"I'm done, Mommy," Sabrina said, slipping down from the table.

Sue glanced at her youngest daughter's plate. Sabrina hadn't even touched the egg Sue had cooked especially for her and had only nibbled the meaty portion of one slice of bacon.

"Breakfast was good," Sabrina added before hurrying out of the room.

"Wasn't it though?" Sue murmured, drinking the juice Kate had poured. "We'll have to have these quality family gatherings more often."

CHAPTER 6

Despite Heidi's misgivings and Kate's nervousness, the two young women hit it off quite well during the long drive to Provo, which gave them time to get acquainted and to get past the barrier of being "Sandi's friend" and "Sandi's sister." Heidi even offered to share her small, beat-up Honda Civic with Kate if the need ever arose.

The first few days in Provo were hectic as both girls adjusted to work schedules, class schedules, and to each other. Certain she would have to make allowances for the younger girl, Heidi was pleasantly surprised by Kate's maturity.

As for Kate, she was relieved to learn that Heidi wasn't as grumpy or austere as she had feared. She quickly discovered that Heidi could be as much fun as Sandi; and although Heidi wouldn't admit it, she enjoyed having Kate around.

"We'll try to get home for most of the major holidays," she told Kate, "but we'll spend most weekends in Provo." Wanting to help Kate ease into college life, she added, "If you get involved in our student ward and in campus activities, you'll adapt quicker."

Kate agreed. She was already falling in love with the large university. At times the size of the campus was overwhelming, but as the days passed, she began feeling more at home.

This was her first experience with being on her own. Her first year away from Bozeman she had lived with her aunt Paige and uncle Stan in Salt Lake. Now, she was an official college co-ed at a full-size university; in fact, she was one of over thirty thousand students attending Brigham Young University that year. After enduring a few twinges of homesickness, she quickly adjusted to handling her own meals, laundry, and housekeeping. She shared dinner responsibilities with Heidi, but because of scheduling conflicts, lunch and breakfast were usually haphazard affairs, each girl eating on the run in between classes and work. Heidi had a part-time job at a local law office and spent a lot of time in the law library on campus studying different legal cases. Kate had to be to work at the Smoot Administration Building, or ASB, by three o'clock on Monday, Wednesday, and Friday afternoons. She worked a morning shift on Tuesdays and Thursdays. She and Heidi rarely saw each other on campus, which was understandable considering the size of BYU. The 638-acre campus included 121 academic buildings, and 81 administration and physical plant facilities. That didn't include the on-campus student housing that was available—281 units.

The single bedroom apartment that Heidi and Kate shared was located in the basement of a small brick home that belonged to a retired couple. Heidi had stumbled across the cozy apartment after returning from her mission. She had hated living in an apartment complex and enjoyed the sense of security and quiet privacy this apartment offered. Only three blocks from campus, it was an ideal location. Small but tidy, the apartment suited the needs of both girls perfectly. Heidi had already established a good rapport with the owners, and they were happy to welcome one of Heidi's friends as their newest tenant.

The street they lived on was lined with tall, leafy trees, making it a pleasant walk to campus. Kate loved the way the scenic Wasatch Mountains seemed to rise up behind the university and the beautiful sunrise that greeted her most mornings. Breathing in the crisp fall air, she was eager for this new phase of her life.

Kate enjoyed her job in the ASB office. The computer skills she had gained the year before proved to be an asset and she soon felt confident with her new responsibilities. Nearly everyone in the office was pleasant to work with and she found that she was constantly making new friends and acquaintances.

BYU offered a variety of educational opportunities, including informative forums that featured specialists in science, art, humanities, government, and the media. From dances, concerts, and plays, to the football games at Cougar Stadium, Kate enjoyed everything about

BYU. She especially looked forward to the devotionals held in the Marriott Center on most Tuesdays at eleven o'clock. General Authorities from the LDS Church and other selected speakers addressed the student body on varied spiritual topics. Heidi usually met her near the Marriott Center so they could attend them together.

On the downside, the amount of homework was often staggering. Still, Kate found that most of her classes were enjoyable. And, as Sandi had suggested, she had been able to challenge two computer courses because of her previous training and experience. After passing both tests with flying colors, Kate had met with a career counselor, who had informed her that if Kate attended two summer semesters and took an extra class each semester, she could graduate with her teaching certificate in three years. In three years she could teach history and computer skills to junior high or high school students, something she had decided on last year.

"I want to work with teenagers," she confided in Heidi. "Maybe I could make a difference with some of them," she added, thinking of the influence past leaders and teachers had been in her own life. "I love history, and computers have become second nature to me—I think I'll really enjoy being a teacher."

Heidi groaned. "You must be into self-torture. I could never be a teacher. I don't have the patience."

"I don't think I could ever be a lawyer," Kate replied, glancing through one of Heidi's thick textbooks. "How do you ever remember all of this stuff?"

Heidi patted the side of her head. "I didn't get looks or talent from our family gene pool. I guess I'll have to settle for brains."

Kate grinned, shaking her head. At first, she had been bothered by Heidi's tendency to put herself down. She'd even argued with her about it before catching on that Heidi loved to tease. She liked to say off-the-wall statements just to see how people would react. Kate was sure Heidi didn't mean most of the derogatory remarks she made about herself—at least, she hoped she didn't. "I guess I'm in trouble then. I didn't get any of those three," Kate said, closing the thick law book.

Heidi snorted in disgust.

"What?" Kate asked.

"You're gorgeous, you have a beautiful singing voice, and I

believe you were smart enough to challenge at least two college classes this semester. I'd say you're adequately blessed."

"Thanks—" Kate stammered, embarrassed.

"For what, pointing out the obvious?" Heidi shrugged, then reached for the book Kate had been looking through. "Now, if you'll excuse me, I have work to do." Opening the book, she thumbed through it and began jotting down a few notes.

Sensing she had been dismissed, Kate moved into the small bedroom to tackle her own pile of homework.

Later that night as she knelt down to pray, Kate expressed her deep gratitude to her Father in Heaven. She remembered how disappointed she had been when she had initially been rejected for admission to BYU during her last year in high school. She could now see that the year she had spent in Salt Lake had been a blessing in disguise. As a result, she had a secure job on campus that would continue during her stay at BYU. The desired teaching degree would be within her grasp in three years. She loved being able to room with someone like Heidi in an apartment that felt safe and homey. As Kate continued to pray, she realized that as her mother had predicted, everything seemed to be falling into place. Randy reappearing in her life still frightened and confused her, but Kate resolved that no matter what the future held, she would place her trust in the Lord.

* * *

As the weeks progressed, Kate found that she had little time for socializing. She went on a few dates, but most were with casual acquaintances. Only one individual seemed intent on making her his own personal conquest—Lyle Jennings, a returned missionary she had met in one of her history classes. Clean-cut and serious-minded, at first he didn't seem to pose much of a threat. She soon learned differently.

"You believe in the priesthood authority, don't you?" Lyle had asked during their first and only date.

Puzzled, Kate had slowly nodded.

"Well, I've received a revelation that you are to become my wife."

Kate immediately shared with Lyle her own revelation that he was very much mistaken, not to mention clueless. After insisting that he take her home, she had closed the door on his sputtering attempts to explain himself. She tried to avoid him as much as possible, but when he learned that she worked as a secretary in the administration building, he wouldn't leave her alone. He left flowers, notes, and gifts that all found their way into the wastepaper basket next to her desk.

Not one to take a hint or give up, Lyle continued in his endeavor to claim Kate as his bride. He tied up her phone lines at work, calling repeatedly to tell her of the great love he had for her. She continued to hang up on him, but he still didn't catch on. When she told him that she was waiting for two missionaries, he merely grinned and said the wait was over. He was here and now, unlike Mike and Randy who were far away and otherwise occupied. At that point in the conversation, Kate fled into the ladies' restroom, making sure the door was locked behind her.

Observing the stress that Lyle was causing in her roommate's life, Heidi decided the time had come to convince him of the error of his ways. She contacted one of her brothers who lived near Spanish Fork and arranged for him to arrive at the administration building at approximately the same time Lyle was due to make his appearance. Making the most out of any opportunity, Lyle always managed to show up in time to escort Kate to the history class they had together on Tuesday and Thursday afternoons.

Heidi's brother Brian took his role as hero quite seriously. He rounded up two good friends, Phillip Yates and Jimmy Bodine, who like himself were both tall and well-proportioned, as well as former college football players. Patiently the trio waited outside the administrative building where Kate worked.

Lyle wasn't hard to pick out of a crowd—he was tall and skinny, and carried flowers. Not realizing the educational moment he was about to have, Lyle walked right past Brian and his friends.

Later that afternoon, Kate waltzed inside the apartment and gleefully announced that she was finally getting her life back. It was the first day in over two weeks that Lyle had left her alone.

"He wasn't waiting outside the ASB and he didn't even try to talk to me in class," she told Heidi. "I wonder what finally sunk in?"

Heidi grinned sheepishly. Seeing her guilty look, Kate immediately demanded, "What have you been up to?"

Heidi stuck her fingers in her mouth and whistled. "It helps to have a few connections," she said to Kate as Brian and his friends wandered out of the bedroom where they had been hiding. "I figured you'd want to personally thank these three for helping out. This is Brian, and his two friends, Jimmy and Phillip."

Kate stared from Heidi to the three large men. "What did you guys do?"

"Let's just say we set Mr. Jennings straight concerning our *little sister!*" Brian said with a grin.

"You what?" Kate asked, looking confused.

"We had a friendly conversation," Brian casually replied. "Stressed what a close-knit brood we are and how we personally take offense if someone troubles a family member. We flexed a few muscles and shared the sad fate of other bothersome boyfriends who had become a nuisance to our kid sister . . ."

Jimmy slugged Brian's arm. "You should have seen him," he said. "Brian had this guy trembling when he assured him that one pushy boyfriend disappeared and his body was never found."

"Brian!" Heidi and Kate exclaimed in unison, their expressions a mixture of amusement and disbelief.

Brian smiled at Kate. "No need to thank me. It's just part of my job as *big brother.*" He turned to his friends. "Well, guys, it's time we headed off to aid other fair maidens."

"Who's next?" Phillip asked.

"Our wives," Brian replied. "They'll be wonderin' what happened to us. Catch ya later, sis," he said, leaning down to kiss Heidi's cheek, "and *little sis,*" he added, winking at Kate before leaving the apartment.

"You guys are great," Heidi hollered after them. "Thanks!"

"I can't believe they did that to Lyle!" Kate exclaimed as Heidi shut the door.

"Hey, it worked," Heidi pointed out. "They didn't harm him—just gave him an attitude adjustment. Something Brother Jennings desperately needed."

"I'll say," Kate agreed, laughing.

CHAPTER 7

Two weeks later, Randy's mother, Jan Miles, called to see if Kate wanted to join the rest of the family at the Salt Lake airport to greet Randy. Kate hesitantly agreed. She hadn't heard a thing from Randy since school had started. Mike, on the other hand, had faithfully sent a letter every other week. His last one had hinted his concern about Randy's return.

Don't let anyone pressure you into doing anything you don't want to do. You're entitled to your own personal revelation. Remember that.

She remembered. But at this point in her life, that knowledge didn't seem to help. Why couldn't things be spelled out clearly? Why was it so difficult to know what it was that she wanted? "Why did I tell Jan 'yes'? I'm not even sure Randy wants to see me again," Kate groaned after Jan's call. Turning in her chair, she glanced at Heidi. "Want to come with me?"

Heidi shook her head, hoping to avoid this event. "You don't want me around for the mushy homecoming scene," she said.

"It may not be as mushy as you think. His mother has already warned me that I can't get too close to him until he's officially released from his mission."

"His mother warned you off?" Heidi replied, looking up from the book she was studying.

"It's not like it sounds. I think she was trying to save me from embarrassing myself." Kate smiled. "Jan's a neat lady. She did a lot to help me when Linda died."

Heidi glanced up from the book, remembering what Sandi had told her about Kate and Linda. Linda Sikes had been a close friend of

Kate's in junior high and high school. A troubled young woman, Linda had led Kate far from Church standards. After Kate had decided to make changes in her life, Linda had angrily planned a party similar to others they had enjoyed in the past. Kate refused to have anything to do with it, and the party had gone on without her. Determined to keep her distance from the crowd Linda chased with, Kate had invited Sandi over to watch a video. Later that night, when Kate had driven Sandi home, the two girls narrowly missed a head-on collision with Linda's car. Drunk and high on cocaine, Linda had plowed into a lamppost. She died a short time later at the local hospital.

"Jan sent flowers for Linda's funeral," Kate murmured. "She called later and helped me sort through some difficult feelings. She even came to see me when I moved to Salt Lake last year."

"Sounds like an okay woman."

"She is. I hope she isn't too disappointed if things don't work out with me and Randy. I get the impression she'd like to see something happen. It might, but then there's Mike to consider. How am I ever going to choose between those two?"

Heidi had been well aware of Kate's confusion as she debated between Mike and Randy. Heidi was tempted to tell her that men weren't worth this amount of stress, but refrained, deciding that it was best to not interfere. Kate would learn soon enough that love was usually a complicated mess.

"I'd really appreciate it if you'd come with me," Kate pleaded.

"I don't know—"

"Please?"

Heidi frowned. This was as difficult as trying to reason with Sandi. "Maybe I can work something out," she finally replied.

"Thanks," Kate said, relieved. "I'm not sure I can do this alone. My aunt Paige would've met me there, but she's tied up with a funeral that day."

"A funeral?"

"She's the Relief Society president in her ward," Kate explained.

"Poor woman," Heidi sympathized. "What time do we need to be there?"

"His plane is supposed to come in around ten."

"Okay," Heidi said, thumbing through her personal planner. "You can plan on it."

"Are you sure this won't mess up your schedule?"

"Don't worry. I'll be fine," Heidi assured her. But from the look on Kate's face, she knew it was the beginning of a worry fest.

* * *

Kate glanced at her watch again. It was nearly eleven o'clock. She nervously paced the floor in the waiting area, glancing periodically at the planes that were visible from the large windows.

"Sit down, you're making me tired just watching you," Heidi complained.

"I can't sit still," Kate replied, moving next to a window.

Smiling, Jan Miles squeezed past a crowd of impatient people to stand next to Kate. "He'll be here soon," she soothed.

Kate forced a smile that looked more like a grimace.

Jan slipped an arm around Kate's shoulders. "I want you to know how much we appreciate you being here. It'll mean a lot to Randy."

"I'm glad I was able to come," Kate managed to squeak out. Excusing herself, she walked down the hall to the nearest drinking fountain. Her mouth had never been drier.

"Is Kate all right?" Jan asked, glancing at Heidi.

"I hope so," Heidi said, trying to smile at the tall, attractive woman who had been introduced to her as Randy's mother, Jan. "I don't think I've ever seen her this nervous before. I'll be glad when Randy's plane finally arrives. She's wearing out the carpet."

Jan returned Heidi's smile, glancing down the hall at Kate. "We sure think the world of that young lady."

"I know she thinks a lot of you," Heidi replied. "The other night she told me how much you helped her when that friend of hers died."

"Linda?" Jan softly asked.

"That's the one. I'm glad she had people like you around to help her through it."

"I didn't do that much," Jan protested.

"You'd be surprised. It meant a lot when you kept in touch with her."

Jan flushed with pleasure. "Thanks for telling me. I sometimes wondered if I was doing more harm than good."

"It was definitely good," Heidi responded.

An announcement over the intercom interrupted. The plane Randy was on had experienced technical difficulties and was being held over in Chicago, Illinois. The flight would be delayed at least three hours.

Moaning, Jan moved back to her family.

"Three hours!" Kate exclaimed, staring at Heidi. "I can't handle this."

"Neither can I," Heidi muttered. "Let's go see if we can round up Sandi for lunch."

"Serious?"

"I am. Go tell the Miles clan that we'll return in about three hours."

Sighing, Kate nodded and walked across the crowded room.

* * *

"I'll bet they'll have to replace the carpet where she paced," Heidi teased, glancing across the table at Sandi.

"Not funny," Kate complained.

"Neither is sitting around an airport for hours," Heidi countered in between bites of her eggplant parmigiana.

"Well, I'm glad you two caught up with me," Sandi said before sipping at her Sprite.

"Thank heavens you're free for the next two hours." Heidi's words were heartfelt. "Maybe you can help me keep Kate from falling to pieces."

Ignoring Heidi's comment, Kate picked at the fettuccine with clam sauce on her plate.

"I thought you liked Italian food," Heidi said, looking at Kate. They had come to the Olive Garden for Kate's benefit, thinking it would cheer her up.

"I do. I'm just not very hungry right now."

"Or very good company," Heidi replied, trying to get Kate to smile. She had learned that Kate usually responded well to light-hearted teasing, but today that technique wasn't working.

"Cut her some slack," Sandi said in Kate's defense. "This can't be easy."

"It's not," Kate admitted. "I wish I could get it over with," she said, rising. "Excuse me, I need to find the ladies' room." Turning, she hurried across the crowded restaurant.

"Can you believe her?" Heidi exclaimed. "She's about to be reunited with the man of her dreams and she acts like she's facing the Inquisition!"

"Heidi, it's more complicated than that," Sandi began.

"What's complicated about a reunion like this? Mr. Returned Missionary gets off the plane, Kate walks across the room to shake his hand, and we leave. It sounds pretty simple to me."

"Kate's life has never been simple," Sandi managed to say before biting into a meatball.

"True." Heidi nodded in agreement. Still, she couldn't believe how jittery Kate had been all morning. As she savored another bite of the eggplant parmigiana, Heidi decided it was time she instructed Kate on the finer points of ignoring men. Sometimes it was the best way to deal with them.

An ironic thought popped into mind. That method had worked for Elena. She had ignored Terry right into wedded bliss. Now they were married college students, so in love they didn't realize how poverty-stricken they were. Heidi had bumped into Elena on campus nearly a month ago. Looking radiant, Elena had tried to initiate a conversation. Heidi had replied by walking away.

Heidi was so lost in her thoughts she only half heard Sandi's question.

"What?" she said, aware that Sandi was giving her a curious look.

"I said, how are you two getting along?" Sandi repeated herself patiently.

At first Heidi thought her sister was talking about Elena and she was annoyed that Sandi could read her so well. "What do you mean?" she stalled.

Sandi stared at Heidi a few moments, then said very slowly, "You and Kate—how are you two getting along?"

Relieved, Heidi shrugged. She didn't want another lecture on reestablishing ties with Elena or Terry. "Okay. She doesn't get in my way very often." She smiled at the indignant look on Sandi's face.

"And here she comes now," Sandi said softly, twirling spaghetti on her fork.

"Did I miss any stimulating conversation?" Kate asked brightly as she sat down.

Heidi gave Sandi a mischievous glance. "We were discussing interesting things like when Sandi's going to make me an aunt," she teased.

Sandi swallowed wrong and began to choke and cough. Kate offered a napkin while Heidi reached around and pounded Sandi on the back. "I . . . don't need . . . the Heimlich maneuver—" Sandi sputtered.

"Breathe in, breathe out, breathe in, breathe out," Heidi teased, sitting back in her chair. "See what a great coach I'd make if you decided to go with natural childbirth!"

Sandi glared at her sister. "*If* and *when* I have a baby, Ian'll be my coach!"

"Meaning the rabbit hasn't died yet?" Heidi quipped.

Sipping carefully at her glass of Sprite, Sandi shook her head.

"Okay, just checking. Mom asks me every time I talk to her. She doesn't think you'll tell her if anything develops that direction."

"And she assumes I'll tell you?" Sandi asked, regaining her sense of humor.

"Of course. We've never kept secrets from each other. There was that one time when I eloped to Spain . . . but I'm sure the details would bore you."

Sandi rolled her eyes.

"I don't know about Sandi, but I'd like to hear this story," Kate said.

For nearly thirty minutes, Heidi kept both girls entertained with her imaginary exploits in Europe. Kate laughed so hard she nearly cried and it proved to be the release she needed. After lunch, the three young women went window-shopping at the Crossroads Plaza. All too soon, it was time for Sandi to head back to campus and for Kate and Heidi to return to the airport.

As Heidi drove Kate to the airport, they were both more relaxed. Heidi parked the car, and it didn't take long for the two young women to make their way back to where Randy's family was anxiously pacing.

"Oh, good, you're here. Randy's plane should be landing any minute," Jan said, relieved to see that Kate had returned.

"I wouldn't have missed it," Kate said, fingering an envelope in her jacket pocket. Puzzled she pulled it out for closer inspection and realized it was Mike's last letter.

"Oh great," she groaned. "Just what I need."

"Kate, are you all right?" Jan asked, concerned by how pale Kate had become.

"I'm fine," Kate lied, pushing the letter deep into her jacket pocket. Then, beginning to feel warm, she slipped out of the jacket, folding it over one arm and holding it tightly against her. An airplane moved into sight, capturing everyone's attention.

"That has to be him," Randy's father muttered. "It's about time."

A few minutes later, a thinner, taller version of Randy approached the small group that had gathered. His sisters squealed and rushed forward, nearly knocking him off his feet. Kate stood quietly in the background, content to watch as Randy's family welcomed him home. Her eyes misted as Jan tearfully embraced her son. Then it was her turn. Both reached as if to hug, then remembering certain restrictions, settled for a handshake. "I can't believe I'm finally here," Randy stammered, releasing Kate's hand. He gazed at her, his blue eyes wandering across her face. "You look . . . wonderful," he said, suddenly flushing.

"I . . . you look good, too," Kate murmured, embarrassed by the way he was staring. As she stepped back, an envelope fell to the floor. Before she could retrieve it, Randy scooped it up.

"Thanks," Kate stammered, reaching for Mike's letter.

Randy nodded and was about to hand it back when he noticed the name in the left-hand corner. Elder Mike Jeffries. He stared at the address for several seconds, then handed the letter back to Kate.

"I'm starved! Let's get something to eat," Randy's younger brother, Devin, announced.

"Good idea," Randy replied. "That airplane food was pretty bad this time around." He glanced at Kate who was still blushing.

"Where to, son?" his father asked.

Randy shrugged. "I'm too tired for decisions." He gazed intently at Kate. "Whatever you want is fine with me."

"You and Heidi come with us," Jan urged.

"I couldn't eat another thing," Kate said, unable to meet Randy's piercing gaze. Why hadn't she checked the pockets of her jacket before leaving Provo? But she didn't have anything to hide. Randy knew about Mike, just as Mike knew about Randy. Keith's face came to mind and she saw again that day at Glen Lake. This was getting complicated. *Why don't I fall in love with every guy I meet?* she angrily thought.

Jan was persistent in her invitation. "Come on, Kate. You can order soft drinks or dessert if you'd like, but come with us. It's our treat. You've waited as long as we have."

Kate looked at Randy's mother. She was certain Jan was well aware of the double meaning of that sentence.

"We won't take 'no' for an answer," Jan continued, leading the way.

Heidi shrugged. "You heard the woman," she said.

"I don't want to tie up your whole day," Kate protested.

"Consider it tied. Besides, this has been fun. I enjoy watching you squirm. Let's go," Heidi replied, pushing Kate forward.

CHAPTER 8

The next time Kate saw Randy was a week later—the Sunday morning he was to report his mission to his home ward in Heber City, a small town southeast of Salt Lake City. Heidi volunteered to drive, and the two girls reached Heber nearly an hour before the meeting was scheduled to take place. With Jan's careful instructions, they had no trouble finding the Miles residence, a large white house with contrasting black shutters.

Randy answered the door and awkwardly invited them into the house. Jan laughed, moving behind her son to beckon both girls into the kitchen. "There's someone here I think you'd like to see," she said mysteriously.

"Mom! Dad!" Kate squealed, rushing forward to hug her parents.

"You'd think *she* was the one who'd been gone two years," Randy joked, grinning at his mother.

"Why didn't you tell me you were coming?" Kate demanded, glancing at her mother.

"We thought it would be more fun to surprise you," Sue said, smiling at Kate, then Heidi.

"Well, this is definitely a surprise. When did you come down?" Kate asked.

"Yesterday. It was so late last night when we got to Salt Lake, we decided not to call you."

"And for the record," Greg interrupted, "we did try to call before we left Bozeman yesterday. No one answered the phone." Greg paused. "You were up pretty early for a Saturday."

"Oh, yeah." Acutely aware that Randy and his mother were

watching her, Kate winced, recalling the reason for her absence. "Heidi and I . . . we—"

Sensing Kate's dilemma, Heidi touched her arm and smiled. "Some friends took us up Provo Canyon for a picnic," she explained. "We wanted to go hiking, so we left around six."

"Where are Tyler and Sabrina?" Kate asked, hoping to change the subject. She looked around the large kitchen. Paper plates, cups, and plastic utensils lined one counter. Cakes and plates of cookies filled the others. From the look of things, a huge feast would follow the meeting.

"Your brother and sister wanted to spend some time with your aunt Paige and uncle Stan in Salt Lake," Sue told Kate, who tried not to show her disappointment. In an instant, her expression changed to one of surprised joy as she heard a familiar voice.

"So it's a good thing we came, too." Paige stepped up behind Kate and wrapped her arms around Kate's middle, giving her niece a tight squeeze. "How's my girl?"

In response Kate whirled around to hug her aunt, who had been like a second mother for the past couple of years. Kate hadn't seen Paige in weeks and was delighted that her favorite aunt had decided to come for this occasion.

Not to be left out, seven-year-old Sabrina ran around Paige into the crowded kitchen and threw herself into Kate's arms. "I've missed you," she said, clinging to Kate as her brother Tyler saluted Kate from across the room.

"I've missed you too, Sabrina," Kate said, returning Tyler's salute and Sabrina's hug. "I still can't believe you guys made it down for this. I thought Dad had to work."

"I was able to trade for this weekend," Greg replied, resting his elbow on Tyler's shoulder. He glanced at Randy, irritated by the way the young man kept looking at his daughter. The main reason he had come to Heber to see for himself what was going on with Randy and Kate. He knew Kate wasn't ready for a serious relationship and wanted to drive home the point that Randy was to give her some space. There was only one problem—Sue had made him promise he wouldn't interfere. He would have to subtly share his personal feelings in a way that couldn't be deciphered by Sue, and yet would be perfectly clear to Randy. He had already telegraphed part of that message in the hearty handshake he had exchanged with the young man upon arrival. Now, he did his best to let Randy know he was continuously watching his every move. He was delighted to see that his probing gaze was enough to cause Randy a certain amount of discomfiture.

At one point Randy tripped, bumping into a plate of cookies that spilled all over the floor. Greg laughed, but Paige and Sue quickly moved to clean up the mess as Randy escaped down the hall. Shaking her head, Jan grabbed a broom out of a nearby closet. "He must be more nervous about speaking today than I thought," she murmured, sweeping up the crumbs from her new vinyl floor.

Sue held the dustpan for Jan and gave Greg a meaningful look. She was well aware of what her husband was doing and she planned to speak to him about it as soon as she could get him alone. Her chance came a few minutes later when the doorbell rang. As Jan rushed to answer, Sue leaned close to Greg and whispered a few well-chosen words. Although he nodded contritely, he had every intention of following through with his plan to make Randy Miles as nervous as possible today.

A few minutes later, Jan brought in another salad made by a neighbor for the dinner that would follow sacrament meeting. "Where in the world am I going to put this?" she complained, opening the fridge that was already filled to capacity.

"Let me help," Paige offered. "I've become pretty good at stuffing fridges."

As Paige moved to assist Jan, Sue led her daughter from the kitchen. "Let's go outside for a bit," Sue suggested.

Kate nodded and followed her mother out of the house.

"They have a nice big home here, but I'm afraid I was feeling claustrophobic with everyone gathering in the kitchen like that," Sue explained as they wandered into the backyard. Tall birch trees and assorted fruit trees provided ample shade for the long banquet tables that had been set up and papered for the occasion. "Besides, I wanted to get you alone for a few minutes now that your dad has promised to behave."

"Dad?"

Sue smiled at her daughter. "Let's just say he's exhibiting signs of being an overprotective parent." She shook her head. "I don't know what I'm going to do with him. As far as he's concerned, you're still his little girl. You probably always will be."

Kate glanced back at the house. "Is it safe to leave him in there alone with Randy?"

"Stan and Paige said they'd keep an eye on things," Sue replied, moving toward one of the banquet tables. Selecting a metal folding chair, she sat down and motioned for Kate to do the same. "Let's talk. Phone calls only reveal so much. How did things really go at the airport?"

"Okay, I guess," Kate replied, sitting beside her mother.

"You guess?"

"It's hard to explain—like today, it doesn't seem real."

Sue nodded. "You seem a little dazed."

"It's because I am."

"I see," Sue replied, studying the worried expression on her daughter's face. "What's bothering you?"

"Everyone's expecting so much." Kate stared down at her hands.

"Honey, you don't need to make any major decisions right away."

"Promise?" Kate met her mother's concerned gaze. "Don't get me wrong—I think the world of Randy's family—I care for Randy, but it's all happening too fast. I don't think I'm ready for this."

"I seem to remember another young lady who felt this same way nearly a year ago," Sue said, thinking of Sandi. "Things worked out quite well for her."

"That's just it, Mom. Everyone assumes Randy and I will go off and get married now!" Kate exclaimed.

"Not everyone," Sue answered quietly.

"Yeah, well, it's intimidating to see Randy's family combined with mine. I mean—I'm glad you guys came down, but can you understand what I'm trying to say?"

Sue smiled. "Yes. That's why I was hesitant to come, but when Jan called to invite us, I felt like it would give me a chance to touch base with you."

"Maybe you can help me figure things out. It's already so crazy." Kate took a deep breath of the crisp fall air. It was a nice day, but a bit chilly. Noticing her mother's jacket, Kate wished she had thought to bring one. "Earlier, Heidi was covering for me. The reason you couldn't reach me yesterday—Heidi and I were on a double date."

"Heidi's dating again?" Sue asked, surprised.

"Yesterday was her first date since Terry and Elena . . . well, you know."

Sue nodded. "This is terrific—Harriet's been so worried."

"She has every reason to be. Heidi informed me it would also be her last."

"Why?"

Kate shrugged. "To quote Heidi, 'All men are scum!'"

Sue winced. She had thought Heidi's mother was exaggerating when Harriet said her daughter would never recover from what Terry had done. "He trampled all over that girl's heart! Why for two cents I'd . . ." Sue smiled, remembering the bodily harm Harriet had threatened against Terry. That young man would do well to steer clear of Bozeman and Harriet Kearns.

Caught up in her own thoughts, Kate absently smoothed her grey skirt. She had pushed up the sleeves of her pink sweater earlier that morning, but now she pulled them down again to cover her bare arms. She hoped it would be warmer during the dinner. "I thought a date would be good for Heidi, but she wasn't ready. She seemed pretty miserable most of the day. The guy she was out with kept trying to put his arm around her to help her up the trail. I thought Heidi was going to deck him. If she'd loosened up, she would've enjoyed it. I was having so much fun—"

"With?" Sue interrupted, suddenly curious. Had Kate met someone else—was that why she was acting so nervous?

"Evan Hillier. He's in our student ward. He's also a law student so he's in a lot of Heidi's classes. Between the two of us, we were able to talk Heidi into doubling with a friend of his."

"Evan, huh?"

Kate pulled a face at her mother. "Don't make more out of it than there is. Evan's a neat guy, we had a blast—but I got the impression he was more interested in Heidi. He asked me all kinds of questions about her."

"Oh? And what kind of impression did you make on Evan?"

"Mom," Kate complained, blushing. "Yesterday was just for fun and yet, today I feel guilty. I stood there in Jan's kitchen and panicked because I thought she or Randy might find out I had dated someone else. Why?"

"Good question. Why do you think you have to hide this from Randy or Jan?"

Kate shook her head. "I don't know," she moaned. "It's not like Randy and I are engaged. We haven't even had a chance to talk. In fact, Randy seems . . . I don't know—distant." She remembered the look on his face after he had picked up Mike's letter. The rest of the afternoon he had been polite but reserved, like today.

"The best advice I can give is to suggest that you take your time. You know how to get answers—get on your knees. Then be honest with yourself and Randy. Neither of you can expect to pick up where you left off. Get to know each other again."

"Kate, Sue, we're ready to leave!" Paige hollered out the kitchen window.

"Be right there," Sue called back. She smiled at Kate. "Now, should we go listen to Randy report his mission?" Sue stood and waited for Kate, slipping an arm around her daughter's waist as they walked toward the house.

"How long are you staying?"

"We'll head back home tomorrow," Sue replied as they rounded the corner to join the crowd of family and friends. "We thought we'd stay in Provo tonight, if that's okay."

"You bet it is," Kate said excitedly. "You'll be staying with us?"

"Actually, we borrowed Stan and Paige's motor home. You probably didn't notice it out front; we had to park it down the street. We thought it would be easier. The way you described your apartment, it didn't sound like there was room for you and Heidi, let alone four more."

"This'll be great," Kate said. "I'll tell Heidi."

Sue smiled as Kate hurried forward to catch up with Heidi. Her gaze shifted to Randy. He looked as bewildered as her daughter. Sighing, Sue walked over to the minivan Stan and Paige had brought down.

"Stan said they have room if we want to ride to the church with them. That way I don't have to make a fool of myself trying to park the motor home again," Greg said, climbing into the minivan.

"Sounds like a plan," Sue replied, noticing that Sabrina and Tyler were already seated in the back.

"Speaking of plans, are there any yet between those two," Stan asked, pointing to Kate and Randy.

"Stan," Paige scolded.

"We all want to know the same thing," Stan defended himself. "Right, Greg?"

Greg nodded and his eyes narrowed as he glared out the window at Randy. Just what made this young man think he was worthy of his daughter? Tall and skinny with no definite plans for the future. What kind of a catch was that?

"There won't be any major announcements for a while," Sue said, easing up inside the minivan.

"Problems?" Paige asked.

"No. They need time to get reacquainted. I don't think either of them is ready for anything too serious right now."

"Good," Greg muttered.

"What?" Sue asked.

"Uh . . . good quality fabric on these seats back here," Greg stammered, patting the car seat.

Sue gave her husband a pained look. *Take your time, Kate,* she thought to herself as Stan started the minivan. *It'll make both of our lives easier.*

CHAPTER 9

Making one last note to herself, Heidi quickly gathered up her books and stuffed them inside of her backpack. As she started to walk across the classroom, someone stepped out in front of her.

"Where are you headed now?" Evan Hillier asked, slipping his own backpack onto one shoulder.

Heidi shrugged, avoiding Evan's inquisitive gaze, much too aware of his tall, muscular build. Evan had never made her nervous before, but since the double-date up Provo Canyon, she had found herself almost drawn to him, something she wasn't comfortable with. They had been friends for over a year, but there had never been anything of a serious nature between them. And yet, for some reason, she had felt jealousy pangs on the hike when Evan had held Kate's hand. For an instant, she had wanted to scream at Kate. Kate who had done nothing wrong. Why should she care if Kate dated Evan? Evan was nothing more that a friend. It's not like he had ever asked her out.

"If you don't have any plans, I thought we might swing by the Cougareat for a bite of lunch. I'm starved. I didn't eat breakfast," Evan suggested.

Heidi lifted an eyebrow. If he had offered this same invitation weeks ago, she might have considered it. But now things were different. Evan had asked Kate out first. Kate obviously liked Evan. Heidi wanted nothing to do with another triangular relationship. "I need to study," she said sharply.

Evan chuckled. "You study enough for three or four people. Take a break," he said. "You deserve it."

Heidi shook her head. "I'm sorry, Evan. I have too much going on right now. I don't have any time to waste. I'll see you later."

Evan stared after Heidi as she walked away. It had taken him months to finally work up enough nerve to ask her out and she had turned him down flat. He had wanted to date her last year before Terry had entered the picture, but Evan hadn't moved quickly enough. He had hated seeing how her breakup with Terry had affected her, how she had withdrawn into a shell of self-pity and pain. Evan had hoped to ease her out by keeping things as casual as possible, finally arranging the double-date a few weeks ago to see if Heidi was ready to date again. Unfortunately, the double-date he planned had backfired.

Originally, he and his friend Jess had decided to ask Heidi and Kate out together. Unfortunately, when Jess had made the call, overcome by his nervousness he had asked for the wrong girl—Heidi. When Heidi had balked at his invitation, Jess had desperately handed the phone to Evan, who had to think quickly to salvage the moment. Asking for Kate, Evan had easily secured her cooperation and the day up Provo Canyon had been the end result. The only problem—Evan had wanted to spend the day with Heidi, not Kate. Since that day, Heidi had been cold and aloof, something he had hoped to remedy this afternoon.

Evan winced as he recalled her words. *I don't have any time to waste?* Was that how she envisioned a date with him?

* * *

"Well, hello there," a voice called across the room. Kate looked around, surprised. She had been wandering around the college bookstore looking for a BYU souvenir to send to Tyler for his birthday. Finally she'd gone downstairs to check out the new shirts that had just come in. She recognized Evan's voice immediately.

"How's it goin'?" Evan asked, walking across the store to stand next to Kate. She noticed that he looked around, as if expecting to see someone else he knew. Kate thought she knew who he was looking for.

"I'm fine. And you?" she answered with a smile.

"Never better," he said brightly. "Where's Heidi?"

Kate shook her head. "I haven't seen her since this morning."

"Actually, I've been meaning to call you," he said. "What would you think about going out to dinner Friday night?"

Kate smiled wistfully. "I'd like to . . . but—"

Evan smacked his forehead playfully. "Oh, that's right, your missionary came home. Heidi mentioned something about that in class the other day. How's he doing?"

"Randy?"

"Is that his name?"

"Yeah. Randy Miles."

"Don't know him, but he must be an okay guy to know someone as great as you."

Kate blushed.

"Has he adjusted to the real world yet?" Evan asked, moving closer to Kate to allow another student to pass behind them in the narrow aisle.

Kate frowned. "He's . . . getting there."

Evan nodded sympathetically. "I remember how hard it was for me. You're on such a spiritual high in the mission field, then wham, you have to come back to earth. I don't envy what he's going through at all."

Kate looked at Evan curiously. "You had a hard time adapting?"

Evan laughed. "My parents thought I was going crazy. So did I until I talked to other RMs. We all make the transition eventually. One way or another."

"What do you mean by that?" Kate asked, gazing at Evan intently.

Evan looked thoughtful. "When you're officially released, it's like going through a grieving process. And Satan's right there to make it as difficult as possible. If you're not strong enough, you can crash pretty hard. Fortunately, most of us come through just fine." He smiled. "See, I'm living proof."

"Yes, you are," Kate murmured, glancing up at Evan, who was much taller than she was. It seemed he was as strong spiritually as he was physically, something she had observed on the hike as he had helped her up the steep trail, much as Keith had done last summer. Keith, with his soft brown eyes . . . his broad shoulders, and . . . what was she thinking? Why did Keith keep coming to mind? He hadn't even answered any of her letters, the jerk. Kate frowned again, then realized Evan was speaking.

". . . so I wouldn't be too worried about Randy. What he's going through is normal."

Kate nodded. "Thanks for explaining this to me. Randy's definitely not himself. I keep thinking it's me, but maybe—"

"He'll be all right," Evan said, glancing at his watch. "But I'd better get cruisin' or I won't be. I'm meeting my roommates for dinner tonight at the Sizzler."

"Isn't that expensive cuisine for a college student?" Kate asked.

Evan grinned. "Conner, one of my roommates, got engaged last weekend. We thought we'd take him out to mourn the demise of his bachelorhood," he explained as he started up the stairs. "By the way, I understand if you'd rather not go out Friday," he added, peering down over the stairway.

"I'd like to, Evan, but I'd better not—not until I understand how things are between Randy and me."

"Okay," Evan sighed. "Hey, it was great seeing you again. Tell Heidi hello for me," he said, bounding up to the main floor.

"Dang it," Kate muttered. Frustrated, she gripped the shirt rack in front of her. There had been no word from Randy since the Sunday she had gone to Heber, and they hadn't had a chance to be alone that day. Most of their conversations had been about Ireland and his adventures as a missionary. They had parted with another handshake. Even Jan had been more affectionate than that. The woman had nearly squeezed her in two as she and Heidi had prepared to leave.

"Keep in touch," Jan had insisted. "Come see us soon."

That was the last contact she had had with the Miles family. She suspected Jan would call before Randy did.

"Maybe he's still upset about seeing Mike's letter," Kate had theorized with Heidi earlier in the week. "I know that didn't go over too well."

"Don't worry about it. It's his problem—his loss."

Part of that was true. It would be his loss, but it was also her problem. She had no idea what to expect, if anything. Trying to distract herself, Kate wandered around the bookstore, closely examining several items before settling on one of the first shirts she had looked at. Imagining Tyler's reaction lifted her spirits briefly—he was an avid BYU fan. But as she slowly made her way home, depression threatened to settle back in. "Maybe I'm the problem," she mumbled. "I don't know what I want." Her thoughts occupied her until she reached the apartment.

"It's about time," Heidi exclaimed, looking up from her notes. Rubbing her eyes, she stretched, trying to eliminate a few kinks. "I'm starved and as I recall, it's your turn to fix dinner."

Kate glanced at her watch. It was nearly six-thirty. "Sorry. I didn't realize it was so late. I swung by the bookstore after I got off work." She was glad she had picked something simple to fix tonight—her version of the classic tuna-noodle casserole. Heidi had seemed to like it well enough when Kate prepared it a few weeks earlier, so she had decided to try it again.

"You went to the bookstore?" Heidi prompted.

"I was trying to find something for Tyler's birthday. Think he'll like this?" Kate held out a bright blue shirt with white trim and the BYU Cougars logo on the front and back.

"He'll love it," Heidi assured her.

"I hope so. I didn't know what else to get him." Kate set the shirt on the kitchen table.

"Is something wrong?" Heidi asked, seeing the troubled expression on Kate's face.

Kate sighed. "I ran into Evan Hillier."

Heidi stared at Kate. Now what?

"He asked me out."

Heidi lifted her eyebrows, amazed by Evan's audacity. So, if one roommate turned him down, he'd just ask the *other*. *Were all men like Terry?* she wondered. Waiting for Kate to continue, Heidi gripped her pencil so hard it nearly broke in two.

"I told him I can't go out with anyone until I know where I stand with Randy," Kate said, unaware of Heidi's inner conflict.

"I think the fact that Randy hasn't given you the time of day is a pretty good hint," Heidi sharply replied. She forced Evan from her mind as she remembered again the private scene she had observed the day Randy had reported his mission. Heidi was sure Kate knew nothing about what she had seen. In Heidi's opinion, Randy belonged on the same list as Terry.

Although Kate was getting used to Heidi's cynicism, she was startled at her bluntness. "Evan said I need to give Randy time, that he's going through an adjustment period," she said somewhat defensively.

Heidi frowned. "Evan—" she paused, unsure of what to say. Taking a deep breath, she tried again. "Randy might be trying to adjust to the real world, but that doesn't give him the right to make you miserable. Forget Randy and forget Evan!" Startled by how protective she suddenly felt, Heidi looked away from the younger girl. She didn't want to see Kate hurt and it was obvious that's exactly what would happen if Kate got involved with either guy. "I'm sure you'll meet someone else who'll make you forget all about those two idiots," she said in a softer tone.

"What's wrong with Evan?" Kate asked, confused. She had thought Heidi liked him. "We had a lot of fun on that picnic up Provo Canyon."

"I know," Heidi stiffly replied. "Look, trust me on this one. Evan's not your type. Men like him think only of themselves! They don't care who they hurt."

Giving Heidi an exasperated look, Kate moved into the hall on her way to the bedroom. Just then the phone rang. Turning, Kate hurried back into the living room and grabbed the phone on the second ring. "Hello?"

"Uh . . . hi. Is Kate there?"

"This is Kate."

"Oh," a deep male voice nervously laughed.

"Randy?" Kate guessed.

"Yeah. How're you doin'?"

"Fine. Good," Kate stammered. She turned her back to Heidi who was making wild gestures and pulling faces at her.

"Uh, I was wondering if maybe you'd like to meet somewhere on campus tomorrow. I'm coming down to get things set for next semester."

"Sure," Kate replied, breathless. "Where do you want to meet?"

"How about the administration building? When do you get off work?"

"I'll be off at five."

"Why don't I meet you then? We could pick up a burger or something. Maybe hit a movie."

"Okay," Kate agreed. "Sounds fun."

"Uh, yeah. Okay. Well, guess I'll see you tomorrow. Bye."

"Bye," Kate said excitedly. Grinning, she hung up the phone.

"Go ahead, do the dance of joy," Heidi said, shaking her head at the elated look on her roommate's face. "Just don't expect me to join in."

* * *

Randy set the phone down on the counter. "There, that ought to make you happy," he said to his mother.

"Randy!" Jan scolded. "I didn't insist that you call her. I was only hinting that you ought to keep in touch with her. That poor girl has no idea where she stands with you."

Randy nodded. "I'm not sure where she stands either. We drifted apart while I was gone. We've both changed. She's dated other guys—" He sank into a recliner.

"That's no reason to hold a grudge. She's only been serious about one of them and he's on a mission now," Jan countered, settling on the couch across from her son.

"Which means it's time I make my move?"

"Only if you want to," Jan said, irritated with her son's attitude. "I don't know why you're dragging your feet, Kate's a wonderful girl."

"I know. I could probably fall for her again pretty easy."

"What's wrong with that?" Jan asked, gazing at her son.

"I'm not sure it's what I want," Randy answered. "Or what Kate wants," he added, remembering the letter she had dropped. What was that anyway, a hint? If she had done it to stir things up inside of him, it had certainly worked. He had come home prepared to start fresh. To date a lot of girls and wait until Laurie came home from the mission field. Until that day at the airport, Randy had been convinced that he and Kate were through. Seeing her in that setting was hard enough—seeing her there with a letter from another guy had been devastating. Feelings he had thought were long dead had revived. This new Kate was more mature, more beautiful than before. And worst of all, this Kate reminded him of Laurie.

"Randy? Have you heard anything I've said in the last five minutes?" Jan asked, shaking her head at her son. "What is going on with you?"

"Mom, I met someone while I was in Ireland," Randy said, confessing the one thing he had hoped to keep secret for a while.

"What?!" Jan said, alarmed.

"It wasn't like that. I was a good boy," Randy hurriedly explained, grinning at his mother. "We met at a zone conference. Then, before I came home, she transferred into my district." He pulled out his wallet and took out the picture he had cut to fit inside one of the plastic protectors. Rising from the chair, he handed the picture to Jan. "Her name is Laurie," he said, sitting down on the couch beside his mother.

Jan stared at the attractive blonde.

"She'll be coming home in February."

"Where's home?" Jan asked.

"Boise, Idaho."

"Oh," Jan said, feeling like the wind had just been knocked out of her. She had sensed something had been holding Randy back. Now she knew what—or rather, who—it had been.

"You'd like her, Mom. She's a lot like Kate. Fun, spunky, but she has a spiritual side, too. There's just something about her—"

"You really care for this girl, don't you?" Jan's concern for her son was evident on her face.

Randy slowly nodded.

"And Kate?"

"I don't know."

Breathing out slowly, Jan handed the picture back to Randy. She stared out the front room window into the darkened street for several minutes. Finally turning, she glanced at Randy. "I have one request. Whatever you do, be honest with Kate. I don't want to see her hurt."

"Give me some credit, Mom," Randy replied, offering a wan smile. "I've decided to go out with Kate a couple of times—see if anything develops. If it doesn't, I'll see where I stand with Laurie when she comes home."

"Does Laurie know how you feel about her?"

Randy blushed furiously. "We didn't talk about it. There was some kind of connection between us, only I'm not sure she felt the same thing."

"I see." Jan gazed thoughtfully at her son. "What happens if you blow things with Kate now because of Laurie and in February you discover that Laurie wants nothing to do with you?"

"It'll all work out somehow," Randy assured his mother. "Who knows, maybe there's a girl out there I haven't even met yet. Maybe she's the woman of my dreams."

"It sounds like you have enough girl trouble as it is," Jan chided, disappointed at his reaction to Kate. She had been convinced that the two were perfect for each other.

"Hey, Mom," Randy said, breaking into her thoughts. "How about we worry about more important things right now, like, what's for supper?"

"What am I going to do with you?" Jan sighed.

"Feed me," Randy said, doing his imitation of the man-eating plant from one of his favorite shows, *Little Shop of Horrors*. Jan was forced to laugh, as she always did when her son reminded her of the bizarre musical she had seen at his insistence.

"Oh, all right. If you'll help, we'll grill up some hamburgers," Jan said, unable to hide her disappointment over her son's confession.

Randy slid a comforting arm around his mother's shoulders. "Deal," he agreed. "And quit worrying. I promise, everything will work out fine."

CHAPTER 10

As Kate walked out of her office, she glanced around for signs of Randy. Disappointed, she looked at her watch. It was fifteen minutes after five.

"Sorry I'm late," Randy said breathlessly, running up behind her. He self-consciously smoothed his thick black hair back into place. "It took longer than I thought to find an apartment." The truth was, he had signed a lease earlier that afternoon. Since then, he had been pacing around campus, trying to figure out what to say to Kate.

"You found one?" she replied, relieved by his appearance. It wasn't like him to be late; the Randy she had once known had been very punctual.

"What?"

"An apartment?" Kate prompted.

Randy slowly nodded. "It's in the same complex I was in before. I checked everywhere else first, but my old place still offered a better deal. I'm into saving money wherever I can these days."

"Same here," Kate responded, struggling to make conversation. "I . . . uh . . . can't believe how much money I've spent on college this semester. Tuition, books, food, rent—"

"Tell me about it," Randy shyly grinned, glancing at Kate, then at the sidewalk. Her look of concern gave him a warm feeling inside, as did the outfit she was wearing. The mint green blouse tucked inside of a pair of dark green dress pants revealed the soft contours of her body, affecting him in ways he wasn't sure he liked. His heart raced, and he felt like a sixteen-year-old on his first date. "So, where would you like to go, courtesy of a poor college student?"

"You say," Kate said, forcing a smile. She wondered if Jan had coerced Randy into this. The only other guy who had acted this nervous around her was Lyle Jennings, although since his experience with Brian Kearns and friends, Lyle avoided her whenever possible. Now, why was she getting the feeling that Randy was frightened of her, too? Sighing, she wiggled into the jacket she had brought with her. The atmosphere suddenly felt very cool.

"How about Shoney's? 'Good food for a decent price,'" Randy said, imitating the commercial. "It's on University Avenue, so we won't have to go too far, which is a plus considering how starved I am."

"Sounds fine," Kate replied, falling in step with Randy as they walked to his car.

During dinner, their conversation drifted toward general topics that included the weather, more of Randy's missionary experiences, Kate's major, Randy's college plans, and the successful season the Cougar football team had been having. Randy found he couldn't bring up the two subjects he really wanted to discuss: Mike and Laurie. Sensing that the timing wasn't right, he made several remarks about the food, but there was only so much a person could say about a dinner salad and chicken-fried steak. Both were relieved to finally leave the restaurant.

After dinner, they drove around trying to find a good movie. Most were rated PG-13 or R. Deciding against that option, Randy drove around BYU, then past the Missionary Training Center. "That place brings back memories," he said, a distant look on his face.

"Good or bad?" Kate asked, figuring she was in for another in a series of missionary experiences.

"Good. I had a hard time adapting to the schedule, but it grows on you. After that, it was great."

Kate stared out the window on her side of the car. "I'm glad you enjoyed your mission," she said quietly. It was obvious he had enjoyed it more than being with her. But maybe it was better this way. If there was nothing left between them, she could quit worrying about it. She had endured too many sleepless nights the past couple of weeks. It would almost be a relief to officially cut the ties. Then she could focus on other things, like getting her degree. She closed her eyes as Mike's face came to mind. Two years. Would he come back as changed and distant as Randy?

"Is Mike enjoying his mission?" Randy asked, finally taking the initiative to find out something about the other man in Kate's life.

Startled, Kate opened her eyes. This was what she had been expecting all night and she still wasn't prepared. "He is now," she stammered. "He didn't at first. After he arrived in Montreal, he ended up with an ornery companion," she nervously rambled. "He was always on Mike's case about something. And when it came to tracting, this guy didn't want to put forth any effort. Mike was so relieved to be transferred to Quebec. It's where he wanted to be anyway. And he gets to use the French he learned in the MTC."

"Good," Randy answered, turning the car toward the temple. "Do you hear from him a lot?"

Kate glanced at Randy, certain he was referring to the letter he had seen. "Randy, about that day at the airport—I had no idea one of Mike's letters was in my jacket pocket."

At this reminder, Randy frowned. Seeing that letter had bothered him more than he was willing to admit. "No problem," he said aloud. "Do you hear from him very often?" he repeated.

"He sends about two letters a month—unlike someone else I could mention." *Touché, Elder Miles*, she silently thought. *Two can play at this game!* She could be as direct as he was.

Randy glanced at Kate, unsure of the tone of her voice. She sounded almost angry. "I was a busy man. I had things to do, places to go, people to see," he said, trying to defend himself. "But, I will admit, I didn't think about the time lapses between my letters until I noticed the ones between yours."

"When you don't get an answer for two or three months, it dampens the letter-writing enthusiasm," she replied, still smarting from that past frustration.

"Among other things," Randy murmured, glancing at Kate. Pulling into the temple parking lot, he shut off the engine. "I hope you don't mind. I like coming here," he said, gazing at the temple.

"No, that's fine." Kate stiffened. This was where Ian had brought Sandi on one of their first dates. Convinced that Randy wasn't after a romantic setting, she wondered what he was up to. Was this a good location to officially end a relationship?

"I'll be honest. I've been more nervous tonight than I have been in a long time," Randy admitted. "I mean, we did have something special for a while. Then, I went on a mission, you went back to Bozeman—things have changed for both of us." He paused. "Maybe it didn't seem like it for you, but I can't believe how fast two years went by."

Kate slowly nodded.

"It's been an adjustment, coming home. Seeing everyone again." He paused, searching for the right words. "It threw me when I saw you at the airport. I wasn't expecting that."

"Your mom invited me."

"I heard. I'm glad you were there. But I didn't know how to react. Especially when you dropped that letter."

Kate gripped the armrest, but refrained from commenting. Randy tried to read the expression on her face, but it was impossible in the darkened interior of the car. "I never meant to do anything to upset you," she finally said.

"I know. But later, when all of your family showed up the day I reported my mission—"

"Your mom called them," Kate interrupted.

Randy nodded. "She wants it to work out between us," he sighed. "My problem is—I don't know if there *is* anything between us."

Kate flinched. Randy certainly wasn't shy about getting to the heart of the matter.

"On my mission—right at first—I couldn't quit thinking about you. Especially after your friend died. I knew that would be rough. I kept your picture on the nightstand by my bed. It was the first thing I looked at in the morning and the last thing at night. The trouble was, I was so caught up in worrying about how you were doing, I wasn't a very effective missionary. Then I attended a special missionary conference. Our mission president gave us a list of things to do to get more in tune with the Spirit. One suggestion was to forget about the people at home—especially girlfriends. He said we couldn't do the Lord's work if we were too preoccupied with what was going on at home. So, I set your picture in my suitcase and replaced it with one of the Savior. After that, my letters to you and home weren't a priority. Ask my mom. Her letters to me were full of hints about my inability to keep in touch." He had been looking out the window as he spoke and now he shifted his gaze to Kate. "So, you see, you weren't the only one I sent short notes to whenever I found the time."

"I tried to understand," Kate replied. "But there were times when I thought you didn't care anymore."

"That wasn't it at all," Randy said quietly.

"I'm glad—I don't want to lose you as a friend."

"Serious?"

Kate slowly nodded.

"What about Mike?"

"I'm not sure," she sighed. "We were very close for a while."

"Close?" Randy asked, trying not to sound as jealous as he suddenly felt.

Glancing at Randy, Kate wondered how to explain her relationship with Mike. She remembered their first date—the senior prom, and all that had followed. There had been a strong physical attraction between them, but there had also been something more. Mike had helped her realize it didn't matter what other people thought, something she still struggled with. He had stood up for her when everyone else had pointed accusing fingers and had treated her like a queen during a time when her self-esteem had hit rock bottom.

"In your letters it sounded like you two dated quite a bit," Randy said, drawing Kate back to the conversation.

"We did. He's a very good friend."

"Friend?" Randy repeated, wondering what her definition of that word was.

"For a while we were pretty serious, but so much has happened since then—I don't know what I'm feeling anymore." As she envisioned Mike, she was disturbed by an image of Keith. Remembering again the day at Glen Lake, she shivered. "I don't know how to figure it all out."

"Same here," Randy said, flipping on the dashboard light. They both blinked to adjust to the glare. Reaching for his wallet, Randy took out the picture of Laurie, gazed at it for several seconds, then handed it to Kate.

"Who's this?" Kate asked, staring at the picture in her hand. This girl was gorgeous. And from the look of adoration on his face, she gathered it was someone pretty important in his life.

"Laurie Spaulding. A sister missionary I met six months ago."

"Oh? She looks . . . nice," Kate said, handing the picture back to Randy. It hit home that she wasn't the only one who had made new friends during the past couple of years.

"She is," he smiled. "She reminds me a lot of you," he added, putting the picture back in his wallet.

"Oh, really?" Kate murmured.

Randy nodded. He reached to flip off the light, then thought better of it. He needed to see how all of this was affecting Kate, to see the emotions in her face. There was a lot riding on her reaction. "I guess that's why I finally called you. I need to know if that's why she attracted me, or if it's something else."

"Like what?" Kate asked, uncomfortable with the way he was studying her face. What was he looking for?

"I'm not sure, but I need to find out if I'm still carrying a torch inside for a certain young lady with long auburn hair." He continued to gaze steadily at Kate. All night he had tried to ignore the attraction he still felt for her. Past feelings were returning with a vengeance and he now felt a sudden urge to kiss her.

Recognizing the look in his eye, Kate blushed. "Randy, I'll warn you, I'm not sure what I'm feeling for you. Two years ago, there would have been no question. But now . . . like you said, things have changed."

"Have they?" he murmured, leaning forward. Kate froze, unsure of herself, unsure of Randy. Mike's face came to mind, adding to the chaos she felt. She wasn't sure she was ready for this, but somehow couldn't pull away. Taking advantage of her confusion, Randy hesitantly kissed her. He pulled back, clearly shaken by the experience.

Dazed, Kate blinked. How could she feel something this intense with Randy when a part of her still loved Mike? She didn't have time to dwell on the question. Grinning, Randy decided to verify what they had both felt. Flipping off the light to enhance the romantic setting, he slid close, kissing her again. This time, Kate was the one to pull away.

"I think we're in trouble here," she said quietly.

"We will be if I don't take you home," he teased, starting the car. They drove in silence to the apartment.

"So, what does all of this mean?" Kate asked when Randy pulled up behind Heidi's car.

"It means we take things slowly. Then there's no pressure. That's what was wrong at the airport and later—the day I spoke in my ward in Heber," he said confidently. Opening his car door, he walked around to Kate's side and helped her out onto the sidewalk. He shyly reached for her hand as they walked to the side door that led into the apartment.

As they stood in front of the door, Randy gazed at Kate, thoughts of Laurie passing through his mind. Blocking them out, he forced himself to remember the night he and Kate first met.

Kate wondered at the odd expression on his face. "What is it?" she asked.

"I was thinking about the first time I saw you," he said, remembering her rebellious anger. Unamused by a family vacation, Kate had hated the idea of eating dinner at the Bar J Ranch in Jackson, Wyoming. Randy had been working there for the summer and had thoroughly enjoyed antagonizing Kate. Convinced she was a spoiled brat, he had seen to it that she was humiliated during the dinner show. She had been spunky enough to track him down and in the process of letting off some steam, had slapped a board, firmly embedding several splinters in her hand. "There were plenty of fireworks that night, too," Randy commented, grinning now at Kate.

Kate blushed, the events of that night playing through her mind. She remembered the horrible scene with her mother. Catching Randy and Kate alone in a cabin, Sue had assumed the worst and had indignantly tried to *rescue* her daughter, unwilling to believe that Randy had taken Kate there to remove a handful of splinters. That incident had led to several heated arguments, including the one that had taken place in Salt Lake City, minutes before Kate had been hit by a car. After the accident, Randy had come by several times to visit while Kate lingered in a coma. He had also come to see her after she had recovered. Now, as she glanced up into Randy's face, she wondered if this was the start of a new stage in their relationship.

"We've shared a lot of wonderful things, including tonight," Randy said, echoing her thoughts. Leaning down, he kissed her, then deciding it was time to leave, began to walk away. "I'll call you in a day or two."

"I'd like that," Kate replied.

Randy grinned, waved, and disappeared into the darkness.

* * *

"I thought you didn't kiss on first dates," Heidi grumbled, rolling onto her side to glare at Kate.

"I don't. This wasn't our first. We had a couple before he left on his mission."

"Oh, I see," Heidi sarcastically replied, stretching out on her bed. "Well, if you can make it down to earth, shut off the light. I have an early class in the morning."

Kate glanced at her roommate, then obediently flipped off the light. She reached for one of her history books and walked out into the small kitchen to study, knowing she was too excited to sleep. But she couldn't study either. Finally shutting the book, she decided to go outside and admire the stars.

* * *

"So, how did things go," Jan demanded, as she tied her robe around her.

"The car ran well. I didn't have a bit of trouble," Randy teased.

"Not the car," Jan said impatiently.

"Oh. The apartment. I'm all set."

"Randy!"

"My college registration is pretty much taken care of, too."

Jan playfully slapped her son on the shoulder. "What about Kate?"

"What about Kate?" he teased.

"I'm counting to ten," Jan warned.

"Okay, all right. The truth is, I think there are some definite possibilities with that young lady."

Jan breathed a sigh of relief. "Did you tell her about Laurie?" she asked, looking worried again.

"You'd be proud of me. I did just what you said. I told Kate everything."

"And?"

"She leveled with me about Mike," Randy said, twirling his set of keys on one finger.

"Good. You two needed to clear the air between you. This is a wonderful start."

"If that kiss was any indication—"

"You kissed her?" Jan exclaimed.

"Settle down. Too much excitement isn't good for someone your age."

Ignoring her son's poor attempt at humor, Jan dragged him into the kitchen to pump him for more details.

CHAPTER 11

"You've been out with him twice and you didn't even call me?" Sandi accused over the phone.

Kate grinned as she sat in an old overstuffed chair, one of the most comfortable furnishings in the apartment she shared with Heidi. "I haven't had time. Between work, school, and Randy, it's been pretty crazy."

"*I* would've worked in a phone call," Sandi emphasized, trying to sound hurt. Secretly, she was tickled for Kate.

"There's just one problem," Kate started.

"Only one?"

"Okay, I lied. There are several. Mike, Randy, and your sister."

"Heidi?"

"That's the one. Attractive blonde law student with a major chip on her shoulder. I think she hates Randy."

"I doubt that," Sandi replied. "What has she done to give you that impression?"

"One example—I was so excited after our first date, but Heidi didn't even want to talk about it. I think I'm falling in love in a major way, and she acts like I've personally offended her."

Sandi pulled a face, sitting down on a hard kitchen chair. "This doesn't sound like Heidi. She was one of my biggest supporters when Ian and I started dating last year."

"I think her attitude has changed since then."

Silently, Sandi agreed. If only things had worked out differently with Terry. "Did Randy say or do something to upset her?" she finally asked.

Kate couldn't think of anything. On the way to hear Randy's mission report, Heidi had seemed almost as excited as Kate. But coming home, she hadn't had a good thing to say about anything, including Randy. "I don't know. I hope not. She seemed fine with him at the airport. But ever since Randy reported his mission—I don't know how to describe it, she's not rude, but she's not friendly either. I hope she doesn't decide to sic your brother on him."

Sandi laughed.

"I'm serious."

"Don't worry, I'll warn Brian to steer clear."

"I wish I could understand what's going on inside of her."

Playing with the phone cord, Sandi sighed. "Maybe she doesn't want to lose another roommate. And we both know she's still getting over Terry."

"Maybe, but I don't understand why she won't give Randy a chance. He isn't a threat to her—is he?"

Considering the question, Sandi picked up a pencil and began doodling on the notebook in front of her. "Who knows. When do I get to meet him?"

Kate leaned back in the chair. "Randy mentioned something about going to BYU's next football game."

"The one here in Salt Lake?" Sandi asked, grinning as she thought of the traditional rivalry between BYU and University of Utah. "The one where the Cougars always get trampled?"

"Hey, you're getting a little personal," Kate warned. "BYU will make mincemeat of the Utes!"

"We'll see. Ian and I could meet you at the game. In fact, why don't you see if you could line Heidi up with someone."

Kate scowled. "Like who?"

"I don't know. There has to be somebody she'd go out with."

This was going to be tough. Kate couldn't think of anyone. Evan Hillier popped into her mind, but she shook her head. Heidi seemed to resent Evan, too, which was a real mystery. Kate thought Evan was a neat guy.

"Are you still there?" Sandi prodded.

"I'm thinking. Only one guy comes to mind and after what she said the other day, I don't think she wants anything to do with him."

Sandi gave a snort of disgust. "We have to start somewhere."

Nodding, Kate decided to go with her intuition. She made a mental note to contact Evan. He was fun-loving and easy to talk to; she couldn't see one thing wrong with him. "I'll try. His name is Evan Hillier. He's a law student and at the first of the year I got the impression he was pretty good friends with Heidi."

"Good," Sandi said. "This sounds perfect. Do you think you can talk him into this?"

"He'll be the easy part. How do I convince Heidi she wants to go?"

"Prayer. Fasting. Stuff like that."

"Real funny," Kate complained.

"Do you want me to talk to her?"

"Yes!" Kate exclaimed. It was only fair. If she had to talk Evan into having one of the worst dates of his life, the least Sandi could do is talk to Heidi.

"Okay," Sandi sighed. "Let's plan on it."

"As long as you and Ian promise not to pout when BYU wins."

"How about a side bet?"

"It's against my religion," Kate quipped.

"Mine, too," Sandi returned.

"What are the stakes?" Kate asked.

"We'll treat you guys to dinner if BYU wins."

"And we'll treat you two if the Utes miraculously conquer. But this sounds lopsided. You'll be treating two couples," Kate pointed out.

"No, the way I see it, Heidi and Evan can buy us dinner, and you and Randy can buy us dessert."

Kate laughed. "All right," she agreed.

* * *

At the game, as the couples good-naturedly cheered for opposing teams, Sandi observed the way Heidi was acting around Randy and Evan. During half-time when Heidi announced she needed to find a little girls' room, Sandi walked with her to the crowded stadium rest rooms.

"How about a friendly discussion?" Sandi asked her sister when they were on their way back.

"A friendly discussion? This sounds interesting."

"I'm curious. Why are you giving Randy such a bad time?"

"Me?" Heidi asked innocently.

"Yes, you, and I'm not the only one who's noticed. Kate mentioned it to me the other day."

"So why hasn't Kate said anything to me?"

"She's hoping it's her imagination. I know it isn't, after today. What's up?"

Heidi paused, then motioned for Sandi to join her away from the crowd headed back to the game. "It was getting too hard to hear back there," she explained as she led Sandi to a deserted corner. "This is my own personal opinion, but I don't think it's going to work out with Kate and Randy."

Sandi stared at her sister. "Why would you think that?" she asked, certain Heidi was displacing her own emotions onto Kate and Randy, something Sandi had recently learned about in a psychology class. Displaced aggression. A condition triggered when an individual can't express what he or she is feeling toward the original source of frustration and instead directs those emotions toward innocent people. This appeared to be a classic case.

"I don't want to see Kate get hurt," Heidi murmured.

"Like you were hurt?" Sandi softly asked. "Heidi, I know it's been rough—if you'll let me, I'd like to help. Talk to me. Tell me what you're feeling."

Heidi shook her head.

"Heidi—"

"I thought we were discussing Kate and Randy. How did I become the main topic?"

"It's all related. You're transferring the anger you've felt toward Terry to Randy."

Heidi stared at Sandi, then burst out laughing.

"This isn't funny!"

"No, you're right, it isn't," Heidi agreed, quickly sobering. "Don't try to analyze me, baby sister. This has nothing to do with Terry. Despite what you think, I'm not on a man-hating crusade."

"Then why aren't you giving guys like Randy and Evan a chance?" Sandi waited for several seconds, but Heidi remained silent. "Evan seems very nice."

"So did Terry."

"I thought you said this had nothing to do with Terry?"

"And I thought we were talking about Kate and Randy," Heidi countered.

Sandi could see this was going to be a long, uphill battle. Something that couldn't be settled in one afternoon. "Okay, fine. Did Randy do something to upset you?"

Heidi sighed. "Did Kate mention that Randy carries around a picture of another girl in his wallet?"

Shaking her head, Sandi waited for an explanation.

"I caught Randy staring at it the day he reported his mission. It's obvious he has some intense feelings for that girl, whoever she is. Is he being fair to Kate—leading her on when there's someone else? I don't think so!"

"What makes you think he would drop Kate for . . . this girl?"

"Let me ask you this," Heidi argued, "Why did Randy drag his feet so long before getting in touch with Kate?"

"Kate said he was trying to figure things out."

"I don't think he has yet. He's not being honest with himself or Kate. That's why I'm concerned and why I can't act excited every time he gets mushy with Kate. Randy's trying too hard. Sure, his mother would love and adore it if he and Kate got married, but Jan'll hate it if and when that marriage fails because it was based on what everyone else expected and not on what Kate and Randy are really feeling." She saw again the look on Randy's face as he had stared at the picture in his hand. "Besides, what about Mike?"

Exasperated, Sandi shoved her hands inside of her jacket, not answering right away.

Heidi pressed on. "You were around those two. Is what they had any less than what Kate seems to have with Randy?"

"You're going to make one heck of a good lawyer."

"Thanks," Heidi angrily responded. She turned and began to walk away.

"Heidi," Sandi called. "Wait."

Heidi reluctantly waited for her sister to catch up.

"I'm sorry. I didn't mean to upset you. I meant—you look at things very carefully. You examine all of the facts. Maybe the rest of us should try to be more like you."

"Maybe," Heidi mumbled ungraciously.

"Truce," Sandi begged. "I don't want to fight with you."

"We're not fighting. We're having a friendly discussion, remember?"

Sandi slowly nodded.

"And I don't think either of us has anything left to say. So should we go watch the rest of the game?" Turning, Heidi walked away.

Sandi looked toward heaven, then followed her sister inside the stadium.

* * *

Twisting her hair around one finger, Kate smiled as her mother pumped her for details about her most recent date with Randy. "It was fun," she sighed into the phone. "Even though I had to promise Heidi I'd do dish detail for two months to get her to go out with Evan."

"It'll be good for you," Sue teased, remembering how her daughter had always hated that chore at home. "Did Heidi enjoy herself at all?"

"Who knows?" Kate shrugged. "We tried. Now it's up to Evan and Heidi." There was a long pause. "Are you still there?" Kate asked, holding the phone closer.

"Yes."

"You should've seen the look on Sandi's face when BYU won. Poor Ian ended up buying dinner for all of us."

"From what I understand, he can afford it," Sue replied. "Harriet is always telling me how well off Sandi and Ian are financially."

"They're not rich, but they're doing okay," Kate replied. She laughed. "But Randy's eating habits could put anybody in the poor house."

"Jan mentioned Randy has quite the appetite."

"He does."

"We are only talking about food, right?"

"*Mom!*" Kate exclaimed, grateful her mother couldn't see the embarrassed look on her face.

"After all, Randy hasn't been around girls for a while—"

"Not true. He came home with a girl's picture in his wallet."

"Not yours?"

"Nope," Kate replied.

"You're kidding?"

"No, it's a sister missionary who transferred into his area before he came home. Her name is Laurie something."

Sue frowned. "Laurie something?" She didn't like the sound of this development.

"I can't remember her last name. Something to do with sports."

Sports? Sue shook her head. Her daughter was definitely one of those if she could sound this unconcerned about a potential rival. "Was there anything serious between them?"

"No. They were friends—"

"Like you and Mike?"

"Hardly," Kate answered dryly. "He only saw her twice. The first time was at a zone conference, the second was just before he came home. She gave him her picture and home address."

"I see," Sue said, trying to keep the worry out of her voice. "Kate—" she started. She could hear a commotion in the background.

"Hello, Mrs. Erickson, this is Randy," Randy said into the phone as Kate protested. "I came by to steal your daughter. She'll call you back later. Tell everyone hi for me," he said before hanging up.

Sue stared at the phone in her hand. "Be careful, Kate," she breathed. "Please, be careful."

CHAPTER 12

The weeks passed quickly and Thanksgiving was soon on the horizon. As it approached, Heidi and Kate made arrangements to travel to Bozeman. Kate had invited Randy to join them, but he had reluctantly declined, explaining that his maternal grandparents from Ohio were coming to Heber for Thanksgiving dinner. They hadn't been able to make it for his homecoming celebration, but now that Randy's grandfather had recovered from a severe bout of pneumonia, they were flying in for the holiday weekend.

"Sorry," Randy said after explaining why he had to stay in Heber. "Maybe for Christmas," he added, grinning down at Kate from the top of the roof, where he had climbed up to shovel the snow that a series of heavy storms had deposited.

Disappointed, Kate moved to the side as Randy continued to shovel snow from the top of the house. The landlords had headed to Arizona for the winter, leaving Kate and Heidi in charge of house maintenance in their absence, with the cost of upkeep to be deducted from their monthly rent. Both girls had happily agreed to this proposal, grateful for the extra money they could now use for other school expenses.

As Kate began to shovel the sidewalk, Randy nailed her with a snowball. "Not funny," Kate complained, wiping snow from her face.

"It depends on who you ask," Randy replied, laughing.

Kate retaliated by throwing a snowball of her own, hitting Randy in the chest. A fierce snowball fight ensued, ending with Randy coming down to wash Kate's face in the snowbank. Kate came up sputtering but before she could avenge herself, Randy kissed her.

"You win more arguments that way," Kate complained.

"It's worth it, right?" he teased, shaking the snow from his hair.

"Maybe," Kate challenged, grabbing another handful of snow. She quickly stuck it down the back of his neck.

"Uh-oh, now you've done it," he threatened, whirling around to grab her. Rolling around together in the snow, they didn't see Heidi walk up. She loudly cleared her throat, and impatiently waited for the couple to notice her presence.

"I'd ask what you two have been up to, but it's quite obvious," she said, giving them an unamused glare.

"He started it," Kate said, squealing as Randy dumped a handful of snow down her back. "That's it," she threatened, going after the scoop shovel.

"You wouldn't dare," Randy countered. He watched with amusement as Kate filled the shovel with snow and threw it in his direction. "Nice aim," he teased when she missed.

"Just wait," Kate promised.

Heidi turned toward the apartment door. "Well, I'll leave you children to play. I, on the other hand, have work to do."

After she left, Randy gave Kate a puzzled look. "Why doesn't she like me?"

Kate leaned on the shovel. She had hoped to avoid this conversation. "She likes you—" she began hesitantly.

"Every time she looks at me she's sending daggers," he countered.

Kate motioned toward Randy's car. Catching on, Randy took the shovel from her and leaned it against the house. He then led Kate to his car. Starting the engine, he turned on the heater so they could begin thawing out.

"I told you Heidi's roommate married her boyfriend last summer?"

Shivering, Randy nodded.

"She isn't over it yet. It's not you, it's men in general."

"She seems to like Evan," Randy replied.

"Maybe, although I think he's getting tired of being held at arm's length. She doesn't trust men. And, after what she's been through, I can't say that I blame her," Kate sighed. "I can't imagine how hard it would be to have the guy you're in love with marry your best friend."

As he listened, Randy brushed the snow from his coat. "Okay, I understand why she's distant with Evan, but that still doesn't explain—"

"Sandi thinks Heidi's afraid of losing another roommate." Kate winced, a warm blush creeping into her face.

"Are you going somewhere?" Randy teased, playing with her hair.

"This conversation has ended. Besides, it's getting late and we need to finish what we started."

"Our snowball fight or our romantic interlude?"

"Neither. Let's go, we have work to do," Kate said, climbing out of the car.

"Slave driver," Randy replied, following Kate out of the car.

* * *

Kate slept most of the way to Bozeman, giving Heidi a chance to quietly absorb the events of the past few weeks. Heidi had never planned on going out with Evan. But, backed into a corner by Kate and Sandi, she had finally given in. Then, instead of enjoying what should have been a wonderful day, she had spent the entire time watching Evan, suspicious that he had eyes only for Kate. She had resisted when he had tried to put his arm around her shoulders and had refused when he offered to share a blanket. She had then shivered through most of the game. Later, adding insult to injury, she had endured a lecture from Sandi, and another one from Kate.

"You weren't even nice to Evan," Kate had accused.

"So," Heidi had countered. "Maybe he didn't deserve it."

"He didn't deserve the way you treated him," Kate had retorted.

Maybe not, Heidi now conceded. Evan had tried to be polite and charming, but she didn't trust him. He had tried to wedge himself between the two roommates and that was unforgivable. As for Randy, she was still convinced it was all an act for his mother's benefit.

As she drove, Heidi continued her mental debate. Beside her, Kate slumbered blissfully, unaware of the emotional struggle that was taking place. Kate had no idea how attracted Heidi was to Evan or how she wrestled with guilt over the way she had been treating Elena. Nor could Kate begin to fathom the pain Heidi was trying to spare her.

When Kate finally woke up, she looked around, aware only that they weren't where she had thought they would be by now. "Where are we?" Kate yawned.

"Outside of West Yellowstone."

"I thought you were taking the interstate to Bozeman."

"I like this way better. The roads have been sanded and there's less traffic. Besides, I love the scenery along highway 191."

Kate nodded sleepily.

"Hungry?"

"Starved," Kate replied, feeling suddenly more awake. She stared out the window on her side of the car as Heidi skillfully drove around the small town. Pulling up next to a familiar-looking building, Heidi smiled.

"Are you up for some of the Colonel's chicken?"

"Sure," Kate responded. She stepped out of the car to stretch, her breath visible in frosty plumes. Shivering, she followed Heidi inside the small building.

It didn't take long for their orders to be processed. Sitting down at a table near a window, they hungrily devoured the chicken dinner.

"This town is so fun," Heidi commented, glancing out the window. "Last year Terry came up and we rented snowmobiles to take through the park . . ." her voice trailed off, pain apparent in her face.

Secretly, Kate was glad Heidi was beginning to open up. She had slipped and mentioned Terry's name several times during the past couple of weeks. Convinced it was a sign of healing, Kate silently urged Heidi to continue as she sampled the small container of mashed potatoes that had come with the chicken. After several silent minutes, Kate attempted to restart the conversation. "I love winter," she murmured, gazing out the window at the white snowdrifts that lined the streets. "I wish Randy could've come. There's so much I'd like him to see."

"Oh, well," Heidi sighed, reaching for her pop.

"What do you mean by that?"

Heidi shrugged, sipping at the root beer.

Kate frowned. The time had come to settle this once and for all. "Heidi, I want you to level with me. What bugs you about Randy?"

Heidi gazed at Kate. "You don't want to hear this."

Kate returned the gaze. "I think I do. Did he do something to upset you?"

Heidi shook her head.

"Then what?"

Heidi frowned. Surely Kate couldn't be this naive. Didn't she realize the risk that existed? Heidi decided it was time to reveal what she knew. "Remember the dinner they held in Randy's honor after he reported his mission?"

Kate nodded.

"I went inside to wash out the punch I'd spilled on my dress. When I walked by the den, Randy was sitting in there by himself. I decided it would be a good opportunity to tell him how much I had enjoyed sacrament meeting." She paused, reluctant to hurt Kate but anxious to convey the concern she felt. "That was when I noticed he was staring at a picture of a beautiful girl." Heidi glanced at Kate. "Kate, it wasn't you. I wouldn't have thought much about it, but you should have seen the expression on his face. He was so preoccupied, he didn't notice me."

Relieved, Kate smiled. "I wish you would've talked to me earlier, I could've cleared this up for you. That picture you saw, it's a girl Randy met on his mission—her name is Laurie. She's a sister missionary from his district. She gave him that picture before he came home. I know all about her, just as Randy knows all about Mike." She gazed steadily at Heidi. "So you see, there's nothing to worry about. We've both decided to take things slowly and see what develops. Right now, it's looking pretty good."

"I hope it still looks that way when Laurie comes home," Heidi said, avoiding Kate's piercing gaze. She was only partially relieved to learn that at least Kate wasn't going to go into this blindly. Still—

Heidi deliberately looked at her watch. "It's after two-thirty already," she exclaimed. "Hurry and eat. We need to get going."

Heidi didn't see Kate's look of frustration as they both silently finished their chicken.

* * *

"That was wonderful, Mom," Kate said, rising to help clear the table. "Oh, yeah," Tyler agreed, wandering from the dining room.

"Now, time for football—what a perfect day!"

Greg shook his head and grinned at Sue. "It's nice to know the boy has priorities. Food and sports."

"Just like his father," Sue teased as she picked up what was left of the turkey.

"Hey, I'm still here! You don't see me parked in front of the TV," he exclaimed as he hurriedly gathered glasses. In his haste to take them into the kitchen, he dropped one, shattering it across the floor.

"Why don't you let Kate and me get this?" Sue suggested.

"But—"

"Go on. We don't mind."

"That way, we'll still have some dishes left," Kate said, grinning at her father.

"All right, I can see when I'm not wanted. Try to do a good turn, see where it gets you," Greg complained as he wandered from the room, holding his stomach.

"Men!" Kate exclaimed.

"Just the subject I had in mind," Sue replied, sweeping up the broken glass.

"Oh?" Kate asked as she gathered the plates. "This wouldn't concern a young man from Heber?"

Sue smiled at her daughter. "As a matter of fact—"

"Mommy, Tyler won't let me watch cartoons," Sabrina complained, walking into the kitchen.

"One crisis at a time," Sue muttered, glancing at the seven-year-old. "Sabrina, how would you like to play on the computer this afternoon? Tyler and Daddy want to watch the football games."

"They're boring!"

"Tyler and Dad?" Kate teased, then jumped when Sue poked her sharply in the ribs with a finger.

"No, those stupid football games," Sabrina answered indignantly.

Sue tried again. "Would you like to play some computer games?" she asked.

Sabrina slowly nodded.

"I'll be right back," Sue informed Kate, handing her the broom and dustpan. Kate obediently swept up the pieces of broken glass as Sue led Sabrina into the study.

"What did you mean—one crisis at a time?" Kate asked a few minutes later when Sue had returned.

Sue gazed at Kate. "What were we talking about before Sabrina interrupted?"

"Randy?"

"That's the crisis."

"Mom!"

"I can't help it, I'm concerned. And I'm not pulling a Harriet," Sue said, thinking of the misery Harriet had caused Sandi and Ian before finally approving of the match.

"I didn't say that," Kate said as she began unloading the dishwasher. "But it is a thought."

"Kate," Sue warned, as she began putting food away. "I'm just curious. How are things between you and Randy?"

Kate smiled at her mother. "Pretty great," she said.

"Translation, please."

"Meaning what?" Kate asked.

"You two have been seeing quite a bit of each other. I'm starting to wonder how serious this is getting."

Kate considered her mother's question as she put away the clean silverware. "I'm not sure," she said thoughtfully. "We have a lot of fun together—but we really haven't talked about . . . you know, things."

"Things?" Sue lifted an eyebrow.

Kate blushed. "Mom," she protested, stacking the clean plates.

"What is your definition of 'things'?"

"You know—things."

"Like marriage?"

Kate nearly dropped the stack of plates she was holding. Gripping them tightly, she finished setting them inside of the cupboard. "We're a long way from discussing things like that," she murmured, glancing at her mother.

"Are you?" Sue probed. "When you mentioned on the phone that you were hoping Randy would come home for Thanksgiving, I started wondering if there was something you hadn't told me."

"I promise, you'll be the first one to know—if things develop that way."

"Why do you keep referring to this relationship as *things?*"

Kate groaned. "Mom, Randy and I are taking *things* one step at a time, just like you suggested."

Sue smiled at her daughter. "Okay. Don't get the wrong impression, I'd be tickled if *things* worked out with you two. I just want you both to be sure this is what you want."

"What is with you and Heidi?" Kate asked, as she rinsed off the stack of dirty plates.

"What do you mean?"

"Why are you both so worried about me?"

Sue stepped into the kitchen with another dish to set in the fridge. "Because we care."

"Mom, I can handle this."

Sue offered her daughter a small smile. "I know. And unlike your father, I also know you're old enough to be on your own, but that doesn't mean I ever stop worrying. If anything, I worry more."

Kate stared at her mother, not completely comprehending.

"You'll see, someday. When your kids grow up and move away, remember this conversation. Remember that you're a mother your entire life and the worries don't stop when your children consider themselves to be adults." She paused, tears filling her eyes.

Shaking her head, Kate moved toward Sue. "I thought we agreed we wouldn't do this to each other this weekend," she said, hugging her mother.

"I can't help it. Especially on days like today. You start thinking about everything you're grateful for. Sometimes you get sentimental." She held onto Kate, tightening her grip. "Do you have any idea how much you are loved?"

"I think so," Kate sniffled.

"Good," Sue said, laughing as she released Kate. "Remember that. Remember I only want the best for you."

"Deal. Now, remember something for me," Kate requested, smiling at her mother. "I'll be fine, I promise. Quit worrying."

Nodding, Sue wiped at her eyes and moved back to the table to finish clearing it.

CHAPTER 13

Kate loved the look on Randy's face when she finally stepped into the apartment's small living room. Offering a low whistle, Randy stared at Kate. "You look great!"

Kate glowed inside. She was wearing the green formal her mother had refashioned for the senior prom she had attended in high school. Green had always been one of her colors and this dress was the perfect shade to bring out the red highlights in her hair. Forest green, it closely matched the emerald tint reflecting from her eyes.

"Mike liked this dress too," Heidi said, innocently studying her nails as she came out behind Kate.

"Don't help me," Kate quietly warned her roommate. She had been plagued by guilt since slipping into the dress. Memories of the dance she had attended with Mike kept coming to mind—as well as phrases from his last letter. She had written, telling him that she was dating Randy, that it looked like things were working out between them. Mike had sent a short note, wishing her well, hinting that he would always be there for her if she ever needed him. He had ended the letter by telling her that if she was happy, he was happy for her. Kate thought it would've been easier if he had sent a letter full of recriminations. Then she wouldn't have cared how her relationship with Randy was affecting him.

When she was away from Randy, she found herself mentally comparing Mike with Randy, which added to the confusion she felt. But when she was with Randy, she didn't think about Mike—the natural chemistry that existed between them was very strong. When she was alone and had time to reflect, she felt ill at ease. Although she prayed for answers, nothing seemed clear.

It was much easier with Keith. Since his departure, she had received only two letters from him. Both were filled with the spiritual experiences he was having. She had written about Randy, hinting for advice. In his last letter he had simply stated that since Kate was the one who would be directly affected by her decision, she would have to be the one to make the choice. Then he had taken himself out of the running by apologizing for overstepping boundaries that day at Glen Lake. He implied that he looked on her as a sister in Zion, a very dear friend that he thought of from time to time.

"Would you like to see their prom picture?" Heidi asked Randy, jolting Kate back to the conversation. "It's on the desk in our room." She grimaced as Kate stepped on her foot.

"I couldn't afford a new dress for tonight. I figured this old thing would do. You guys look sharp," Kate said, eager to change the subject. It was true. The two young men were wearing their best suits. Randy was sporting a black pinstripe; Evan had selected dark blue for the occasion.

"Thanks," Evan replied, his gaze settling on Heidi. She was wearing a pale pink dress that fit her perfectly. "We'll have the prettiest dates at the dance," he said, offering Heidi the corsage in his hand.

Kate frowned as Heidi nodded her thanks and took the corsage from Evan to pin on herself. As Kate pinned Randy's boutonniere to the lapel of his suit, he leaned in for a quick kiss, and she saw Heidi turn away, evidently remembering Evan's boutonniere was still in the fridge. When Heidi had retrieved it from the refrigerator, she casually tossed it to Evan.

Kate shook her head, offering Evan an apologetic smile. As he pinned the small white carnation on his lapel, he returned her smile ruefully. Going into the kitchen to grab her shawl, Kate put an arm around Heidi's shoulders. "Behave yourself tonight," she whispered.

"I could say the same thing," Heidi countered.

"True. But you don't have anything to worry about. So relax."

"Don't I? With you looking like that, there isn't a man alive who could think straight, including Randy."

"Thanks. You look wonderful tonight, too," Kate replied, walking out of the kitchen.

"Should we go?" Randy suggested, taking Kate's arm, determined to dispel the hold Mike already seemed to have on the evening. He chuckled to himself. By the time this night was over, Kate would be asking *"Mike who?"*

* * *

Heidi resisted the temptation to roll her eyes as she walked through the door behind Kate and Randy. To her dismay, Evan took hold of her hand and led her away from Randy's car.

"I thought we were all going together," Heidi protested as Evan tried to help her into his own small car.

"We'll meet at the restaurant for dinner," Evan hastily explained. "And later at the Christmas dance." He smiled at Heidi. "Randy wanted some time alone with Kate tonight."

Heidi stared at Evan. "No. He wouldn't," she moaned to herself as Evan shut the door. She closed her eyes in frustration. The only reason she had agreed to go to the Christmas dance with Evan was to keep an eye on Kate. "Randy, you jerk," she muttered as Evan walked around to his side of the car.

* * *

"Where did Heidi and Evan get to?" Kate asked, glancing around the large room. Christmas lights were strung across the ceiling, giving it a soft, romantic look.

"They'll be here. I told Evan which ballroom we'd be in," Randy replied. "Want to dance?" he asked, eager to hold Kate. This was the first dance they had attended together and he could hardly wait to begin.

"I'm not sure I *can* dance after all that food," Kate commented, patting her stomach.

"Those steaks were good, weren't they," Randy agreed, leading her onto the dance floor. It had been Evan's idea to head to the Sizzler for the steak and shrimp special that night.

"Aren't we going to wait for Heidi and Evan?" Kate asked.

"We shared dinner. The rest of the evening is ours," he said, thoroughly enjoying the slow number with Kate. Her light, flowery perfume heightened the attraction he felt. Inhaling deeply, he realized he could be perfectly content to hold her like this forever.

* * *

After a couple of songs, Heidi stormed into the ballroom, followed by an out-of-breath Evan. "Heidi, I'm sorry," Evan panted.

Heidi only increased her speed and moved to the other side of the room. She still couldn't believe Evan's nerve. Kissing her on the way to the Wilkinson Center!

"Actually, I'm not sorry," Evan said, catching up with Heidi. "That's something I've wanted to do for a very long time."

"Well, I hope you enjoyed it because it won't happen again!" Heidi snapped.

"Oh, yeah?" Evan challenged, moving close. He was only an inch taller, but at the moment, he seemed to tower over Heidi. Taking her in his arms, he kissed her again. When he finally released her, the sound of applause echoed around the room. "See, everyone else thought it was wonderful, too," Evan said, grinning.

"They're clapping for the band," Heidi protested, reeling from what Evan had just done.

"Maybe. Maybe not. Should we find out?"

"No!"

"Want to go for a walk?" Evan asked. "I think we have a few things to discuss."

Still in a state of shock, Heidi didn't protest as Evan led her from the crowded room.

* * *

"Did you see those two?" Kate asked as the couple disappeared from sight.

"I did. Most atrocious," he replied. When Kate turned to look at him in surprise, he grinned. "Most atrocious that Heidi hasn't let him do that before."

"Agreed," Kate said, laughing. "I think it's wonderful."

Randy nodded, leaning down to kiss Kate. Then, holding her close, he wondered briefly what it might have been like to have held Laurie. But Kate was too real. He couldn't even see Laurie's face anymore. Kate was inside his heart now.

* * *

Reluctantly Heidi let Evan lead her to a secluded corner of the student center. Finding a couple of empty chairs, he invited her to sit down. Giving him a skeptical look, Heidi took a seat. Pulling the other chair close, Evan sat down, facing her.

"Heidi," he said, trying to take her hand. Unwilling to cooperate, she folded her arms. "We have a problem," he continued.

Heidi lifted her eyebrows. "We?"

Evan nodded. "One of us has fallen in love."

Heidi's heart thudded in her chest. If Evan was going to tell her that he had fallen for her roommate, she was ready for him. She had seen it coming ever since the hike.

Looking somber, Evan moved his chair closer. "Heidi, I love you," he admitted.

Heidi's mouth was dry. She hadn't anticipated this. "What?" she said. "You don't even know me!"

He gazed at her steadily, until she looked away. "I know enough," he said softly. "I know you're a headstrong woman who likes to get her own way." Before she could offer a rebuttal, he hurried on, gathering his courage. "I know you love learning . . . you enjoy good food and the great outdoors—"

Heidi closed her eyes. "Evan, stop," she said. She couldn't give in to this, no matter how inviting. There was still the matter of Kate. Now that Randy was hogging the picture, Evan was settling for second best. *Not this time,* she angrily thought, assuring herself she wouldn't go through this again. She was certain that when Kate finally saw through Randy, Evan would be waiting to pick up the pieces.

"I know you served a mission in California and you're this close to becoming one of the best lawyers this generation has ever seen," he emphasized, pinching two fingers together.

Heidi shook her head. Why was he doing this to her?

"I love how you always stand up to Professor Moss, how you know things off the top of your head that the rest of us have to look up. And I love how you can be so serious one minute and a riot the next."

"Evan—" she whispered.

He ignored the interruption. "This semester we've been in the same student ward and I've seen another side of you. You're a great gospel doctrine teacher and when you share your testimony, I feel like we're kindred spirits. And now that we've kissed—"

Gripping the sides of her chair, Heidi shook her head. "Stop it!"

". . . so I think if we talk this thing out—"

Heidi took a deep breath. "What about Kate?" she demanded at last. "You two were quite an item before Randy took over."

"We went out one time and that was by accident!" Evan exclaimed in frustration, turning to face her. Then he looked at her, as if seeing her for the first time, and suddenly smiled.

Misinterpreting the smile, Heidi rose to face him. "That's right, grin. I know exactly what kind of guy you are!"

"The kind who won't let you walk out of here before you know the whole story," Evan countered, compelling her to sit back down. Surprised by his forcefulness, Heidi remained in her chair. Evan spoke rapidly. "Jess was supposed to ask Kate out, so I could ask you and we could double. But he got nervous and asked for you instead. So all I could do was ask Kate, and make the best of it."

"You wanted to ask me out?" Heidi repeated, stunned.

Nodding, Evan continued. "I like Kate as a friend, but you're the one I'm interested in. I wanted to ask you out last year, but Terry blundered into the middle of things and you were so wrapped up with him you didn't even notice me."

Heidi blushed. She didn't want to discuss Terry with Evan. "But you asked Kate out again—that day I turned you down—"

Evan loosened his tie. "I thought she could help me get closer to you—that she might shed some light on how to break down the barrier between us. Later, it was so aggravating knowing Kate was twisting your arm to make you go out with me." He shook his head, then gazed sadly at Heidi. "I'm sorry about the mix-up. I was hoping tonight would change things between us."

Heidi remained silent.

"Can we call a truce and start over?"

Heidi closed her eyes and tried to make some sense out of everything Evan was saying.

"Heidi," Evan said as he took her hands in his, "can't you let go of your pain and try to feel something for me?"

Slowly raising her chin, Heidi met Evan's searching gaze. If he only knew. Tears made an unwelcome appearance. Biting her lip she tried to toughen up, but it didn't work. She offered no resistance when Evan tenderly held her, allowing her to cry all over the suit he had just picked up from the dry cleaners.

* * *

"Did you have fun tonight?" Randy asked as he helped Kate out of the car.

Kate nodded. She was almost afraid to speak, fearing light conversation would ruin the magic that had been between them at the dance. Several times she had felt like she was floating. She shivered, reliving the intense emotions of the final dance.

"Here," Randy offered, taking off his suit coat. He quickly placed it around Kate's shoulders. "I forgot how chilly it was tonight." He took Kate's hand.

"I'm not cold," Kate replied, following Randy to the sidewalk. She glanced up at the temple. Randy had driven here after the dance, claiming he wanted to go somewhere special. She liked how it felt when he placed an arm around her shoulders as they walked together to the front of the temple. Randy motioned to a nearby bench. He brushed off the light covering of snow and helped Kate sit down. Then he nervously sat beside her.

"Kate, I was going to wait until Christmas, but I brought this along tonight, just in case."

Kate's eyes widened. She tried to speak, but Randy silenced her by placing a finger on her lips. He stood, removing a small box from his pants pocket. Slowly kneeling in the snow, he opened the box, revealing a diamond ring. "Kate Erickson, I love you. Will you marry me?"

He didn't get the reaction he had anticipated. Instead of squeals, there were tears as Kate embraced Randy.

"I love you so much," she said when she could speak again.

"It's a good thing 'cuz you're stuck with me now," he assured her, pulling her to her feet. Sliding the ring onto the appropriate finger, he sealed their engagement by kissing her in front of the temple.

* * *

They decided to notify Kate's parents first and drove back to the apartment to make the call. They were surprised that Evan and Heidi weren't around, but hoping that was a good sign, concluded there was nothing to worry about. Kate glanced at her watch. It was nearly two o'clock in the morning.

"Go ahead, I'm sure they'll forgive you when you tell them why you're calling this late," Randy encouraged.

Smiling, Kate quickly dialed and then impatiently waited for someone to answer. After three rings, she heard her dad's muffled voice.

". . . ello."

"Hi, Dad—"

"Ummmm?"

"Dad, it's me, Kate."

"Kate who?" Greg mumbled.

"Your daughter."

"Hmmmmmm."

"Dad, I know it's late, but I have something to tell you."

"Greg, who is it?" Sue asked, forcing her eyes open.

"Here's your mother," Greg murmured, sleepily handing the phone to Sue. "It's someone named Kate."

"Kate?" Sue said, instantly alert. "Is everything all right?" she asked, gripping the phone.

"Everything is wonderful," Kate said brightly.

Sue sat up, glancing at the clock by the side of the bed. "Where are you?"

"Here in Provo, in my apartment."

"Weren't you going to a dance tonight . . . I mean, last night," Sue added, glancing again at the clock. Her eyes widened. "Kate, why is everything wonderful this time of morning?"

"Because I'm engaged to the most marvelous man in the world," Kate answered.

Sue stifled a squeal. "Greg, wake up," she said, shaking her husband. "Our daughter's engaged! Greg, did you hear me?"

"Whaa . . . ?" Greg asked, sitting up.

"Kate's engaged!" Sue tearfully revealed.

"To what?"

"Not what, who. She's engaged to Randy." The phone slipped from Sue's hand, falling onto the bed. She quickly picked it up and held it to her ear. "Oh, Kate, I'm so happy for you!" she said, ignoring the look on her husband's face.

"Me too," Kate agreed.

"I wish Provo was closer," Sue continued, choking up. "I'd hug the stuffings out of you. Oh, wow! A wedding! Congratulations! Is Randy there with you?"

"Yes. He's standing right here," Kate answered, handing the phone to Randy.

"Hi," he stammered nervously.

"Randy? Kate tells me you two got engaged tonight. That's great!" Sue exclaimed.

"We think so, too," Randy replied.

"Kate and Randy are engaged?" Greg asked again, reaching for his glasses. He didn't hear clearly without them which was odd, considering they were designed to improve his vision. Everything seemed fuzzy without them on.

"Yes, dear," Sue said, glancing at her husband. "Randy, Kate's father is going into shock, why don't you let Kate talk to him for a minute. Maybe she can convince him this is real." Sue handed the phone to Greg before moving into the bathroom to cry.

* * *

Too excited to sleep, Kate agreed to travel home with Randy to break the news to his parents. There was still no sign of Heidi or Evan, so Kate left a quick note and placed it on the table where Heidi would be sure to notice.

Heidi,

Sorry we missed you. We're on our way to Heber. We'll have something to tell you later today.

Love,
Kate & Randy

P.S. We hope you and Evan behaved yourselves tonight. We were a little concerned after what took place at the dance.

During the thirty-minute ride to Heber through Provo Canyon, Kate and Randy began making plans.

"How soon do you want to get married?" Kate asked.

"As soon as possible," Randy replied, smiling at her. "For reasons that a true gentleman like myself would never reveal in mixed company."

Kate was glad it was still dark so Randy couldn't see the blush in her cheeks. "I guess waiting until the school year's over is out of the question then."

"Pretty much. I was thinking, oh, maybe right after Christmas."

"Randy! Our mothers will have a fit."

"Let 'em. We're the ones getting married."

Shaking her head, Kate wondered how she could explain this to Randy. "Randy, my mother has been planning my wedding since I was about eight years old."

"Sounds like she's had plenty of time to prepare then."

"That isn't what I meant," Kate countered.

"We could elope," Randy suggested. "It would save time and money—time being the operative word here."

Kate blushed again. "You'll just have to learn to control yourself, Elder Miles," she said firmly.

"Easier said than done, especially when you look like you do tonight," Randy observed, reaching with one hand to caress her cheek.

"You'd better watch the road," Kate said.

"You're more fun to look at," Randy assured her, obediently gripping the steering wheel with both hands. "How many kids should we have?" he asked.

"Kids? Already?"

"I can't help it—I want a large family. We'll have to get started right away."

Kate studied the amused look on his face. "Just how many are we talking here?"

"Oh, I don't know, twelve or thirteen."

"Not this girl—I'd never survive!"

Randy laughed. "You, the epitome of patience? You'll make a wonderful mother."

"Maybe." Kate said. "How about we continue to take things—" she thought of her mother and grinned—"one step at a time, okay?"

"If you insist," Randy replied. "Let's see, we covered the wedding plans, children, what's left? Silly me, how could I forget, there's still the little item of the honeymoon."

Again, Kate felt her cheeks grow warm. "Randy, has anyone ever told you that you have a one-track mind?"

"Oh, yes," he chuckled, as they pulled into Heber. "Well, are you ready to face the music? You do realize what we're in for when we tell Mom what we've done tonight."

"What we've done?"

"We've merely fulfilled her lifelong ambition. Do you realize how long she has waited for this moment?"

"Almost as long as I have," Kate teased.

Randy parked the car in his parents' driveway and shut off the engine. "Was it worth the wait?" he asked, kissing her.

"Definitely," Kate replied.

A few minutes later, they entered the house. "Dad, Mom, I'm home," Randy called out, glancing at the clock in the living room. It was 3:40 a.m.

"Mom!" Randy sang out. "Oh, Mother!"

"I'm coming," Jan said tiredly, wrapping a robe around herself. She had tried to wait up for Randy but had given up around one-thirty. "Why are you so late?" she started to ask as she walked into the spacious living room. Her eyes grew huge as she stared at Kate. Patting her hair self-consciously, Jan smiled at Kate, then at her son. "All right, you two, what's going on?"

"This is all Kate's fault," Randy replied. "Look what got stuck on her finger," he continued, pulling Kate forward. He reached for Kate's hand and waved the ringed finger in front of his mother's face.

"Oh, Randy!" Jan squealed, hugging her son, then turning to hug Kate. "I'm so happy for you," she cried as she clung to Kate. "I knew you two would work things out." She pulled back for a better look at the ring on Kate's finger. "It's beautiful. You have excellent taste, son," she said, wiping at her eyes.

"I know," Randy admitted, putting an arm around Kate.

"What's all the commotion?" Randy's father sleepily demanded as he walked into the room.

"Randy has an announcement to make." Jan smiled at her husband, then at her daughters who had poked their heads around the corner. "Julie, Alisha, one of you go get Devin up. Your brother will want to hear this."

Randy grinned. "See what you're getting into," he murmured into Kate's ear as the rest of his family gathered in the living room.

"I can hardly wait," Kate replied.

CHAPTER 14

Heidi wandered out to the kitchen and poured herself a small glass of apple juice. Moving to the table, she sat down and stared at the note she had first seen earlier that morning. Studying it, she smiled. "They went to Heber—that can only mean one thing," she said, feeling incredibly happy. "As soon as I saw that look in his eye, I knew he was going to ask her."

Sighing contentedly, Heidi sipped at her juice and thought about the events of the night before. Yesterday, she would've been furious at Randy for proposing. Today, she wanted to dance at their wedding. The way Evan had been talking, she might even be dancing at her own.

As she remembered the sensitive way he had understood her needs, a thrill of ecstasy went through her. After encouraging her to have a good cry, he had gently led her from the building, taking her to his apartment where she had been able to pour out her heart in privacy. They had talked until early this morning, agreeing to take things at her pace. Unaware of the passage of time, it had startled them both when two of his roommates returned from the dance.

On the way back to her apartment, Evan had assured her it had been a wonderful evening and had thanked her for finally letting him inside of her shell of privacy and pain.

Smiling now, Heidi quickly rose and walked into the living room. There sitting on the top of the small television was the seashell Evan had given her. A souvenir from his mission, he had made her promise that whenever she felt discouraged or depressed, she would hold this beautiful, pink-tinted shell and think of him. "Remember I can crack your shell anytime," he had teased, kissing her lightly at the door before leaving.

Picking up the shell, she sank into the overstuffed chair and held it close to her ear, laughing at the distant roar that echoed.

* * *

Elena shifted around in her chair, intently watching people as they hurried past. Glancing at her watch, she frowned. There was still no sign of Heidi. Closing her eyes, she offered another in a series of silent prayers. Heidi had finally called. Unsure of the reason, Elena was determined to make the most of it. They had agreed to meet for lunch at the Cougareat before Heidi had to work.

"Elena?"

Elena turned her head and nervously waved as Heidi approached. When Heidi smiled, Elena hoped it was a good sign.

"Sorry I'm late. I had some questions that took Professor Moss a while to explain," Heidi said, sliding into a chair across from Elena.

Smiling politely, Elena searched Heidi's face. Heidi had always asked hard questions. She was still struggling with the last one Heidi had asked her—"Why?"

"Elena, before we eat, would you mind if we talked?"

"That's fine," Elena replied, hoping this wouldn't be a repeat of the last emotional scene they had shared.

Heidi lowered her eyes. "I can't eat a thing until we settle this." She hesitated for several seconds, searching for the right words. Deciding to keep it simple, she gazed at her former friend. "Can you ever forgive me?"

Surprised, Elena stared. "That's my question," she said in a choked voice.

"No, it isn't. I behaved terribly and I'd like to explain why. I was angry, hurt—and just stubborn enough I wouldn't let myself deal with what happened," Heidi admitted. "I thought I was in love with Terry and the night I found you two—"

"Heidi—"

Heidi shook her head. "I wanted to hate both of you, but I finally realized the person I hated most was me."

Elena's eyes widened.

"I thought I'd driven Terry to you—that I wasn't attractive enough—that I couldn't hold his interest—"

"Heidi, it wasn't that at all," Elena said tearfully. "There's nothing wrong with you—we fell in love. We never meant to hurt you, but when we fought against how we felt, we were miserable." She wiped at her eyes. "It was nothing compared to the misery I felt when I realized we had broken your heart." She gazed steadily at Heidi. "You'll never know how much I've missed you . . ." Unable to continue, she rose to meet Heidi in a fierce embrace.

Several minutes later, Heidi pulled back to look at Elena. "So, when is Junior due?"

Elena self-consciously patted her stomach. "In about four months." Sitting down, she smiled shyly at Heidi. They spent the next hour catching up on each other's lives. Elena invited Heidi and Evan to dinner later that week, anxious for Terry to be a part of this healing process. Parting with another intense hug, they went their separate ways lighter inside than they had felt in months.

* * *

As the weeks progressed, wedding plans were made and set. Kate managed to talk Randy into waiting until April. "Mom wants at least four months to pull this off," she tried to explain. "Besides, good things are worth waiting for, right?"

Randy teasingly groaned his displeasure. "I can't believe you're using my own words against me," he complained. It was the same thing he had told Kate just before leaving on his mission.

"Well, it's true. Besides, we'll have all of eternity together. four months will seem like a drop in the bucket."

"A big, long drop," he countered.

"Maybe. But it gives us something to look forward to."

"Don't remind me," Randy said, pulling Kate outside for another enthusiastic snowball fight.

* * *

Things went very smoothly until the first week of March. Saturday afternoon Kate and Randy decided to go in search of something cold to drink and ended up in the Twilight Zone. Set up like a miniature convenience store, it offered a variety of drinks, snacks, and study materials.

"What do you want?" Randy asked, looking over the selection.

"I don't know. Creme soda, I guess."

"Sounds good to me," he replied, opening the glass door to reach inside the refrigerated cooler.

"Randy?" a soft voice called.

Randy turned his head, nearly dropping both bottles. "Laurie?" he stammered, staring at the beautiful, blonde young woman.

Kate glanced from Randy to Laurie. She hated to admit it, but Laurie was even more attractive in person. Stunned, she stared.

"I . . . uh . . . how are you?" Randy stuttered nervously.

"Fine. Mom and I came down this weekend to check out BYU." She glanced around the small convenience store. "This place is bigger than Ricks, but I think I'm going to love it."

Randy nodded, handing the bottles of pop to Kate. He wiped his right hand on the side of his pants and extended it to Laurie. "You look . . . wonderful," he said, shaking Laurie's hand.

Kate's eyes narrowed. "Nice opening line," she muttered, remembering that he had said the same thing when he greeted her at the airport. She cleared her throat loudly.

"Oh, yeah. Uh . . . Laurie, this is Kate . . . Kate . . . uh—"

"Erickson," Kate helpfully supplied.

"She's my . . . uh . . ."

"Fiancée," Kate provided.

"Uh, yeah," Randy stuttered.

Laurie smiled warmly at Kate. "You're engaged. That's wonderful."

Kate blinked. Was it her imagination, or was Laurie really being sincere about this?

"I knew he wouldn't last long," Laurie continued, moving closer to Kate. "He's a great guy," she confided. "I'm happy—for both of you."

Kate forced a smile.

"Laurie?"

Laurie turned her head. "Over here, Mom," she said, motioning to a petite, dark-haired woman. She waited for her mother to approach.

"Mom, this is one of the elders I met in Ireland, Randy . . . uh . . ."

Kate suppressed a smirk. Laurie didn't even remember Randy's last name?

"Miles," Randy offered.

"Miles, that's right. I kept thinking it was something like Giles, I don't know why," Laurie smiled brightly. "And this is his fiancée, Kate Erickson."

Kate lifted an eyebrow. Laurie couldn't remember Randy's full name, but had immediately locked onto hers? Disturbed by this, Kate forced a smile at Laurie's mother.

"I'm glad to meet both of you," Mrs. Spaulding replied. She glanced at her watch. "How would you two like to join us for lunch? We were just on our way to grab a quick bite before we head back to Boise."

"Well . . . I . . . that is . . ." Randy stammered.

"It will give you a chance to visit," Mrs. Spaulding added.

Kate waited for Randy to politely refuse the invitation. Instead, he grinned shyly at Laurie and her mother and told them that would be fine. Kate waited to hit him until they climbed into the back seat of Mrs. Spaulding's car. Startled, Randy glanced at Kate, who pretended she had accidentally bumped into him.

* * *

Kate walked into the apartment, slamming the door behind her. "That was the most miserable afternoon I've ever endured in my life!" she exclaimed to Heidi.

"What happened?" Heidi asked, alarmed by Kate's behavior. She had never seen her this upset before.

"Does the name Laurie Spaulding ring a bell?" Kate asked, her eyes flickering with anger and pain.

Heidi let out a slow rush of air. This didn't sound good.

"We ran into her today at the bookstore," Kate continued as she paced around the living room. "There she was, big as life, in the Twilight Zone—an accurate setting for this bizarre event. You should've seen the look on Randy's face! He couldn't even function. We're supposed to get married next month—and he can't even remember who I am! I had to introduce myself to her! And then, get this, Laurie's mother invites us to lunch. Just 'a quick bite' because they're heading back home later today. Does Randy get the hint that they're in a hurry? Oh, no, he's too busy gawking. He accepts the offer for lunch, and he and Laurie talk all afternoon!" Kate ran an aggravated hand through her hair. "I mean, I try to be as patient as the next girl, but would you enjoy hanging around a girl your fiancé is practically drooling over?"

Heidi slowly shook her head. She remembered what it had felt like those last few weeks after Terry and Elena had started dating.

"We spent the entire afternoon listening to Laurie and Randy as they wandered down memory lane. 'Oh, Randy, do you remember how green everything was in Ireland?'!" Kate mimicked.

"I'm seeing something pretty green right now," Heidi said wryly. "You are one jealous lady."

"I have every right to be," Kate fumed. "You don't know how tempted I was to knock Randy's plate of spaghetti into his lap. I'm still so angry I don't know what to do with myself!"

Seeing a little of herself in Kate, Heidi flinched. "Kate, Randy loves you," she soothed, rising from the kitchen chair. "He wouldn't have proposed if he didn't."

Kate glanced at her roommate. "I never thought I'd hear you say that."

"Well, here's something else you probably never thought I would ever say—I was wrong—about a lot of things. Don't let my fears and frustrations drag you down. Trust yourself, but more important, trust Randy," Heidi pleaded, fearing the doubts she had planted in Kate were finally taking root. "Did you tell Randy how you felt?"

"I think he finally caught on when he walked me home. He was so thrilled about running into *her*, it took a while for him to realize he was having a one-sided conversation."

"So, you talked?"

Kate shook her head. "I couldn't. I knew if I said anything, I'd regret it later. I just told him that I hadn't enjoyed the afternoon, I wasn't feeling well, and I wanted to go home." She glared at Heidi. "And here I am."

Heidi gazed at the ceiling. *And now, what do I do with you?* she thought. Almost on cue, Kate burst into tears.

"I can't lose him, Heidi. Not now. Not after everything we've been to each other."

Shaking her head, Heidi walked toward Kate, opening her arms to the distraught young woman. "It isn't over," she stressed several minutes later as she led Kate to the couch. "So quit acting like it is. After the shock of seeing Laurie has worn off, Randy will come to his senses."

"I hope so," Kate tearfully responded. "I don't know what I'll do if he doesn't."

CHAPTER 15

Randy scowled at Kate. He couldn't believe how upset she had been since they had spotted Laurie at the bookstore two weeks ago. "Kate, we were just talking," he tried to explain. He glanced around, hoping to avoid an emotional scene. The campus sidewalks were crowded as students rushed to their next class. A few of them gave Kate and Randy a curious glance as they walked past, but most were in too big of a hurry to care.

"You and Laurie are always talking!" Kate accused, referring to the conversation she had just interrupted. The minute Laurie had seen Kate coming, she had quickly hurried down the sidewalk, disappearing in the swarm of students who were bustling past. "Why did Laurie run off when she saw me? If these are such innocent chats you two are having, why can't I be a part of them?" she pressed.

"She had to hurry to work," Randy said. "She told me that ten minutes before you showed up."

Kate reluctantly admitted that part could be true. Laurie had recently been hired as a waitress at Chuck-a-Rama. "Okay," she said, trying to calm down. "What were you talking about?"

Randy glared at Kate. "Does it matter? We served in the same mission—"

"Knew the same people, traveled through the same area, I know. I've heard all about it several times!"

"Why are you so angry?"

"Gee, I don't know. Maybe seeing another girl with my fiancé bothers me. Call me silly—"

"If you keep it up, I may call you something else!" Randy threatened, his own temper flaring into existence.

"Spoken like a true gentleman!" Kate challenged.

Randy sighed. He didn't want to fight with Kate, but he was as frustrated as she was. Feelings he didn't understand were tearing him apart. The last thing he needed was for Kate to jump all over him. "I think we both need some time to think things over."

"I see," Kate said sullenly.

"No, you don't see. That's what's so aggravating about all of this."

"I'll tell you what's aggravating—watching the man you're about to marry make goo-goo eyes at another girl!"

"Laurie is a good friend."

"Is she, Randy? Is that all she is to you?" Kate asked, feeling sick inside. Since Laurie's arrival, Kate's life seemed to be propelling out of control. Fear was her constant companion as she helplessly watched Randy struggle with emotions she couldn't fathom.

"This isn't getting us anywhere. I think we both need to do some thinking and praying."

"Especially one of us," Kate snapped as she turned and walked away.

* * *

Clint Miles gazed at his son. Uncomfortable with Randy's tears, he nervously coughed, shifting behind the desk in his study.

"Dad, I don't know what to do," Randy stammered.

"Too bad polygamy was banned," Clint said, trying to lighten the conversation.

"Yeah, right," Randy said morosely. "They'd claw each other's eyes out. Correction. Kate would drag Laurie backwards through a knothole, and Laurie would let her because she feels guilty."

"Why does Laurie feel guilty?"

Randy focused on his hands. "Because she feels something for me. Something pretty strong. I could tell when we kissed."

"You kissed her?"

Randy slowly nodded. "I didn't mean for it to happen. We were walking around the temple grounds and—"

Clint sighed. "Son, why did you take another girl to see the temple—"

"When I'm engaged to someone else," Randy said, finishing the sentence. "Kate and I had just had another major fight. I bumped into Laurie—"

"That seems to be happening on a frequent basis," Clint observed.

"Tell me about it," Randy agreed. It was almost eerie. They hadn't made arrangements to see each other, but every time he turned around, there was Laurie. Something Kate didn't appreciate at all. True, he had called and talked to Laurie a few times on the phone, but it was just to touch base with her on how she was doing or to ask a question about their former mission that he had forgotten to ask before.

"You bumped into Laurie," Clint prompted.

"Yeah. One thing led to another and I invited her to attend a temple session with me. I thought it would help me figure things out. Instead, I'm more confused than ever. I sat in the celestial room for almost an hour, praying about what's happening to Kate and me."

Clint picked up a pen and began playing with it. "Maybe that's part of your answer."

"What?"

"The confusion. Remember the advice Oliver Cowdery was given years ago concerning answers to prayers?"

"You mean that part about studying it out in your mind?" Randy replied. "I memorized that scripture in the MTC."

Clint reached for the triple combination sitting on his desk and turned to the ninth section of the Doctrine and Covenants. "That's the one." He cleared his throat, then began to read out loud. '. . . You must study it out in your mind; then you must ask me if it be right, and if it is right I will cause that your bosom shall burn within you; therefore, you shall feel that it is right. But if it be not right you shall have . . . a stupor of thought . . .'"

"Stupor of thought?" Randy exclaimed. "That's me—I don't know what to do. I thought I loved Kate, but now . . . Dad, I'm feeling something for Laurie too."

"I suggest you pray—a lot," Clint advised. "And it wouldn't hurt to fast. I might even join you."

"You'd do that for me?"

"Yes, but I'm also doing it for me. You and I both know how this whole thing is going to affect your mother."

Randy nodded miserably. He knew his mother absolutely adored Kate. This decision would not be taken lightly by Jan Miles, especially if he decided to break up with Kate.

"Don't give up hope. The answer will come. Your challenge is to be in tune enough to decipher what that answer is."

Randy met his father's concerned gaze. "I don't want to hurt anyone, Dad."

"I don't think it can be avoided," Clint answered somberly.

Picturing Kate and Laurie side by side, Randy nodded. There were things he loved about both girls. It killed him to think he might have to hurt one of them. Why had he rushed things with Kate? Why hadn't he waited? Had he been so obsessed by his jealousy of Mike that he had misjudged the entire situation?

As he thought about Laurie, Randy realized he wasn't certain of her feelings for him. The kiss they shared had been wonderful, but then she had burst into tears and run away. If he pursued that route, would he throw away the love he had for Kate only to chase a phantom dream?

"What should I do?" he asked his father, pleading for help.

"Son, that is a question only you and your Father in Heaven can answer."

* * *

It was a rough couple of days. Randy opted to spend the weekend in Heber. Fasting, he spent the majority of the time in his room. His mother worried over him until Clint finally made it clear that Randy needed to spend this time alone.

"Why? Is there something wrong?" Jan grew pale as a horrible thought came to mind. "Oh, Clint, he and Kate—they didn't—"

Quickly assuring his wife that nothing improper had taken place between their son and Kate, Clint refrained from revealing Randy's true source of distress. When he explained that Randy had some decisions to make about his future, Jan automatically assumed he meant career choices. Clint didn't think there was any harm in letting her believe that. There was a good chance Randy would decide to leave things as they were with Kate. Until their son made his choice, Clint wanted to avoid upsetting his wife. The strong bond Jan shared with Kate might tend to sway things that direction and Clint knew Randy needed to make this decision on his own.

As the hours passed, Randy alternated between reading the scriptures and prayer. Struggling for an answer, he carefully studied his patriarchal blessing, fervently scanning its contents, hoping to discover a clue. It promised that if he made righteous choices, a remarkable young woman would come into his life, an eternal companion.

"Eternal companion?" Randy mumbled. "Why doesn't it say what her initials are?" As he agonized over his inability to make a decision, he remembered the advice the bishop had given him when he was first called to serve a mission. "The greatest quests cause us to search deep within our souls, requiring tremendous effort and sacrifice." It wasn't until he was out in the mission field that he had fully appreciated that counsel. The harsh climate of Ireland, at times as harsh as the attitudes of its people, compelled him to reach further and try harder than he had ever done before. And in the end, it had been worth it. Marvelous things had transpired. Lives had changed for the better, including his own.

The personal quest he now faced was one of significant importance. His eternal fate hung in the balance. Kate or Laurie. He knew he loved both girls, but in different ways. Both had the potential to be wonderful wives and mothers. Mother. He groaned at the thought of his own mother. Was she partially responsible for this mess? Shaking his head, he knew he had only one person to blame—himself.

Exhausted, he slept for nearly an hour, then awoke with a start after a vivid dream. Quickly kneeling beside his bed, Randy began to pray. After nearly thirty minutes of prayerful meditation, an interpretation of the dream came to his mind. Randy slowly opened his eyes as an intense inner burning pushed doubt away. Rising to his feet, he reached for the phone next to his bed and dialed a number he had memorized weeks ago.

CHAPTER 16

Kate followed Randy down to the shore of Utah Lake. For several minutes, Randy stared out across the shimmering water. Puzzled by his continued silence, Kate moved up behind him, slipping her arms around his waist. "I've missed you," she murmured, giving him a hug. Randy pulled away from her. "Randy?"

"We need to talk," he began.

"Obviously," Kate replied, confused.

He motioned to a large rock. Taking off his jacket, he placed it on top of the rock and helped Kate sit down.

"There's room for two," Kate invited.

Randy shook his head.

"Okay," she replied, trying to read the expression on his face. "What's up?"

"Kate, I've made the biggest mistake of my life and now I have to try to make it right."

Her heart began racing. This was it. He was finally going to level with her. "Does this have to do with Laurie?"

Randy slowly nodded. "I don't know how to say this—"

Taking pity on him, Kate realized she had never seen Randy this scared before. "Maybe I can help you out."

"What?"

"I know you've been seeing Laurie. Heidi saw you two kiss in front of the temple—something that really ticked me off at first, but now that I've had time to cool down and you've realized you've made a mistake—"

"Heidi saw us?"

"Oh yeah. She had decided to hit a temple session after her last class that afternoon. As she walked up the sidewalk—"

"She saw us coming out," Randy supplied. "She must really hate me now." Frustrated, he kicked against the rock.

Kate touched his face. "She doesn't hate you and neither do I. Randy, I *can* forgive one kiss, okay?"

"But—"

Kate placed a finger on his lips. "Your turn to listen. I want you to know that I *am* capable of understanding. It hasn't seemed that way lately, but I'm not angry anymore. Heidi and I had a long talk and I realized my anger has been driving you away."

Randy leaned against the rock for support, letting her speak.

"I've been thinking things over and I've decided it's important for you to get Laurie out of your system. It's the only way it'll work between us. If it took a simple kiss to help you realize—"

"Kate, this is about more than a kiss."

Kate's eyes widened. "How much more?"

Randy clenched his fists and took a deep breath. "It's pretty serious between Laurie and me," he tried to explain.

"You just said you'd made a terrible mistake. What have you done?" Sensing his agitation, she panicked, thinking the worst. "Tell me it didn't go further than that. You didn't—"

"Kate, I'm sorry—"

"I'm going to be sick," Kate said, slipping down off the rock. She breathed in deeply. "You'd think two returned missionaries could at least keep themselves under control!" Turning, she raced to the edge of the lake.

Perplexed, Randy stared after her. Then it dawned on him what Kate was implying. He hurried after her. "Kate, wait up!"

"How could you?" Kate demanded, turning to stare at him.

"It isn't like you think."

"Oh? Tell me what I'm thinking!" she demanded, waiting impatiently for an explanation.

Randy blushed.

"Then I'm right."

"No! You couldn't be more wrong!"

Kate gazed intently at him, trying to calm down. It was difficult, forcing the image of Laurie and Randy from her mind, but she made a valiant effort. "You really had me going for a minute. I was afraid you were trying to tell me something like now you *had* to marry her."

Randy nearly choked. Turning to the side, he coughed violently.

"I mean, it's not like Laurie's pregnant or anything, right?" Kate pressed.

"NO! And I wish you'd quit saying things like that about the woman I'm going to marry!"

Kate gaped at him.

Randy cringed. "Kate . . . I'm sorry . . . I didn't mean to tell you . . . not like this."

"Marry? You're going to *marry her?"* she asked, staggering under the intensity of this bombshell.

Randy slowly nodded. "Kate—"

Kate closed her eyes. "This is a nightmare. It isn't real. Any minute now I'll wake up screaming and none of this will have happened," she murmured.

"I'm sorry, Kate. I've been trying to figure out how to break this to you without hurting you—"

"You're not doing a very good job," Kate said. Opening her eyes, she stared at him. "This isn't a dream, is it?"

Randy shook his head.

"I didn't think so," Kate faltered, sinking to her knees. The pain was too intense to be an illusion. Gasping for air, she wrapped her arms around herself.

"Kate?"

"Don't touch me!" she warned.

"I'm sorry," Randy said, helplessly dropping his hands to his sides.

"Everyone tried to tell me this would happen. Why didn't I listen?" she moaned, rocking back and forth.

"Kate—" Randy pleaded, kneeling in front of her.

"Did I drive you away?"

"It wasn't anything you did or said. It was me. I should've paid more attention to what I was really feeling. Then none of this would've happened," he stammered, wishing he could take her pain upon himself. He hated the wounded look in her eyes.

"How could you do this?"

Tears glimmered in Randy's eyes as he said, "I'm in love with Laurie. That's what I've been trying to tell you. I have been all along, but I was so confused—"

Kate blinked, stung by his confession. "You said you loved me."

"I still do, as a friend."

"A friend?" Kate exclaimed. "We were supposed to get married in three weeks!"

"Kate—"

"Why?"

"It's my fault. If I'd been more in tune I would've caught on to what was really going on between us. I thought I loved you, but what I loved was how you reminded me of Laurie."

"You said Laurie reminded you of me," Kate mumbled.

"I had it backwards," he answered, reaching to wipe a stray tear from her cheek. He flinched when she pulled away. "It took me a while to figure things out."

"Are you sure you have?"

"Yes. For the first time in weeks, I'm sure," he said, remembering the dream he'd had Sunday afternoon. Hesitantly, he tried to describe it to Kate. Walking along a path, he had suddenly been joined by Kate. They had walked together until reaching a crossroads. Kate longed to take another path, but sensing Randy's indecision, stayed by his side. In the distance, Laurie had appeared. Her path was linked with the one Randy felt he should take. "The prompting that came later when I prayed about it was so strong," Randy tried to explain. "I know Laurie's meant to be my wife."

"You seemed pretty sure the night you proposed to me!" Kate accused, rising to her feet.

"We did have something special," Randy admitted.

"I thought so, too. What I don't get is why you suddenly think it's over!" Was this her reward for doing things the right way? For adhering to Church standards? She wanted to scream!

"I wish you could understand—that I could explain it better. What I'm feeling for Laurie is different—"

"Different?!"

"I don't know how to put it into words." He slowly stood, facing her.

"Try, Randy! Try really hard, because I'm not understanding any of this!" Kate demanded.

"I know and I'm sorry—"

"You keep saying that," Kate accused. "It doesn't mean anything! Feeling sorry won't change what you're doing!" Turning her back to him, she began to walk away.

"Kate, listen to me."

"That's what got me into trouble in the first place!"

"Kate—"

"Don't expect me to be gracious about this!" Kate exclaimed. "We've already mailed half of the wedding invitations. My wedding dress is nearly finished—"

"Kate, look at me." He hurried forward to grab her, turning her around. "I *do* care about you— I didn't want to hurt you!"

Kate refused to look at him.

"I thought I was in love with you. But, what we had—the fun, the laughter, the memories of what we shared before—it wasn't enough. If it had been, Laurie never would've come between us." He gestured between them. "It's over, Kate. I know that now."

"Oh? How convenient for you!" Kate pulled away from him. "The one I feel sorry for is Laurie. Does she realize that you'll drop her when someone else comes along?"

"I'm not that kind of guy."

"You're talking to the wrong person. You just did it to me, remember?"

Randy gazed steadily at Kate. "I know Laurie's the one. I think it's something I've known all along, but I let doubt creep in. Mom mentioned that I might lose you waiting for a girl who would want nothing to do with me. That possibility frightened me. Laurie and I had never talked about how we felt, not until she came to Provo. You were here and real, there was a strong attraction between us. I convinced myself it was love."

"You convinced me, too," Kate said tersely.

"But when I saw Laurie that day, something went off inside of me. Big-time promptings that I still tried to ignore because we were engaged."

Kate closed her eyes.

"Kate, if I could go back and change things, I would. Then none of this would've happened." He waited, but there was no response. "I guess we both should've listened to Heidi. As much as I hate to admit it, she was right, and when I fasted and prayed about it this week—"

"I've prayed about us too, Randy. Doesn't that count for anything?" Kate asked, glaring at him.

"It does . . . but—"

"I'm in love with you, you jerk!"

"It isn't love, Kate—not the way you think."

Kate's eyes flashed dangerously. "Our relationship meant something to me!"

"I didn't mean—"

"Well, I mean this—take your ring, take me home, and take yourself out of my life! I never want to see you again!" Pulling the ring from her finger, Kate threw it at him. Then she stomped back to the car, fury curbing the tears that ached for release.

CHAPTER 17

Kate finished the semester in a daze. It helped, having Heidi to talk to. Heidi understood the betrayal she felt and seemed to know exactly what to say. Kate's mother came down the day after the breakup and stayed a week. Her words of soothing comfort went a long way toward softening the emotional blow Kate had suffered. Aunt Paige stopped in for several lengthy visits, lending another form of solace. Sandi tried everything she could think of to cheer her up, but they all knew it would be a long time before Kate would smile and mean it.

As Kate struggled through each day, Jan suffered her own personal heartache. She had been prepared to accept Kate as a daughter, and it had come as a terrible blow to learn of the breakup. At first she had been furious with Randy and hurt that she had been left out of the decision. It took a while for her to understand this was something Randy had needed to do on his own. As Clint reasoned with her, Jan softened and by the time Randy brought Laurie by for a visit, she was almost ready to accept her.

After she had had a chance to absorb the shock herself, Jan went to see Kate. They spent the entire visit crying, but afterwards they both felt surprisingly better.

Randy sent an apologetic note with flowers, all of which ended up in the garbage. Heidi was alarmed at first, but was glad to see that Kate was getting some of her spunk back. Heidi knew in time Kate would be ready to forgive and she hoped to pave the way for her by helping her avoid the mistakes she had made.

"If you don't let go of the anger, the bitterness can eat you alive," she said soberly, anxious to help Kate avoid that pitfall. Kate knew that Heidi spoke from experience and it helped, but she was relieved when the semester was finally over, and only too glad to escape to Bozeman for the summer.

Randy and Laurie were married in June. Aware of her limitations, Kate avoided the reception although she did mail a nice gift for the new couple—a framed picture of the Provo Temple. She then tried to forced their wedding out of her mind by putting in long hours as a secretary in her father's computer company.

* * *

About the middle of July, Kate was finally ready to start thinking about her future. Deciding there must've been a reason for the way things had turned out, she prayed in earnest to discover what that was.

Although she was still determined to get her teaching degree, Kate had the nagging sense that there was something else she needed to do. As she refocused on her patriarchal blessing, one phrase seemed to leap off the page. It concerned the sheaves she would bring to the Lord. As she pondered that line, two words came to mind: missionary work. Stunned, Kate considered the possibility. In one year she would be twenty-one and old enough to go, but a mission? She'd never considered it before. She thought of how she had loved hearing about Heidi's missionary experiences and wondered if that had been an influence. A few nights later she drove to the Kearns' house to talk to Heidi.

Seeing immediately that Kate had something important on her mind, Heidi led her out onto the front porch for some privacy. Both of her brothers were up with their families and it seemed like the house was bursting at the seams with children.

As they sat together on the steps, the two friends took a minute to enjoy the pleasant evening. A cool breeze played with their hair as the sun began to dip behind the mountains.

"I love it here," Kate exclaimed. "Every time I come home it's harder to leave."

"I know what you mean," Heidi sighed.

"I wonder if I could stand to be away for eighteen months."

At first it didn't dawn on Heidi what Kate meant. "Eighteen months? You'll be home again in less than four."

"I'm not talking about school."

Heidi's eyes widened. "What are you trying to say?"

Kate's eyes sparkled with mischief. "Take a guess."

"A mission?"

Kate nodded. "That thought hit me so strongly the other day. I can't explain it, but it feels right. I've been wondering if maybe that's why . . ." Her voice trailed off as she thought of Randy. "He mentioned a dream he'd had when he called off our engagement. Something about a different path I was supposed to explore."

"Could be," Heidi softly replied. "Have you prayed about it?"

Kate nodded. "It feels like the right thing to do."

"Have you told your parents?"

Kate shook her head. "I haven't decided for sure and I have a year to think about it."

"A lot can happen in a year," Heidi responded, holding out her hand, finally drawing Kate's attention to the ring on her finger.

Kate squealed with excitement as she hugged Heidi. "When did this happen?"

"A week ago," Heidi said, grinning.

"Why didn't you tell me?" Kate accused.

"I thought about calling, but I wasn't sure you were ready for this kind of news yet."

Grinning, Kate grabbed Heidi's hand for a closer look. "It's gorgeous," she breathed, staring at the sparkling diamond.

"I know. I about died when Evan first showed it to me."

Kate reached for another hug. "I'm so happy for you," she said. As she returned the hug, Heidi was thinking the same thing of Kate. It was good to see Kate excited about life again.

* * *

On her next day off, Kate rode her ten-speed to Glen Lake for some private meditation. After finding a place to leave her bike, she approached the lake's edge and reached for a flat stone. She managed to skip it a couple of times before it sank from sight.

"Not bad," a husky voice commented. "Of course, I've never been one for skipping rocks."

Startled, Kate glanced around, staring at the broad-shouldered man behind her.

"Again, I'd have to say, not bad. Not bad at all. You've grown into a beautiful woman, Kate."

Kate stared at the bearded man in the expensively tailored suit. His eyes were hidden by his sunglasses. "I'm sorry, but I'm afraid you have the advantage—"

The man grinned. "That's how it should be, Kate. How it always should've been, and how it is now."

Puzzled by a growing sense of uneasiness, Kate continued to stare, but still couldn't place who this was. "Look, I have no idea who you are—or how you know me—"

"I'm hurt, Katie. Truly hurt. Has it been that long?" He removed his sunglasses and gazed steadily at Kate.

"Jace?" Kate ventured, gaping at her former boyfriend. She had dated him most of her junior year, before Church standards had begun to appeal to her. He had been exciting, dangerous, and exactly the kind of guy her parents had hated. "Jace Sloan?"

"The one and only," Jace said, grinning.

Kate continued to stare. She had pictured Jace in her mind several times the past two years, but never like this. She had always imagined him drunk with unkept hair, a straggly beard, and disheveled clothes. The man she saw now was far removed from that image.

Jace laughed, enjoying the shocked look on Kate's face. "I can see you're surprised at how well I've turned out."

"I . . . you've changed so much," she finally stammered.

"Have I?" Jace questioned, stepping closer. "Or, is this the real me, hidden all those years by lack of funds."

"You must be doing well," Kate said weakly, still trying to comprehend what she was seeing.

"You might say that, yeah," Jace said gleefully.

"How . . . what I mean—"

"How did I go from a simple drunk to this," Jace asked, a sneer curling his upper lip. "It wasn't easy, Katie. It was all uphill from where you left me."

"From where I left you? Now, just a minute, Jace—"

"You turned your nose up at me. Suddenly, I wasn't good enough for you. You ruined everything for me, then walked away."

Kate eased back a step, glancing around the park for help. She noticed two teenage boys throwing a football. If she screamed loud enough, they would probably come running. Kate remembered only too well the last time he had tried to touch her. He had grabbed her the night of the senior prom, making several lewd threats. Fortunately, Mike Jeffries, her date for the evening, had come to her rescue. When Kate had disappeared a few minutes earlier, Mike had searched for her and found her just before Jace tried to force her into his car. Mike effectively stopped Jace by plowing his fist into Jace's face and stomach. Mike had been proclaimed a hero while Jace had ended up in juvenile court with a stiff sentence.

"Don't worry, Kate, I've learned my lesson. I won't lay a finger on you," he snapped. "I heard you were back in town and just wanted to stop by to see how you were doing."

"Jace—"

"You do look good. Real good." A hungry gleam appeared in his eyes. "Amazing, isn't it, that you weren't good enough for your cowboy friend."

"What?"

"You know, that imbecile who broke up with you to marry someone else. I guess he didn't want damaged goods after all."

Kate's eyes narrowed. "I'm not 'damaged goods'! It just didn't work out between us. And anyway, what business is it of yours?"

Jace shrugged. "Everything you do is my business. I've kept track of you. It's been a fun hobby. That's why I came by, to renew old ties. I saw you from the other end of the park and decided we needed to have a chat. It's been too long, much too long."

"I don't know what you're after, but—"

"Just wanted to say hello." Jace grinned. "I'll admit, during the time I spent in juvenile detention, I had big plans for you. Big plans," he emphasized, his eyes wandering along her body.

Kate blushed. "Jace—"

"But I finally caught on that if I came after you, it would only get me into more trouble. So, I decided to chase a different dream. I decided there were better ways of evening the score. When I got out of detention, my parents sent me back down to stay with my uncle in Wyoming. You know, the one who owns the ranch, the one I stayed with before when you first stirred up trouble for me."

"You have no one to blame for what happened but yourself," Kate said angrily.

"Did you know I had to repeat my senior year of high school? Everyone thought going to a smaller school and working on my uncle's ranch would shape me up. Well, guess what, it did. I decided right then and there that I would never allow myself to be put into that kind of situation again, that I would never have to dig cow manure out from under my fingernails." He held up his hands for inspection. "I have my nails treated by a manicurist once a week now," he said proudly. "See that Porsche over there, the bright red one? That's mine."

Kate glanced across the park at the fancy sports car.

"Remember when you and Linda and I were talking about what kind of car we would have after high school? We all agreed on the same thing, a Porsche. Well, we all know that isn't possible for Linda anymore. I see you're still getting around town on a ten-speed. That leaves me. I'm the only one living our dream."

"My dreams have changed—" Kate began.

"So have mine." He turned and motioned to someone in the Porsche. A tall, beautiful brunette climbed out of the car. She hesitated, glancing at Jace for guidance. "No, that's okay, stay there. I'll be right up. Just wanted to show you off," Jace hollered at her. The woman obediently climbed back inside of the sports car. "I have her trained, don't I," Jace bragged. "And the best part is, she'll do anything I tell her to—unlike someone else I know," he added, his eyes burning as he gazed steadily at Kate.

Kate had had enough. "I'm *tickled* things have worked out so well for you, Jace, but I really have to be going now," she said.

"Don't you even want to hear how I've managed all of this?" Jace asked.

"I'm not interested in you or your life," Kate said as she turned her back to him.

"You don't care that it all started with some contacts I made while I was in that detention center? That I have you to thank for all of this?"

Kate turned to glare at Jace. "What is it you're trying to say?"

"Well, Katie, you'd be proud of me. I made it in life the old-fashioned way. I started with nothing and through hard work, made my fortune."

"Doing what?"

"I'm much too modest to brag, but I will tell you this—I'm probably one of the most popular guys around, especially with kids. I give teenagers what they want, they have a good time, and they have me to thank for it."

Horrified by what she was sure Jace was hinting at, she gasped. It all made sense—his newfound wealth, the car, his clothes. "You're dealing drugs," she finally managed to say.

"You always were a sharp one, Katie," Jace said, smiling. "It's such a rewarding profession. I bring joy and happiness into so many people's lives."

"You make me sick!" Kate said, closing her eyes.

"It's especially the smaller children that I enjoy helping. They even have a cute nickname for me. Something to do with candy, I'm sure it's because I'm so sweet."

"You're the candy man," Kate accused, opening her eyes. "I've heard Sabrina talk about you. She said something about a real nice man at the park who hands out candy and stickers."

"We start them out slow," Jace commented. "Those stickers have been quite popular, actually. Your sister has been one of my best customers."

Kate fought the urge to panic. She had to be able to think clearly, especially if what Jace was saying was true.

"We save the special stickers for customers like Sabrina."

"You dirty—"

"Ah, ah, ah, you don't say those kind of things anymore, remember?"

"Why are you telling me this? You know I'll go straight to the police!"

Relishing the terrified look on her face, he grinned. "And say what?"

"Everything you've just told me."

"It'll be your word against mine. And, presently, I'm a model citizen. I'm above reproach. You, my dear, have no proof, and I'll simply deny everything. Besides, I really don't think you'll want to bother the police with this trivial matter."

Her temper flaring, Kate glared at Jace. "Name one reason why I wouldn't!"

"Your family," Jace said menacingly. "We'd hate for anything to happen to your dear mother, for example."

"You wouldn't!"

"Try me," Jace countered. "By the way, that incident with your brother's car—"

"The one he's trying to fix up?"

"That's the one."

Kate stared at him. "You're the one who vandalized it!"

"One and the same, although someone else did the actual work. I was merely the brains behind it all."

Stunned by what she was hearing, Kate shook her head. "Do you realize how hard he's worked on that car?"

"That's what made it fun."

Enraged, Kate slapped Jace across the face.

"That was uncalled for," Jace warned, rubbing his face. "In fact, you'll be really sorry you did that," he added, his eyes dark and menacing. "Now, if you don't mind, I'm needed on the other side of the park. Customers await." Whirling around, he headed for his Porsche. As he drove away, Kate ran to her bike and pedaled furiously toward her home.

CHAPTER 18

"Sabrina—why didn't you answer when I called?" Kate asked breathlessly as she hurried downstairs to the family room.

"I'm watchin' cartoons," her younger sister lisped.

Kate walked across the room and hugged her eight-year-old sister tight. Overwhelmed by the fear that had haunted her on the way home, she clung to Sabrina, relieved that the younger girl was all right.

"Kate," Sabrina complained. "I'm tryin' to watch—"

"Cartoons, I know," Kate said, fighting tears as she released Sabrina. She gazed at her younger sister. Sabrina had recently been baptized. She had been so excited about becoming an official member of the Church. "Now I'm a real Moron," Sabrina had lisped to her amused family. Kate had stepped on Tyler's foot to keep him from commenting on Sabrina's slip of the tongue. "She meant Mormon. She didn't realize what she said," Kate had told him later.

"She never does," Tyler had good-naturedly quipped.

As Kate reflected on Sabrina's innocence, she pulled her sister into another hug.

"What's wrong with you," Sabrina asked, squirming away. "Why are you huggin' me and cryin'?"

"Breeny—"

"Sabrina!" the eight-year-old insisted.

"Sabrina—sorry." Kate forced a smile. "Where's Mom?"

"She went to visit the teachers."

"What?"

"You know, with Sister Humphreys."

"Oh, visiting teaching," Kate guessed.

"That's what I said."

"Who's here with you?"

"Tyler," Sabrina said, wrinkling up her nose. "He's out in the garage with his old car. He told me to come watch cartoons."

Kate slowly stood, motioning to the couch. There would have to be a few changes around here. Sabrina couldn't be left on her own until this entire mess was resolved. "Sabrina, we need to talk."

"About what?" Sabrina asked, suddenly suspicious. When grown-ups wanted to talk, it always meant trouble.

Kate turned off the TV and moved to the couch. She waited patiently for her younger sister to join her. "I want to talk to you about this candy man you've been telling me about."

"I already told you," Sabrina started.

"Tell me again, I think I missed part of what you said."

Sabrina glowered at Kate. She wondered if anyone ever listened to what she said. But, Kate was paying attention now. Sighing, she decided to try again. "He's a nice man—"

"Why do you think he's nice?"

"'Cuz he gives me stuff."

Kate nervously swallowed. "What kind of stuff?"

Sabrina shrugged. No one had seemed to care before. In a way, she had been glad. It had been a fun secret to keep to herself. Whenever she'd mentioned the stickers, everyone said things like, "That's nice," totally ignoring her.

"Sabrina, this is important."

"Why, do you want some candy and stickers too?" Sabrina sullenly asked.

Kate prayed for patience. "Is that what the candy man gave you?"

Sabrina nodded.

"Did you eat the candy?"

Again, Sabrina nodded. "It was wrapped. Mommy told me not to eat candy that isn't wrapped."

"Mom also told you to never take candy from strangers."

"He's not a stranger, he knows you. He said you were his friend."

Frustrated, Kate ran a hand through her hair. "He's not my friend. He isn't anybody's friend."

"He is so. All my friends like him."

"I want you to promise me that you'll stay away from him," Kate said.

"Why?"

Noting the pouting lip, Kate knew she had a fight on her hands. "Sabrina, I don't know how to explain this to you." Rising, she paced the floor. "Have you ever listened when they've had those assemblies in your school about drugs?" she finally asked.

"Drugs are bad!"

"Yes, they are. And if anyone ever offered you drugs, what would you do?"

"Scream real loud and run away. Then I'd tell my teacher or Mommy."

"Good answer," Kate said, relieved. She sat down next to her sister, placing an arm around her small shoulders. "Sabrina, the candy man is selling drugs to older kids."

Sabrina's eyes widened. "Uh-uh," she said, shaking her head.

"Yes, he is. I found out about it this afternoon."

"No way!" Sabrina argued, pulling away from Kate.

"Sabrina, he told me about it. He's trying to get you younger kids to like him so you'll buy drugs from him too."

Sabrina looked like she was about to cry. "But he gave me neat stuff. It was free."

"I know, but he's a bad man." Kate frowned. "Do you remember a guy I used to go out with, a guy named Jace?"

Sabrina shook her head.

Kate sighed. "Just as well. He was a loser then and an even bigger loser now. Jace is the candy man."

"You dated the candy man?"

Kate slowly nodded. "It wasn't the smartest thing I've ever done, but it was a long time ago. Before I caught on to what a cretin he was. I ran into him today at the park."

"He gave me candy and stickers," Sabrina said mournfully.

"Could I see the stickers he gave you?"

"Why?"

"I want to see what he's been handing out."

"Okay," Sabrina finally said. Then, looking up at Kate, she murmured, "If he sells drugs, he's not a nice man."

"No, he isn't, Breeny. You need to stay away from him. Jace is a very bad man."

* * *

Sue glanced at the stickers and shook her head. Unable to speak, she reached for her husband's hand.

Greg squeezed Sue's hand, then gazed at Kate. "I knew I should've taken that boy out when I had the chance," he grumbled.

"I don't think the children would've enjoyed seeing you in prison," Sue replied.

"I'd like to see him in prison!" Greg exclaimed.

"Me, too," Kate sighed. "I'm sorry—I feel like this is my fault."

Sue stared at her oldest daughter. "How is this your fault?"

"If I hadn't gone out with Jace—"

Greg shook his head. "We don't hold you responsible for any of this. I'm just glad you found out what he's up to."

"Are any of these stickers laced with drugs?" Sue asked, staring again at the stickers that were laid out on the kitchen counter.

"I don't know," Kate admitted. "Jace hinted that he had given special stickers to Sabrina. I'm not sure what he meant by that."

"They could be laced with drugs?" Greg asked slowly.

Sue nodded. "It was brought up at a special meeting the school district held last fall. In some areas, stickers laced with drugs like LSD have been handed out to grade school kids."

"I'll kill him!" Greg said angrily.

"I'm sure you're not the only one who'd like to," Sue replied. "But right now, we need to think clearly and decide what we're going to do."

"Is there any question—we're going to the police!"

Kate glanced at her father. "What about his threat against the family?"

"She has a point, Greg. Look what he did to Tyler's car."

Greg brought a fist down on the counter. "I will not be intimidated by a two-bit punk!"

"And I won't have my family placed in danger," Sue said just as stubbornly.

"So, what do we do, allow Jace the freedom to sell drugs to anyone, anywhere? Do we stand idly by while he hands out drug-laced stickers to kids?"

"I don't know what the answer is," Sue moaned, rubbing her temples.

"What if we give an anonymous tip?" Kate offered.

"Wouldn't Jace be able to track it down?" Sue asked.

"I doubt it. He's not that smart," Greg replied. "I still say we turn this over to the police."

Sue breathed deeply. "I'd feel better about it if we prayed first. Maybe then we'll know how to handle things."

Greg slowly nodded. "Kate, go round up your siblings. I think it's time we held a family council."

* * *

It was decided that Kate and Greg would drop by the police station to report what Kate had learned. They brought along the stickers as evidence. After explaining why they had come, they were turned over to Detective Frank Bart, the police officer who had already been working on this case.

"We've had our eye on Mr. Sloan for quite some time," Detective Bart revealed. "We're just waiting for him to lead us to the bigger fish in this polluted pond of scum. He's working for some big boys out of Los Angeles. That's where he's gotten all of his fancy toys. Actually, it was his newly acquired wealth that attracted our attention. We knew it wasn't a case of hometown boy makes good."

"More like hometown boy makes a mess out of things," Greg grumbled.

"Exactly. He must think we're stupid." Detective Bart shook his head. "There's no way he could be making that kind of money running the video store he manages. And we know that's where he distributes most of the drugs. Kids go into the store under the pretense of renting a video and come out with a video case containing cocaine, crack, maybe even heroin."

Greg shook his head.

"We've nabbed a few of those kids. They've been a big help in gathering evidence. We're getting quite a collection of those specially prepared video cases. As soon as we can tie it all together with California, Mr. Sloan is out of business."

"What about these stickers?" Greg asked, pointing to Sabrina's collection.

The police detective carefully picked up one of the sticker sheets, then shrugged. "We'll have them tested. As far as we know, none of the drug-laced stickers have turned up in Bozeman. We've kept a close eye on that end of things. Sloan might think it's coming, but he's wrong."

"How long until he's arrested?" Kate worriedly asked. She knew Jace too well to believe he wouldn't retaliate against them for reporting this.

"Like I said, we're just giving Mr. Sloan time to hook himself good, then we'll reel him in. His days of so-called glory are coming to an end. He'll end up in the can with the rest of his associates."

Kate's head was pounding when she finally returned home with her father. As she recalled the detective's words, she shuddered, picturing Jace in prison.

"Kate, are you all right?" Sue asked worriedly as Kate and Greg walked into the house.

Kate's voice was subdued. "Yeah," she said quietly.

"You look a little pale," Sue pressed.

"I have a headache. I think I'll go lie down for a while," Kate responded, heading upstairs.

"Let her go, Sue," Greg counseled as Sue prepared to follow. "We learned some pretty awful things this afternoon." He quickly filled Sue and Tyler in on what was taking place. They decided to keep things low-key for Sabrina's sake. She was upset enough as it was.

"Eventually, they'll put Jace out of commission," Greg assured Sue and Tyler.

"What do we do in the meantime?" Sue asked.

"Until they finish this sting operation, we keep a low profile and sit tight," Greg replied.

"What about Jace's threat?" Tyler asked.

"I don't think anything will come of it. Detective Bart said they would patrol this street to keep track of us. We'll take some precautions of our own, too. None of us are to go anywhere alone, especially you, Kate, and Sabrina."

Sue gazed at Greg. "We'll be prisoners in our own home."

"It won't be forever. The police talked like they were close to wrapping this one up."

"I hope so," she sighed, leaning her head against her husband's shoulder. "I can't live this way for very long."

CHAPTER 19

Five days went by without mishap. Deciding that Jace had been bluffing, the Ericksons began to relax. Greg still insisted on escorts for Sue, Kate, and Sabrina, but even he had concluded that Jace's threat had been idle. What they didn't know was how patient Jace had become in recent years. He had learned that some things were worth waiting for. As he bided his time until he was certain that the Ericksons' initial alarm had passed, he devised a plan to teach them all a lesson. He had heard through a reliable source at the police station that Kate and her father had stopped by for a visit. It was time to show them who had the upper hand.

Two days later, he got his chance. Tired of being cooped up in the house, Sabrina decided she wanted to go to a nearby park to play. Sneaking out while her mother was on the phone, she grabbed her bike and pedaled quickly down the street.

A few minuter later, Sabrina contentedly played on a slide with three other little girls. The three were sisters who were staying in Bozeman with their grandmother for part of the summer. They were tickled to meet Sabrina and had a nice time until the candy man made an appearance.

Sabrina didn't see Jace until the last possible moment. He busily handed out candy and gum to the other girls, purposely ignoring Sabrina. He knew her curiosity would eventually get the best of her and it did. She watched for several seconds before approaching him.

"You want something?" he asked, slowly looking at her.

Sabrina shook her head.

"Wow, look Sabrina," one of the other girls exclaimed. "I got heart stickers."

Pretending indifference, Sabrina walked away. This was a bad man—Kate had said so. He sold drugs and it was his fault she had been grounded for over a week. Her parents had told her she couldn't even talk to her friends about him. It made her mad. Heading for a swing, Sabrina sat down and began to pump herself high into the air.

Jace watched her out of the corner of his eye. Lingering near a group of trees, he waited until Sabrina was alone before making his move.

* * *

"Where's Sabrina?" Kate asked, coming back upstairs after a long day at work. Certain that Sabrina was tiring of what she called *house-resting,* her interpretation of house arrest, Kate had decided to take Sabrina for an ice cream cone.

"She was playing on the computer when your grandmother called," Sue replied, walking out of the kitchen. Busily preparing supper, she hadn't thought to check on her youngest daughter after the phone call.

"I want to take her out for an ice cream cone," Kate said, heading down the hall to check in the computer room. "I know she's getting tired of staying in the house."

Sue nodded, not caring if an ice cream run spoiled Sabrina's dinner. It would do the eight-year-old some good. "Take Tyler or your dad with you," she requested when Kate reappeared. "They're both out in the garage working on Tyler's car."

"Why don't we all go?" Kate suggested.

The idea appealed to Sue. She was tiring of house arrest, too. "Let me pop this lasagna in the oven to keep it warm and I'll be ready to go. You get Sabrina."

"Where is she?"

"In the study."

"No, she isn't," Kate replied, "I already looked there."

"She's not in her room?"

Kate shook her head. She had glanced in there on the way back from the study. "And I already checked the family room. I figured she'd be downstairs watching cartoons."

As a vague uneasiness settled in, both Kate and Sue hurried upstairs to search through the other rooms of the house.

* * *

Jace grinned. This was too easy. Earlier, when no one was watching, he had slashed a tire on Sabrina's bike. Waiting until the other girls left, he then approached Sabrina again, offering candy. Sabrina stubbornly refused, marching to her bike to head home. Dismayed by the flat tire, she had burst into tears. All sympathy and kindness, Jace promised to help her. He knew she would be too upset over her bike to remember anything Kate or her parents might've said about him. When he offered to take her bike to a place where it could be fixed, Sabrina eagerly agreed.

Loading her bike into the small utility van he had brought, he then helped Sabrina up inside the van, instructing her to stay in the back with the bike to keep it from sliding around. The back portion of the van was closed in so no one could see in and Sabrina couldn't see out.

Grinning, Jace started the engine. "Let the games begin," he muttered under his breath.

* * *

Detective Bart arrived at last, and Sue leaned against Kate for support while Greg answered his questions. Tyler stood somberly in the corner of the living room, watching out the window. They had already tried all of Sabrina's known friends and everyone in the neighborhood. No one had seen her.

* * *

Jace's original plan had been to keep Sabrina just long enough to allow panic to set in. He had no intention of hurting the young girl; he just wanted to get his point across. The Ericksons needed to learn an important lesson, one that he was only too willing to teach. Pulling in behind his video store, he quickly helped Sabrina from the van and led her through the back entrance of the building.

"Hey, Larry," he hollered from the back room. "C'mere a minute," he said, motioning for Sabrina to sit on a chair behind a cluttered desk.

"I wanna go home now," Sabrina said, suddenly scared. She had an uncomfortable feeling inside and wondered if it was the Holy Ghost her parents had talked about. "If you feel bad in here," her mother had explained, pointing to her heart, "that's the Holy Ghost trying to tell you that whatever you're doing, it's wrong or dangerous." Now, as Sabrina glanced around the messy room, that feeling of wrongness intensified. Tears welling up in her eyes, she glanced back at the door.

Jace smiled at her. "It's okay, squirt. I'll have Larry go get a new tire for your bike. Then I'll see to it you get home. If we fix your tire, you won't even get in trouble. You can tell your parents that I helped you, that I was looking out for you." Grinning as he thought of their reaction, he pulled a wrapped lollipop from a vest pocket. "Here, suck on this while you wait. I'll set up a movie for you to watch back here. Want to watch *Bambi*?" Without waiting for an answer, he called out again, "Larry!"

Sabrina took the sucker, but didn't unwrap it. Instead she set it on the desk and watched with widened eyes as a tall, skinny man entered the small room.

"It's about time," Jace snapped. Then, remembering Sabrina, he changed his tone. "I need you to do a quick favor for this pretty little girl."

Larry glanced from Jace to Sabrina. He wasn't sure what his boss was up to, but he didn't like the looks of this.

"Her tire went flat at the park. Take a look at it—it's in the van. Run across the street and get her a new tire. When it's all set, come tell me and we'll see to it that Sabrina gets home okay."

Larry glanced back over his shoulder. "Uh, Jace, we got a problem."

"No, we don't, not as long as you hustle out that door and do like I say," Jace snarled. Then, calming, he turned to smile sweetly at Sabrina. "Sometimes Larry is a naughty boy. I have to show him who's boss."

"We got company," Larry said, motioning toward the front of the store.

Annoyed, Jace scowled. Now what?

"California's here and they're plenty nervous."

Swearing under his breath, Jace reevaluated the situation. "Okay, here's what we do, you take the kid with you to fix her bike. Then send her on her way and get back here pronto," he said, pulling a wad of money out of his wallet. "That should take care of the tire," he added, handing the money to Larry. "Now get her out of here quick."

"Get who out of here, Sloan?" A tall man in an gray silk suit stepped through the door, and two large men moved in behind him.

"Blake, what are you doin' here, man?" Jace asked, trying to act surprised. He turned to his employee. "Larry, why didn't you tell me Blake was here?"

"Cut the crap," Blake said, unimpressed with Jace's act. "We came to check on our investment. We understand there's a cause for concern in this *hick town*," he said, emphasizing his distaste for Bozeman. His gaze drifted to Sabrina, who was sinking down in her chair. "Good-looking kiddie you got there," he commented, giving Jace a meaningful look. "What kind of racket have you got goin' here, Sloan?"

"Nothin' like that, Blake. She's a neighborhood kid whose bike broke down. We try to be good neighbors. It gives us a good name. Makes people happy. Larry here is gonna help her fix the tire, isn't that right, Sabrina?" Jace asked, eager to get her out of here. He didn't trust Blake or his men. He motioned for Larry to take Sabrina out the back door. "Go on now, Sabrina, Larry will help you with your bike," Jace insisted.

"Sabrina, huh?" the tall man said as the frightened young girl tried to move past him. "What's a pretty young thing like you doin' with a slime-ball like Mr. Sloan?"

Terrified, Sabrina froze. Jace grabbed her arm and pulled her toward him. "We'll talk another time, Sabrina," Jace said, pushing her into Larry.

"Now why are you so eager to get rid of this cute little girl?" Blake asked, signaling to one of his men to block the door. "Is this why you've got the feds breathin' down our necks?"

Jace began to perspire. He hated it when California sent someone to check up on him. He enjoyed playing the role of big boss; it made him nervous to have anyone else giving the orders.

Blake moved closer to Sabrina, who tried to hide behind Jace. Kneeling until he was eye-level with the girl, he softly whistled. "Hey, now, pretty young thing," he crooned, "tell Uncle Blake why you're really here."

"Hhheee ssaid he wwwould ffffix myyy bbike," Sabrina stammered as she started to cry.

Blake glanced up at Jace. "Let's see the bike," he growled.

Jace nodded to Larry who quickly moved out the back door to the van. When he returned with the bike, Blake visibly relaxed. Rising, he inspected the tire.

"Well, Jace, for once it seems you're on the level," he muttered, examining the slashed tire. "I see now why you're so concerned about this little girl's safety." He turned and was about to forget the entire matter when a nameplate hanging from the bike caught his eye. "Erickson?" he asked, glancing at Jace who began perspiring again. "Now where have I heard that name before?"

"It's mmmmy nnname," Sabrina stuttered.

Blake grinned. "You know something, that name sounds very familiar," he stated, reaching into his pocket. Pulling out a small notebook, he flipped to a page and scanned the contents. His eyes narrowed. "What a coincidence. It says right here that some people named Erickson have been stirring up trouble for us." With a perverse smile to Sabrina, he returned the notebook to his suit pocket. "I don't suppose you know anyone named Kate or Greg?"

Jace managed to muffle Sabrina's answer with his hand. "Blake, don't be ridiculous. Do you know how many Ericksons there are in this town?"

Blake eyed Jace thoughtfully. "No, but I'm sure you'll tell me. You'll tell me everything I want to know, right, Mr. Sloan? It occurs to me that if we had access to say, a relative of Greg or Kate Erickson, we might have a bartering tool, don't you think, Sloan?" he asked, motioning to the large man standing behind him. As the man obediently reached for Sabrina, Jace pushed her to Larry who quickly bolted out the door with her before the other man could stop him. The large bodyguard chased after them, but came back a few minutes later winded and empty-handed.

"That was stupid, Sloan," Blake said, motioning again to his two companions. "Gentlemen, teach Sloan here how stupid that was." Backing out of the way, he watched as the two large men began Jace's lesson.

* * *

Larry didn't have the keys to the utility van so he picked Sabrina up in his arms, running with her to his old beat-up truck. Outracing the goon who tried to follow, he threw Sabrina into the truck and tore out of the back alley. Fearing he would be pursued, he took several back streets, turning the curves so sharply, Sabrina began to cry.

"I wanna go home," she sobbed.

Cursing Jace, he finally turned up the Ericksons' street. The last time he had come here, he had helped vandalize Tyler's car. Now here he was, attempting to return Sabrina safely home. He wondered if one act canceled out the other but didn't have time to dwell on that thought. Spotting the cop cars, Larry shifted into reverse. Calling Jace everything he could think of, he slowly backed up, hoping no one would notice.

"Let me out! That's my house," Sabrina sobbed.

Deciding that was his best option, Larry stopped the truck, quickly opened the door on his side, and lifted Sabrina out onto the street. "Run like you've got a fire behind you," he ordered as he began easing the truck backwards. Backing out of the street, he quickly drove away, vowing to drive until he reached Billings. He had a brother-in-law there who would put him up for a while. He had no desire to continue his employment with Jace Sloan. As far as he was concerned, that business venture had been permanently dissolved.

* * *

As Kate sat next to her mother, a sense of comforting peace surrounded them. Sue glanced at Greg and saw that he, too, was experiencing the same sensation. Tyler still looked white as a sheet, nervously gripping and releasing the sofa pillow he had in his hands. The branch president had just offered a word of prayer in their behalf and the comfort he had prayed for had been almost immediate.

"Sabrina will be fine," President Randolph said, looking around the room. "The Spirit dictated that to me quite strongly."

"Thank you, President," Greg managed to say. He glanced into the kitchen where the police had set up temporary headquarters. They had respectfully given them a few minutes of silence during the prayer. Now, it was business as usual as they set about trying to figure out where Sabrina had gone. Several reports had come in—Sabrina had been seen at a local park. Giving her disappearance first priority, teams made up of police, neighbors and friends were all out searching. It was where Greg longed to be, but he had been asked to remain at home where they could protect him. Greg hated sitting here. He didn't want to be protected, safe while Sabrina . . . He shook his head, trying to ignore his fears.

Another thirty minutes dragged by. Greg joined Tyler near the window. Sue and Kate were still sitting together on the couch. Sue held Kate's hand so tightly that Kate thought the circulation had been cut off. Still, she didn't complain, sensing her mother's great need as she did what she could to offer comforting support.

Suddenly the front door banged open and an officer carried a sobbing Sabrina into the house. The minute he set her down, the entire family knelt around her in a fierce group hug.

CHAPTER 20

Greg stared in disbelief at the detective. "You're kidding?!" he exclaimed.

Detective Frank Bart shook his head. "As much as it pains me to say it, Jace Sloan died a hero. When we finally caught up to Larry Miter, we got the whole story. Everything your daughter described took place. I still have my suspicions about how that bike tire got slashed, but Larry claims that the minute Jace knew those men from California were in the video store, he wanted Sabrina out of there quick." The detective gave Greg a grave look. "I'm sure I don't have to tell you how serious it would've been if Jace hadn't come through like he did."

Giving Greg time to absorb this news, Detective Bart glanced at Kate and Tyler. He had been told that Sabrina was safely tucked in bed with her mother. Sabrina had had nightmares the past three nights, and Sue was determined to restore the sense of security the little girl had once known. Detective Bart sighed, knowing it would take quite a while for the effects of this trauma to wear off.

"And after Sabrina escaped they killed Jace?" Kate asked, still in shock. She had heard two days ago that Jace had died. At the time, she had felt he had deserved it for taking Sabrina. Now, as all of the pieces of this jumbled puzzle came together, she experienced a twinge of remorse for the spiteful thoughts she had had. Jace had saved her sister. When it had really counted, he had finally done the right thing.

Detective Bart nodded. "I don't think they meant to. The coroner said he died from brain trauma—his head connected pretty hard with the file cabinet. I think the original plan had been to rough him up a bit." He shook his head. "Jace must've put up quite a struggle—all three of those men from California looked awful when we picked them up near Billings. They were trying to track Larry down to permanently silence him after Jace died. They knew they couldn't leave any loose ends behind."

"And they're all in jail?" Tyler worriedly asked.

"Yes, and singing like canaries. They'll turn state's evidence without doubt." He gazed around the room. "This should be the end of the trouble for you folks. We're already working with the California authorities to shut this operation down permanently. And we finally discovered our weak link on the force here in Bozeman. I'm not at liberty to reveal his name, but he's a new guy, young, thought he could make a lot of money by jumping on Sloan's wagon." He sadly shook his head. "It's too bad—he would've made a fine officer."

Slowly rising to his feet, the police detective shook Greg's hand, then Tyler's. Teary-eyed, Kate nodded to him before leaving the kitchen.

"Will she be all right?" Detective Bart asked Greg, who glanced quickly at his daughter before he turned back to the man who had seen them through this nightmare.

"Eventually. This whole thing has hit her pretty hard. I'm just glad she has a couple of weeks before school starts. I don't want to send her down to Provo until she's had a chance to work through what's happened."

Nodding, the detective left the room and quietly let himself out of the house.

* * *

Upstairs, Kate knelt beside her bed and poured her heart out to her Heavenly Father, pleading for answers, for comfort. Images of Jace and Sabrina haunted her dreams an hour later when she finally cried herself to sleep.

Greg came up to check on Kate and finding her asleep, picked up the folded blanket on the end of the bed and covered her with it. Her low groan and the tortured look on her face troubled him. Leaning down, he softly kissed her cheek, wishing he could somehow ease her pain. A thought came to mind. Nodding, he gently shook her awake and then gave her a father's blessing. Afterward, he quietly held her as she sobbed against his shoulder.

* * *

The summer flew by for Heidi and Evan as wedding plans were made and carried out. Evan spent most of the summer working for his father's Salt Lake law office as he tried to save money to help cover their future living expenses. Heidi had decided to take the summer off and spent the time preparing for the wedding.

They were married the last week of August, which proved to be a timely distraction for Kate. Heidi had asked her be one of her bridesmaids at the reception, and Kate was only too happy to stand in line with Heidi's sisters. Two days later, it was back to BYU. The steady pace kept Kate busy enough that she didn't have time to dwell on thoughts that threatened to tear her apart. It was difficult for her to leave home, but she sensed it was time to get on with her life.

Heidi turned the apartment they had shared over to Kate; she and Evan had an apartment in the Y's married housing complex. Everything seemed to be falling into place. Evan still had a couple of years to go to earn his degree and Heidi would be working with a small law firm in Provo. It would give her the experience she desired and in her opinion was a wonderful opportunity, even though her income wouldn't stretch very far. The happiness and love Heidi and Evan shared cushioned the minor hardships that would be endured for what they knew would be a brief but wonderful time in their lives.

Within days of posting an ad for a new roommate, Kate was contacted by a junior who was looking for housing. Quiet and extremely reserved, Elizabeth "Buffy" Knighting proved to be an ideal roommate. The two girls became good friends even though their interests and personalities differed greatly.

Kate's classes and her work kept her occupied. She dated periodically, but made it clear she wasn't looking for a serious relationship. Mike still kept in touch, but as had happened with Randy, his letters became infrequent and impersonal. Somewhat relieved, Kate realized she didn't want any binding ties. By the end of the school year she had made up her mind to serve a mission. She would turn twenty-one in August and made plans accordingly.

When she first learned of Kate's new aspiration, Sue wondered if her daughter was running from Mike, who would be coming home in June. She tried to tactfully bring up the subject when Kate returned home for the summer.

"Honey, it's not that we don't want you to serve a mission, but are you sure it's the thing to do right now? With Mike coming home—"

Kate nodded. "Mom, I've given this a lot of thought and prayer. I know it's the right thing for me." She smiled sadly at her mother, sensing her concern. "If it's meant to work out with Mike, then I guess he'll still be around when I come home," she said softly. "Regardless, I know I'm supposed to serve a mission."

Sue studied her daughter's face. "If it's what you really want, you know we'll support you one hundred percent."

"I know and I appreciate that," Kate replied, giving her mother a hug.

"I'd better get in a healthy supply of these while I still can," Sue murmured, returning the hug. "Eighteen months seems like a long time."

"I'll break you in for Tyler," Kate teased, pulling away.

Sue watched Kate leave the room, an expression of sorrow and pride evident in her face.

* * *

Mike arrived at the airport in a flurry of excitement. He scanned the crowd at the airport for Kate's face, but was disappointed to see that she had not come to welcome him home. Thanks to his mother's letters, he had been informed about Kate's broken engagement. He understood why she hadn't come, but he was still disappointed.

Kate did come to hear him report his mission in their home branch. Thrilled to finally see her, Mike impatiently made his way to her side after the meeting. But when he finally reached her, he suddenly found himself tongue-tied. The girl he had left behind was now an attractive, confident woman.

"Uh . . . hi," he stammered, gazing at Kate. Had she been this beautiful before?

Smiling, Kate reached for a handshake. She had been impressed with the experiences he had shared and was eager to share her own excitement for the mission field.

Accepting the handshake, Mike longed for a hug but sensed the barrier between them. "It's . . . so good to see you," he said at last, his soft brown eyes revealing his nervousness.

Kate suppressed a smile, sensing his discomfort. "It's good to see you, too, Mike," she replied. "I enjoyed the meeting. You had some wonderful experiences."

Nodding, Mike ran a nervous hand through his short brown hair. Several people passed by, clapping him on the shoulder. He smiled at them briefly, but remained in front of Kate. There was so much he wanted to say, but none of it seemed appropriate now. "I'd like to get together with you sometime," he finally said.

"We do need to talk," Kate agreed.

"How about tomorrow afternoon?" he offered. "I've been dying for one of those juicy burgers at the Grill," he added, referring to a former favorite hangout. Decorated with memorabilia from the forties and fifties, it served some of the best hamburgers in town.

"Sounds good," Kate said.

"I could pick you up at noon," he suggested.

"I'll plan on it," she replied, amused by the outraged look on his younger sister's face. Spotting the two of them together, Jennifer Jeffries scowled. Obviously still holding a grudge, the sixteen-year-old forced her way through the crowd to her brother's side. She had hated it when Kate and Mike had dated in high school. Unwilling to let go of Kate's past mistakes, she was still convinced that Kate Erickson wasn't good enough for her brother.

"Mike, Mom has been looking for you everywhere," Jennifer snapped. "C'mon—remember the dinner?"

Mike ignored Jennifer and continued to smile at Kate. "Want to come with us? Mom fixed enough food to feed a small army."

Glancing at the indignant expression on Jennifer's face, Kate shook her head. She had no desire to endure another uncomfortable family setting, and under the circumstances, felt it would be inappropriate. "I'll see you tomorrow," she said to Mike, enjoying Jennifer's frown. Turning, she moved from the crowded room.

* * *

"This place has changed a bit," Mike complained, glancing at the menu. The prices had gone up in the time he had been gone.

"I think you'll see that a lot of things have changed," Kate murmured, dropping a subtle hint. She glanced around the busy diner, wondering if this would be a good setting to fill Mike in on her plans. He had hinted about going for a drive around town after lunch. That might be a better time to break the news to him about her mission.

The hamburgers were as wonderful as Mike remembered. Washing them down with thick chocolate shakes, they were both extremely full when they made their way back to Mike's car. "That was excellent," he said appreciatively as he helped her into his car. Kate wondered if he would still feel that way after she had told him about her future plans.

They drove around Bozeman for several minutes as Mike pointed out the changes that had taken place in their hometown during the past two years. They were changes Kate had been aware of, but hadn't noticed as much as Mike. "Two years. They went by so fast and yet, so many things happened," he said.

Deciding this was a good lead into what she needed to say, Kate cleared her throat. "You're right, Mike, a lot of things happened—a lot of things have changed. I've made a decision that's going to affect both of us. There's something I need to tell you."

Disturbed by the gravity in her voice, Mike glanced at her. Pulling into a nearby park, he coasted to a stop and shut off the engine. "Let's go for a walk," he suggested, pulling her out of the car. They walked in silence for several minutes, then headed to a picnic table and sat down. "So, the rumors about you going on a mission are true?" he asked, catching Kate off guard.

"Yes. How did you know?"

Smiling sadly, Mike brushed a few pine needles from the wooden table. "There isn't much that goes on in this town that my kid sister doesn't know about," he replied. "She let me know yesterday that you were heading out of here in about three months."

Kate nodded. A chittering squirrel in a nearby tree expressed his opinion.

"I agree with him," Mike teased, glancing at Kate. "But for purely selfish reasons." Turning, he faced Kate. "Yesterday, the news caught me by surprise, but now that I've had time to think about it, if it's what you really want, I think it's a wonderful idea. Serving the Lord can be one of the best experiences you'll ever have."

Stunned by his reaction, Kate stared at him.

"I'm serious. I've seen the miracles that sister missionaries can generate." He grinned. "I think your mission president will have his hands full with you, but I also think you'll make a great missionary." Tiring of its harangue, the squirrel finally ceased its verbal barrage. "I think I convinced him," Mike said, pointing toward the squirrel. "Have I convinced you?"

Smiling, Kate nodded. "Thank you . . . for understanding . . . for being so sweet. I know this is what I'm supposed to do right now, but I'm having a difficult time convincing the people around me. Mom thinks I'm running away, that I'm scared of getting into another relationship." She blushed. "It's not that at all. It's just not the right time."

Letting out a slow rush of air, Mike nodded in agreement. "I understand perfectly. I'm really not sure what I want to do with my life right now. I need some time myself to figure out things like what I want to be when I grow up," he said with a shy smile.

Kate smiled, realizing how much Mike had matured in the time they had been apart. He seemed to understand her decision and she respected him for that.

"Eighteen months should give me plenty of time to figure everything out," Mike continued. "And if some other fair maiden hasn't made off with me, I'll be waiting at the airport when you come home." Reaching down, he took one of Kate's hands in his. Raising it to his mouth, he gently kissed it. "Do we have a deal, m'lady?"

Nodding, Kate willingly moved into the hug he offered.

CHAPTER 21

The summer passed by quickly as Kate worked full-time at her father's computer company. She carefully saved most of her earnings for her mission, determined to pay for part of it. Her parents had assured her of their financial support, but she didn't want to burden them with the entire cost. Soon Tyler would be heading off to college and, she hoped, on his own mission. Kate knew that whatever she could contribute would help reduce future monetary strain.

In August her twenty-first birthday came and with it a surprise party thrown by her family and friends. Mike brought his sister, Jennifer, to the party, determined to end what was threatening to become a permanent dispute. After the cake-cutting ceremony, while everyone was busy eating and visiting, Mike arranged for Kate and Jennifer to have a few moments alone in the study. Mike had already talked to Kate about it, wanting these two to clear the air between them once and for all.

"I won't have my favorite sister—"

"Your only sister," Kate pointed out.

"And my favorite girl—"

"Friend," Kate inserted.

Mike grinned, a mischievous light in his eyes. "If you insist— girl*friend,"* he said, hurrying on before Kate could argue with him, "I won't have you two feuding anymore. I'll go get Jennifer and you two talk this out." He smiled brightly. "It's my birthday present to you."

"Gee, thanks," Kate muttered, although in reality she was grateful for Mike's intervention. She didn't want hard feelings hanging over her head in the mission field and knew it was time to declare a truce with Jennifer. She hoped Jennifer would be willing. If Mike had to force her to cooperate, it wouldn't work.

A few minutes later, Mike dragged Jennifer into the study to face Kate. He had plagued his sister with guilt all summer, insisting she make things right with Kate. Some of what he had said had sunk it. Getting Jennifer to this party was nothing short of a miracle. Mike had been pleasantly surprised when Jennifer had finally agreed to come. Suspicious at first, he now sensed that both girls were anxious to get this behind them.

"Now, you two get this out of your systems and then we'll really party," Mike promised, closing the door.

At first, Jennifer refused to look at Kate. She wasn't angry anymore, but ashamed of how she had treated Kate in the past. She knew in her heart that jealousy had led her to say things she really hadn't meant. She had always idolized Mike and had resented anyone who stood between herself and her big brother.

Well aware of Kate's past exploits, she had judged her more harshly than most. The resulting rumors Jennifer had spread had been a constant source of irritation and pain for Kate. This summer, Mike had been able to pry through Jennifer's thick shell of resentment to get his sister to see the damage she had done. It wasn't something she was proud of, and her guilt had continuously nagged at her to make things right, to somehow atone for the misery she had caused Kate in high school concerning Mike, and then later with Keith Taylor.

Now, here she stood, alone in the room with the person she had hurt the most, and Jennifer found that she couldn't face Kate.

"Jennifer," Kate began, perceiving the other girl's struggle, "I want you to know that I don't hold anything against you. I know coming here today wasn't easy for you, but I appreciate the effort you're making. I'd like us to be friends."

Jennifer slowly met Kate's supportive gaze. "Even after everything I've done?" she asked.

Kate nodded.

"Kate, I've been rotten—I admit it. I wouldn't blame you if you never wanted to speak to me again." She searched Kate's face for anger and found only loving concern. Choking up, Jennifer moved to a window. "Having Mike around this summer—it's like living with

Jiminy Cricket," she finally stammered. "He keeps challenging me to let my conscience be my guide. He's annoying, but he's right." Jennifer turned to look at Kate. "I don't know why I said some of those things—I knew they weren't true. I guess I was trying to hurt you—to keep you away from Mike."

Kate patiently waited, realizing Jennifer needed to be the one to control this conversation.

"Then, after he left on his mission, when you started dating Keith, I knew that would hurt Mike." Suddenly it all came out in a rush, the anger she had felt, the sense of betrayal, and everything she had ever said against Kate.

". . . this guilt thing is killing me—I can't take it anymore. Kate, I'm sorry. Can you ever forgive me?"

Unable to find the right words, Kate expressed herself with a heartfelt hug. When the two of them left the study, Kate knew she had finally gained a friend.

* * *

The temptation to open Kate's mission call was almost irresistible, but Sue restrained herself, waiting for her daughter to come home from work. When Sue finally had everyone gathered around the dining room table, she handed Kate the envelope. Kate jumped to her feet, squealing with excitement, and hurriedly opened it. As she silently read her destination, tears began to roll down her cheeks, and she handed the letter to her mother.

"What does it say?" Greg asked impatiently.

"Dear Sister Erickson," Sue read aloud, "You are hereby called to serve as a missionary of The Church of Jesus Christ of Latter-day Saints to labor in the Scotland Edinburgh Mission." Clapping her hand over her mouth, Sue dropped the letter. Greg retrieved it, read it for himself, then handed it to Tyler.

"Where's Scotland?" Sabrina demanded to know. She glanced around the room for an answer but could see everyone was too busy crying to reply. Even Tyler had slipped from the room claiming he had something in his eye. Shaking her head, Sabrina finally went to find the world atlas by herself.

* * *

"So, you'll be serving in the same country some of your ancestors are from," Marie Sikes Ross observed.

Kate nodded at the pretty blonde woman who was the mother of her friend Linda. Marie had stayed in touch with her since Linda's death, and her life had steadily improved since that painful time. Reactivated in the church, Marie had married a wonderful man named Stephen Ross, and their marriage had been sealed a year later in the Idaho Falls temple.

Linda had been Marie's only child. Now she and Stephen had a cute, blond-haired boy, and Marie was expecting again. Kate knew they were hoping for a girl, but she suspected they would be just as thrilled to have another son.

"When do you leave?" Marie asked, smiling warmly at Kate.

"The middle of October," Kate replied.

"That's not too far away," Marie commented. "If you don't mind me asking, when are you planning on going through the temple to take out your endowment?"

Kate considered the question. She had been hit with so many different dates, she couldn't remember. "I'm not sure, but it'll be on the calendar. I'll go look," she offered, rising from the couch.

Marie lightly touched Kate's arm. "We can find out later. Right now I want to ask you something." From the serious look on her face, Kate knew it must be important and sat down beside her. "As you know, I've wanted to take care of Linda's temple work for quite some time."

Kate nodded.

"But for some reason it never felt right. I don't know why—maybe Linda wasn't ready to accept it. But now—"

"You think she is?" Kate excitedly interrupted.

"Yes," Marie said, smiling. Tears came to her eyes. "I can't explain it, but somehow, I know." She blinked, sending two tears down the sides of her face. Wiping them away, she continued to smile at Kate. "I was wondering—would you mind if I went through for Linda the same day you take out your endowment?" Kate started to speak, but Marie stopped her. "I don't want to intrude on your day, but I would like you to be a part of this—I think Linda would like that, too."

Unable to speak, Kate tearfully nodded.

"We were also thinking of having our entire family sealed together after the endowment ceremony. Toby was born before Stephen and I went through the temple." She patted her stomach. "This one will be born under the covenant, but I want all of my children sealed to me forever—including Linda." She gazed intently at Kate. "Would you be willing to stand in proxy for Linda during the sealing ceremony?"

"Yes," Kate managed to stammer before Marie embraced her.

* * *

The day Kate went through the temple was one of the most beautiful she had ever known. As she went through the endowment ceremony, she was struck by a deep sense of reverent love. Spiritually overwhelmed, she knew it would take several return visits to fully comprehend the symbolism representing this life and the next.

Surrounded by family and friends, Kate realized how fortunate she was to have all these wonderful people in her life. Her parents had come, as well as her uncle Stan and aunt Paige with their two oldest children, Tami and Kyle and their respective spouses. Sandi had brought her husband, Ian, and Heidi came with Evan. Fred and Harriet Kearns were there as well, along with Kate's branch president and his wife—President and Sister Randolph and Kate's former Laurel leader, Lori Blanchard. Stephen and Marie Ross were there, as were Mike Jeffries and his parents. All had made the trip to the Idaho Falls Temple for this special occasion.

The day progressed and finally it was time for the sealing of the Ross family. There were no dry eyes in that beautiful room as three-year-old Toby dressed in white was reunited with his family. Marie reached for her son and for Kate, drawing them close to her as they gathered around the altar. As Stephen reached for her hand, Marie experienced a joy she had never felt before. She sensed that Linda was close and felt certain her oldest daughter approved of this eternal bond.

Afterward, Kate sat and gazed into the mirrors that seemed to go on forever in a powerful symbol of eternal families. Convinced Linda had been with her, Kate closed her eyes, remembering the slight warm pressure she had felt across her shoulders. "I love you, Linda," she whispered, letting go of a pain that had been tucked away for too many years. A comforting peace filled her heart as she continued to gaze into the mirrors.

CHAPTER 22

Kate thrived on the hectic pace of the MTC, and it wasn't long before she was on a flight destined for Edinburgh, Scotland. It had been difficult, telling everyone goodbye again at the Salt Lake airport, but now that she was finally on her way, Kate could hardly wait to reach Scotland.

At the Edinburgh airport, Kate was met by the mission president and his wife, President and Sister Everson. Impressed by the warm, positive attitude of this loving couple, Kate knew she was in very good hands.

As they drove through town, President Everson pointed out famous landmarks, like Edinburgh Castle, and Greyfriars Kirk, whose churchyard contained the bronze statue of Greyfriars Bobby, the faithful terrier who followed his master's remains to Greyfriars churchyard. The loyal dog guarded his master's grave for fourteen years until his own death.

"That's the kind of loyalty we expect from our missionaries," President Everson lightly teased after relating this story to his newest charge. When he laughed, Kate relaxed, grateful the mission president had a sense of humor.

It didn't take long for Kate to discover that President Everson was also a spiritual giant. As he met with her in his office, he instructed her to look up several scriptures that had to do with missionary work and spoke of the importance of touching lives through the miracle of the gospel. He then went over several of the local customs and explained the rules he had established for this mission. He asked several pertinent questions about her life and the reason she had chosen to serve a mission. When she revealed a strong desire to serve the Lord, he beamed and introduced her to her companion, Melissa Larsen.

A petite brunette, Melissa quickly gathered Kate up in a hug, establishing from the beginning that they were sisters in the gospel. Melissa was from Tennessee and Kate loved her soft, southern accent. Already on their way to becoming good friends, they spent the first night together getting acquainted, sharing a room in the house the mission president and his wife were living in. The next day, President Everson and his wife drove them to their assigned location, Dumbarton, a medium-sized town about sixty-one miles from Edinburgh.

Their three-room flat, located in an old rock building, was small but tidy. The kitchen also served as the living room, and the tiny bedroom the girls would share led into an even smaller bathroom. Compact, but clean, it was home for now.

That night as Kate knelt in prayer, she thought about all that had led her to this beautiful country. She had never seen so many different shades of green in her entire life. The grass, the trees, the moss, the hillsides, bushes—everywhere she looked there was vibrant color. The Eversons had assured her that she had been called to the best mission on earth. "Possibly one of the most challenging, but the best," President Everson had added.

Kate had already been told how missionaries were sometimes treated in Scotland. The Scotch were a proud people who held fast to a colorful heritage and timeworn traditions. Some were offended by the presence of American missionaries and would often advise the eager young men and women to return to their own *heathen* land to preach. Such statements were at times punctuated by rocks or waving fists. But there were others who were more receptive, those who were seeking answers—golden contacts who were waiting to hear a sincere testimony of the gospel of Jesus Christ.

Coming to Scotland was both exciting and frightening for Kate. She feared rejection, but was thrilled to be standing on ground her ancestors had walked. She hoped to meet some of her distant cousins while serving and prayed daily that she might be guided to find them.

* * *

One of the biggest challenges Kate faced was catching onto the local dialect. Melissa frequently assured her that she was hearing the English language, but at times it was spoken so quickly and with such a strong Gaelic accent, whole sentences went right by her. It amused, then annoyed the local people if Kate asked them to repeat what had been said.

"Why can't they understand how hard this is for me?" Kate complained one day to Melissa. "And why wasn't I prepared for this in the MTC?"

"You'll catch on soon enough," Melissa soothed. "If I can pick up the local lingo, so can you."

"I hope so. Take that last woman. What was it she said? 'Fit you on a boot.' I wasn't asking about shoes. Why can't they understand me? I don't talk near as fast as they do."

Melissa laughed. "That woman wasn't talkin' to you about shoes. She was askin' what y'all were going on about—in other words, what is it you're tryin' to say?"

Kate groaned. "I'll never get the hang of this!"

"Sure you will—give it time." Melissa glanced at her watch. "Now, are you ready to check out Loch Lomond?"

"The big lake I saw the day we climbed Dumbarton Rock?" Kate excitedly asked. The large volcanic rock that seemed to rise up out of the River Clyde on the outskirts of Dumbarton had been the site of a strategic fortress for nearly fifteen hundred years. Melissa had taken Kate on a quick tour during last week's prep day, and both had enjoyed exploring Dumbarton Castle. During the eighth and ninth centuries it had served as the seat of the British kingdom of Strathclyde, a kingdom that had included land from the head of Loch Lomond, to Lancashire. One legend rumored that the castle had been the residence of King Arthur, and that the surrounding area had been known as Camelot. William Wallace had been imprisoned there, and young Mary Queen of Scots had stayed there for five months before sailing to France.

As the two companions admired the souvenirs from past ages that were now on display at the castle, Kate felt like she was in heaven, seeing firsthand this place of history and tradition. She wanted to memorize every detail and looked forward to the day she could share it with her future students.

"With Great Britain surrounded by ocean waters, Loch Lomond is the largest body of fresh water in Britain," Melissa said. "It's absolutely beautiful and the best part is that it's only about four miles from here." As she spoke, a member of the Dumbarton ward pulled up in a small car to give the missionaries a ride to see the loch.

"Sister Geillis, we sure appreciate this," Melissa said, smiling her thanks to the middle-aged woman as they climbed into her car.

"Nae trouble. Glad tae dae it," Sister Geillis replied.

"If you don't mind, could we stop at Balloch Castle on our way back?" Melissa asked, eager to show it off to Kate. A love of history was shared by both girls, and Melissa enjoyed seeing Kate's excitement each time they explored a treasure from the past.

"Aye," Sister Geillis replied cheerily.

"Balloch Castle?" Kate asked.

Melissa grinned. "You'll love it. It's in the middle of this slopin' park—you don't even realize it's uphill till you get to the top. You can see clear across Loch Lomond from there." Melissa glanced at the camera Kate had brought. "You'll get some good shots this afternoon. Especially if the sun keeps shinin'."

"Aye. But it's still pretty when it rains," Sister Geillis pointed out, taking pride in her native land.

"True," Melissa agreed with Sister Geillis. Turning, she smiled at Kate. Scotland's stormy weather had been one of Kate's biggest complaints. "No matter what the weather does, you'll still love the castle, the loch, and the gardens in the park. The whole area's gorgeous."

"Sae, have you broken in this new companion of yers yet?" Sister Geillis asked, smiling at Melissa.

"I'm sure tryin'," Melissa replied, her southern accent more evident when she was teasing.

"More surprises?" Kate asked, thinking of the expressions Melissa had already cautioned her against using. Harmless American phrases were often obscene in this country.

"No. Just a few things we need to talk about sometime," Melissa said, glancing at the small bag of chips Kate had brought along for a snack. "Don't worry about it now. Let's enjoy what's left of our prep day," she added, pointing out the window as she caught the first glimpse of Loch Lomond.

* * *

"So, what was it we needed to talk about?" Kate later asked as she finished towel-drying her hair. They had been caught in a major downpour at Balloch Country Park.

"Just some advice I try to pass on to my companions."

"Advice?"

"I'll tell y'all what Sister Everson told me when I first arrived," Melissa said brightly. "First, she said it was wise to avoid bright colors. She said that sister missionaries shouldn't dress like flowers tryin' to attract bees."

Kate nodded, relieved that most of her skirts and dresses were dark colors.

"She also said that the sister missionaries need to be careful, that we should take extra precautions—you know what I'm sayin'?"

"Not make ourselves walking targets?" Kate supplied.

"Exactly," Melissa agreed. "And we shouldn't do anythin' that might give the wrong impression of why we're here. We're representatives of the Church and we should always remember that people are watchin' us constantly." She smiled warmly at Kate. "But I think we'll be fine. You are one neat lady and I'm glad we have this chance to serve together." Giving Kate a big hug, she then led her to the small kitchen table to finish this discussion. As they each took a seat, Melissa hoped the compliments she had given Kate would soften what she now had to say. "There's somethin' else I need to mention."

Kate looked at Melissa expectantly.

"We have to watch out for the food in this country."

"Will it make us sick?" Kate asked, puzzled.

"No, but it's easy to put on weight in this mission," Melissa responded. Kate had only gained a pound or two since arriving, but Melissa knew it would get worse if she didn't say something now.

"Why?" Kate asked, glancing down at herself. She was well aware that she had gained five pounds in the past three weeks, but didn't think it was a cause for concern. At first she was slightly offended by Melissa's words, but when she saw the concern in her companion's eyes, she realized that no insult had been intended.

"Kate, I'm not tryin' to upset you. I'm just passin' on the same advice I was given when I first arrived." She laughed, patting her stomach. "In one month, I gained ten pounds."

Kate stared at her slender companion. In her opinion, Melissa could stand to gain another ten.

"Here in Scotland, they deep-fry everythin'. And when the local ward members feed us, they believe in heapin' the plate. They especially enjoy servin' dessert, and they like to use real butter or that rich chocolate they make here. Their custards are especially fattenin'."

"Oh," Kate replied, understanding why Melissa had politely refused a second helping of custard the other night at a ward activity, unlike herself. She made a mental note to restrict the portions offered in the future.

"And you'll want to avoid those *crisps,* as they call 'em around here," Melissa continued.

"But they're so cheap and I love them," Kate protested.

"True, but those little bags of potato chips are full of greasy calories."

Kate sighed. "So, what do we eat?"

"Cereal, veggies, fruit, bread, temptin' things like that."

"Pretty much what we've been eating," Kate sighed, glancing around the kitchen.

"Yep. Now you know why." Melissa glanced at her watch. "Speakin' of food, how about some dinner? I'm starved."

Kate agreed, and together she and Melissa prepared a simple but nutritious meal.

* * *

As the weeks passed, Kate and Melissa became a successful missionary team. Their district was difficult due in part to the indifferent attitudes of the local people, but they were making slow progress. Whenever possible, they offered service in a variety of different ways. They carried groceries for some of the older residents and baby-sat for their landlady when a family emergency called her to Glasgow. When a fund-raiser was held for family who had lost everything in a fire, Kate and Melissa spent hours working in a food booth. Their willingness to serve had impressed several people. Now, instead of biting comments and gestures, there was the occasional smile. "On yer way, hen," most of the older women now told them when they approached. Melissa later explained that it was considered a term of endearment.

"The elders are the only ones who mean it in a derogatory way," Melissa continued.

"I've noticed," Kate replied. She had been surprised by the antagonism that existed between the elders and sister missionaries in their district. "What's their problem?" she finally asked after a run-in with two particular elders in their district.

"They consider us to be poachers."

"What?"

"It started with Emily Stewart."

"What does Emily have to do with this?" Kate asked, picturing the middle-aged woman who had recently been baptized. Filled with a zest for life, Emily had been a delight to work with.

"Elder Peterson and Elder Frank had been meetin' with her. But, in order for them to teach a single sister, they have to have a chaperon. When you and I were asked to finish the discussions with her, they resented it."

"But she accepted the gospel. She was baptized. Isn't that what we're here for?"

Melissa slowly nodded. "Sometimes people forget what it's all about." She smiled. "Not all elders are like that though," she added. "Most aren't that competitive—just the two we happen to be workin' with in this district."

"Tell me about it," Kate replied, thinking of an upcoming missionary conference in Edinburgh. It had been rumored that a general authority would be speaking. Upon learning of the conference, Elder Frank and Elder Peterson had challenged Kate and Melissa to a round of GQ-ing on the bus trip.

"What is GQ-ing?" Kate asked.

"GQ-in' stands for the 'Golden Question.'"

"What?"

"They want us to split up, sit with different people, and ask the golden questions."

"What do you mean?"

Melissa thought for a minute before answering. "Oh, like— have you ever wondered about the purpose of life? Things like that."

Looking dismayed, Kate shook her head. "Serious?"

"Uh-huh. Sometimes it leads to a contact."

"I don't think I like this," Kate said, frowning.

"You never know—you might find someone who's interested. What I don't like about it is this competition thing. Those two are challengin' us to a duel. They want to see who can have the most success."

Kate couldn't help but feel disgusted. "There can't be much spiritual guidance behind this," she mumbled.

"It might not be so bad."

Kate gave her companion a pained look. "Can't we talk them out of this?"

"Maybe. We'll have to see. It's become a matter of pride. This might be a graceful way to make things up to them."

"You're kidding?" Kate exclaimed.

"No, I'm not. You know how fragile the male ego can be. If we let them think they've gotten the best of us, it might make things easier around here."

Kate scowled.

"I know what you're thinkin', but maybe we need to be the first to swallow some pride."

Studying her companion's face to see if she was serious, Kate was not happy to see that Melissa was.

"Sister Erickson, you and I know we didn't do anything wrong, but in their eyes, we stole a contact."

"But we were asked to—"

"You'll see," Melissa said. "It'll be better this way."

* * *

The day finally came for the special conference. As Kate and Melissa made their way to the bus stop, they were joined by Elder Peterson and Elder Frank.

"Well, if it isn't our two favorite sister missionaries," Elder Frank said snidely.

Kate bristled, enraged by this short, stout elder. She was about to offer a sharp retort when Melissa touched her arm and shook her head.

"How are you two this mornin'?" Melissa politely asked, trying to set a good example for Kate.

"Fine," Elder Peterson replied, avoiding her eyes. Taller and painfully thin, the only thing he seemed to have in common with his companion was an attitude problem.

"Are you sisters up for a round of GQ-ing?" Elder Frank asked.

"Sure," Melissa replied, giving Kate a warning look.

"Just so you know, when we start talking to someone, that isn't your cue to take over," Elder Frank continued. "C'mon, elder, I see some prospective contacts. We'd better hurry before these two latch onto them." As the two elders hurried off, Kate's eyes flashed dangerously.

"It's okay, Kate," Melissa said quietly.

"No, it's not!"

Melissa smiled encouragingly at Kate. "It will be if we handle this right. Remember, we're older, wiser, we're more in control of ourselves. It's up to us to handle this delicately."

Rolling her eyes, Kate knew that part of what Melissa had said was right. They were both two years older than the elder missionaries who were just nineteen. "Okay, *senior companion*, what should we do?"

"I hate it when you call me that," Melissa complained, then closed her eyes briefly, offering a silent prayer.

"On yer bike, Jimmy," a loud voice protested.

Melissa opened her eyes, following Kate's amused gaze. The elders had approached a rather large man who was not happy about being disturbed while waiting for the bus. Bus stops were often a good place to tract. People waiting for a bus weren't as apt to run off and would sometimes listen to the missionaries. It wasn't the case this day.

"We just want to ask you a question," Elder Frank began.

"Are ye daft as a ha'penny watch?" the large man asked, "I said, on yer bike, Jimmy."

"We didn't bring our bikes," Elder Peterson replied. "We're waiting for the bus."

"Then keep yer questions tae yerselves y'pure waste o'space or y'might find yerselves doon the road wi'oot the bus!" The group that had gathered around applauded.

"Nice," Kate observed. "Let's get them all to hate us right off the bat."

"At least we didn't cause the problem," Melissa pointed out. Kate nodded. She and Melissa kept a low profile until the bus pulled up. As the eager crowd pushed forward, they were the last to get on. Only two vacant seats were left. The first by a young mother with a baby, the other beside a young woman who appeared to be sleeping. Smiling, Melissa took the seat next to the young mother, allowing Kate to make her way back to sit beside the other young woman.

When Kate sat down, the young woman opened one eye and glanced at her. Shaking her head, she curled up next to the window and tried to go back to sleep. Sensing the unspoken hostility, Kate remained silent.

"Och, y're one o'them," a loud voice charged.

Turning, Kate saw that the man who had given the elders such a bad time was sitting in the seat behind her.

"Sure y'are. Look at the tag." His frown turned into a smile as he gazed appreciatively at Kate. "If ye'd been the one to ask questions, I might've answered differently," he said, grinning slyly and lifting his bushy eyebrows.

Uncomfortable with his scrutiny, Kate looked toward Melissa for help, but her companion was busy holding the baby, talking to the woman beside her. Kate glanced around for the elders who were sitting in different seats toward the front of the bus. They too were speaking to the people beside them and with their backs to her, couldn't see her predicament.

"What's a charmin' young lassie like yerself doin' oot preachin' to those who dinna want tae hear?"

Kate silently prayed for guidance.

"Are y'deaf as that pair o'insolent pups?"

Taking a deep breath, Kate slowly turned to face her antagonizer.

"That's better. Tell me, are they all as lovely as yerself back home?"

"Thank you for the compliment, but isn't there something else we could talk about?" Kate asked. If she could convince him that Mormon missionaries weren't as annoying as he believed, it might go a long way toward establishing good rapport with some of the local residents.

The man laughed. "Sure now there is," he answered, gazing intently at Kate.

Kate blushed, realizing her mistake.

"Y'listen to old Jock, I'll educate y'plenty. We'll get tae know each other. I'll teach ye m'own religion—wine, women, and song!"

"Leave 'er alone," a stern voice demanded.

"What's it to ye?"

The young woman sitting beside Kate fired off a fiery retort using language that caused Kate to blush even more. Overhearing the loud argument, Melissa glanced back at Kate. Taking in the situation, Melissa tried unsuccessfully to get the attention of the elders. She gave Kate a helpless look. Finally, the bus driver interceded.

"That will do," the burly driver insisted. "Or y'can walk the rest of the way!"

The two elders finally turned around to see the cause of the commotion. They were delighted that the man who had given them such trouble was in the middle of it. Elder Peterson glanced at Kate, finally catching on that she had been having a difficult time. He gave her an encouraging smile, unlike Elder Frank, who seemed to be gloating.

Frowning his displeasure, the man seated behind Kate shot one final glare at the young woman by the window before shifting back in his seat.

"Thank you," Kate stammered quietly to the young woman sitting beside her. As she gazed at her, she was struck by a sense of déjà vu. "Have we met somewhere before?"

The young woman violently shook her head, her long brown hair cascading down her back.

"But you look so familiar."

"I came to yer aid, now heed me and leave me alone." Her green eyes flashed a warning.

Slowly nodding, Kate remained quiet the rest of the trip.

"Are you all right?" Melissa later asked when Kate stepped off the bus to join her.

"Yes. Luck of the draw, as they say. I didn't realize who I'd sat in front of until it was too late."

"And there weren't any other seats available," Melissa commiserated. "I should've been the one to head back there. But when I saw that woman with the baby, somethin' clicked."

"I noticed you two visited most of the way. How did it go?"

"Good. She came today to visit a sister." Melissa smiled sadly. "She's all alone, tryin' to raise that sweet baby. She has a lot of questions about life right now. I think maybe we can help her." She held up a card she had written an address on. "She told me to come see her when she gets back to Dumbarton."

"That's great," Kate said.

"Elder Peterson and I both made contacts to follow up on," Elder Frank interrupted, moving toward Kate and Melissa. "Too bad you two didn't do as well," he added, daring them to contradict him. Melissa quietly slipped the card she had shown Kate into a pocket in her skirt. "Incidentally, Sister Erickson, haven't you been instructed not to flirt with the natives?" he smirked.

Kate glared at the district leader. It was all she could do to remain silent. Glancing at Melissa, she saw the pleading look on her face and made a valiant effort to calm down.

"I think Sister Erickson handled herself as well as she could under the circumstances," Elder Peterson countered. "Hey, President Everson sent his A.P.'s to pick us up," he added, pointing to the other side of the street.

Grateful that Elder Peterson had taken her side, Kate glanced at the two young men who were approaching, Elder Taggart and Elder Styles. Relieved to no longer be the focus of the conversation, Kate followed as the two assistants to the mission president led them to a waiting car.

CHAPTER 23

As Jenny MacTavish hurried from store to store, she choked back the fear that threatened to engulf her. The phone call from her father had unnerved her, breaking through the layers of self-reliance and fortitude that normally kept her going. "This cannae be happening," she mumbled quietly, repeating the phrase as she searched for gifts. Buying things on impulse, she refused to see the futility of her self-imposed task.

A saleswoman in one shop sensed the young woman's distress. Concerned, she placed a hand on Jenny's shoulder and asked if all was well. Unable to convey her grief, Jenny bolted from the store, crashing into two young women.

As the packages went flying in every direction, Kate and Melissa scrambled to help Jenny, brushing off the snow as they apologized, although it hadn't been their fault.

"Naw, naw. It's nae trouble," Jenny said as the two young women piled the packages in her arms. "Nothin's broken. Nae harm done." Her green eyes sparkled with unshed tears.

Kate gasped, realizing that this was the same young woman who had sat beside her on the bus to Edinburgh. As before, she was struck by how familiar the girl seemed.

"You have a lot to carry," Melissa said, glancing at Kate. She too had noticed the reddened eyes.

"We'd be glad to help you out," Kate said. "It's the least we can do."

Although Jenny refused at first, Kate and Melissa insisted, and Jenny finally allowed them to ease the packages out of her weary arms. They quietly followed as she led them to the building where she lived. "I c'n take it from here," she said at the door. "I thank ye but there's nae need for further aid."

"Are you sure?" Melissa asked as she shifted the packages she was carrying to open the door that led inside the stone building. Jenny eyed them suspiciously, certain they wanted a handout of some kind. Holding out her hands, she took back her packages.

"If you'd rather we didn't come up, that's fine," Kate assured her. "We just want to make sure that you're all right."

"And do y' really care so much?" Jenny asked, glancing from Melissa to Kate. She had never had many close friends—she had never felt the need of that until now. She desperately wanted someone to ease what she was feeling, but pride prevented her from revealing her distress. Her associates at work had noticed something was wrong, but had refrained from asking, certain Jenny would resent their interference. Ordinarily this was true, but today was different. The one person who had reached out to her was the salesclerk who had unwittingly set off this chain reaction.

"Yes, we really care," Melissa said firmly, heeding a prompting to stress that point.

"And why would that be?" Jenny challenged. They didn't know her at all. How could they possibly care? Their answer surprised her.

"Because you're a child of God," Kate answered. She glanced at Melissa who smiled her approval.

Jenny frowned, reminding herself that these two were missionaries. They probably thought they had a quick conversion on their hands. It would be best to set them straight right away. "Wouldn't you two be the bothersome missionaries I've heard complaints aboot 'round town?"

"No, that would be the elders," Kate said mischievously. She ignored the look Melissa gave her.

Jenny studied their faces, trying to place where she had seen them before. "Wait now, I know where I've see ye—y're the young woman who caused so much trouble on the bus to Edinburgh aboot two weeks ago," she said, pointing to Kate.

"*I* caused the trouble?" she sputtered.

"Of course y'did," Jenny replied firmly. "A wee bonnie lass like yerself has nae business traipsin' aboot a foreign land. Nae tellin' whit mischief will abound."

Melissa laughed. "That's Sister Erickson, all right—mischief does abound with her."

"Now, just a minute, Sister Larsen," Kate said indignantly.

"Y'two are sisters?" Jenny asked, puzzled.

Both girls shook their heads.

Jenny nodded. "I wondered. Y'look nothin' alike and yer accents aren't the same." She shifted the packages in her hands.

"I told you that around here, we're the ones who sound funny," Melissa told Kate.

"Y'are indeed," Jenny replied. It was somehow comforting to hear the lighthearted banter between these two young women who seemed to be about her age. "Seen's how y've been so kind, y'may as weel come up to m'flat," she invited. This gesture was unusual for her, but she didn't want to be alone right now—as long as these two didn't get any ideas about converting her.

A few minutes later, they entered Jenny's sparsely furnished flat, and Jenny gestured to a worn-out couch after they had deposited the packages on a tiny kitchen table.

"I dinna have much t'offer," she said, nervously flipping her long hair over one shoulder, "but I kin brew some tea."

"No, thanks," Melissa said brightly. "But you go ahead if you'd like." Unbuttoning her coat, she smiled at their hostess.

"Aye. I'm aboot freezin'."

Kate grinned, excited that she had understood Jenny's phrase. She was starting to understand the Scottish-flavored language more all the time. "I'm nearly frozen myself," she replied. It was true, despite the sweat pants and thick socks she had worn under her dress. Even the heavy coat her parents had sent didn't keep out the bitter wind. Her left leg often throbbed with the cold, reminding her of a past injury. Scotland's turbulent weather inspired appreciation for the bright sunny days that infrequently appeared.

"Would y'care for tea?" Jenny asked, directing her question to Kate.

"No, thank you," Kate replied as she took off her coat.

Annoyed by the refusal, Jenny shook her head as she put a kettle on to boil.

"Sister Erickson and I don't mean to offend you," Melissa said. "We just don't drink tea. It's part of our religion."

"S'nds like a religion I want nae part uv," Jenny scoffed.

"We believe caffeine is harmful to our bodies," Kate added.

Jenny shook her head. "Ye dinna ken whit y're missin.'" She looked at them, wondering a second time at the curious way they referred to each other. "Y'two are nae sisters. Then why dae y'call each other sister?" she asked, confused.

"We believe that we're all brothers and sisters," Melissa began.

Jenny frowned. "How dae y'marry then?"

Kate smiled. This girl was quick-witted. "We don't take it that far," she said. "What Sister Larsen means is, we try to treat each other as we would a brother or a sister because we're all children of God."

"Y'said that b'fore. Whit does it mean?"

"It means we believe that we're all sons and daughters of our Heavenly Father and that we all have the potential to someday become like him," Melissa answered.

Jenny had been so busy entertaining her guests that she had completely forgotten why she had been so upset earlier. Now she felt a new surge of anger and pain shoot through her chest. "Tell me this, if we're all so verra special, why's it some are gi'en mair in this life than others? Why dae some of us suffer wh'le others gae unscathed?"

As Jenny pulled a kitchen chair closer to the couch, Kate could see that the sadness had returned to her eyes. After moving the chair, Jenny retrieved her cup of tea and sat down, blowing at the cup in her hands. Kate glanced at Melissa wondering how to handle this turn in the conversation. Jenny didn't give them time to respond.

"C'n y'tell me what y'r real names are?" she said. "I dinna go f'r this sister thing m'self."

"Okay," Kate replied. "I'm Kate and this is Melissa."

Kate looked at Melissa, who gave her a reassuring nod. This was a bit unorthodox, but sometimes that was what this mission called for.

"Kate and Melissa. That sounds better." Nodding her thanks, Jenny continued sipping at her cup of tea. Aware that her guests had nothing while she had her tea, she thought of something else she could offer them. "I've a few bags of crisps if ye'd like," she said.

Kate accepted the offer before Melissa could respond. She feared another rejection would insult Jenny and she was starved. To borrow a Scottish phrase, she felt as though she could eat "a scabby dug."

"Thanks, we'd like that," Kate said.

"All right, I'll fetch them for ye," Jenny said, pleased that her attempt to be a good hostess had finally been appreciated.

As Jenny moved back to the small kitchen, Kate glanced at her companion.

"It's okay," Melissa mouthed before smiling. She too had felt that another negative answer would come across as rude.

"Can I help?" Kate politely asked.

"Naw, I kin manage." As Jenny moved back to the small kitchen, she had another question for them. "If y'dinna mind me askin', why's it y'two traveled 'cross the world to preach in Scotland?"

"We can answer both of your questions," Melissa began.

"Both?"

"You asked why some people seem to have more trials than others."

"Sae I did," Jenny replied, handing each young woman a small bag of crisps. "M'own fault then. I've always been tae curious for m'own good." She sat down across from Kate and Melissa.

"I think being curious is a good thing," Kate replied.

"Dae ye?"

"Yes. I've always asked a lot of questions," Kate continued. Jenny was amused to see Kate give her companion a slight elbow jab when Melissa vigorously nodded to confirm this.

"And did y'find the answers?" Jenny asked intently.

"Most of them," Kate responded.

"And how did y'come to know?"

Kate looked at Melissa, hoping for a clue on how to proceed. Both felt like they had been led to Jenny. Instead of relying on their own intuition, they offered silent prayers for guidance. Jenny was obviously searching for answers. It was unclear why, but this young woman was very upset. If they could answer her questions, it might bring Jenny the comfort she seemed to be seeking.

Prayer. That was the answer Jenny needed to hear. Kate eagerly leaned forward. "Jenny, I'll tell you how I receive answers—it's something everyone can do."

"It is?" Jenny asked.

"Yes. Do you ever pray?"

Jenny rolled her eyes.

"What's wrong?" Melissa asked.

"For a minute, I thought y'were goin' to gi' me a real answer." She pulled another face. "Prayer!"

"It does work," Melissa countered.

Jenny shook her head. "I've tried it b'fore. It doesna work."

"Sometimes we don't get the answer we want," Kate began.

"Whit good does it dae y'tae pray then?" Jenny argued. Remembering that these were her guests, she forced a small smile. "Dinna look as though yer face is trippin' ye. Nothin' against ye, but I dinna believe in it."

"Do you believe in God, Jenny?" Melissa asked.

Jenny shrugged. "There was a time . . ." Her voice trailed off and a distant look came to her eyes.

"Jenny—" Kate started, but Jenny suddenly stood up.

"I ken ane thing now, God doesna have time tae listen tae me," Jenny said bitterly. "Speakin' o'time, I've little of that and I've taken up tae much of yer own this day." She wasn't in the mood for a religious discussion, and she hoped they would pick up the hint and leave.

Kate also rose to her feet. "Jenny, we don't want to pry, but you seemed pretty upset when we bumped into you earlier." She took a step toward Jenny, and behind her, Melissa also stood up. "What's wrong?" Kate asked softly.

"Something that's oot of m'hands," Jenny quickly replied, turning her back to Kate and Melissa as her fragile emotions threatened to get the best of her again.

"Jenny," Melissa said softly, "you asked why we came to Scotland—it's to help people like you."

"People like m'self?" Jenny asked, whirling around to glare at Melissa.

"People who are searching for answers," Kate added.

"I suppose ye have all the answers tae life's problems?" Jenny snapped.

"We have the fullness of the gospel of Jesus Christ—" Kate began.

"Are y'sayin' what m'church has is any less?"

Kate sighed. She hated the contention that was so quick to rise on this subject. President Everson had suggested that they steer away from religious comparisons and focus on what the LDS church had to offer.

"The Bible isn't common ground, it's a battleground. Use the Book of Mormon. If they'll prayerfully read it, they'll know for themselves that the Church is true," the mission president often advised.

Kate looked intently at Jenny as she spoke. "There's good in most churches, but the LDS church has much to offer a troubled world. For instance, we know the trials that we have in life are to test our obedience to God. They're not always easy, but, speaking from personal experience, those are the times when we can grow and learn."

As Jenny listened, she had a feeling that she didn't know how to describe. She had never known such a feeling of comforting peace, particularly in the last few weeks.

Kate continued to speak. "We're all tested. We all face temptations, choices, heartaches, and at times, physical pain. It sometimes seems like other people never experience those things, but their trials might not be as visible."

"Sae, y're sayin' everyone goes through hard times?" Jenny asked.

Kate nodded. "Yes. But we're also here to find joy and love."

Jenny shook her head, thinking of her mother. "And how is it possible?"

"By rememberin' who we are and why we're here," Melissa responded. "Jenny, Sister Erickson—that is, Kate and I are messengers of Jesus Christ. We came to Scotland to help people understand how the gospel of Jesus Christ can bring peace and the strength to overcome their trials." A tingle went down Jenny's spine as Melissa bore a simple testimony of the truthfulness of the gospel of Jesus Christ. The room became very quiet as she finished.

Jenny's chest felt like it was on fire, and yet there was no pain, only a comfortable warmth, like a mother's embrace. "Whit is it I'm feelin'?" she asked, perplexed.

"The promptings of the Holy Ghost," Kate softly answered.

Jenny wasn't quite sure what that meant, but as she looked at Kate and Melissa, she was suddenly overcome by the feeling of love that she felt from these two women. Two women who had been strangers only an hour before. Earlier that day she had been consumed with fear and sorrow, never expecting that she could feel the peace and love that pervaded her small living room now. Tears came to her eyes, and overwhelmed, she fled to her room and shut the door behind her.

Kate and Melissa exchanged a worried glance. Heeding a strong prompting, they went after Jenny and found her lying across a bed, sobbing.

"Jenny, what is it?" Kate asked, slowly sitting beside the young woman.

"M'mother," Jenny sniffed. "Faither phoned me at work. She's dyin' o'cancer. We've known for months. She's in the infirmary in Edinburgh. They don't think she'll last the night."

Melissa rested a hand on Jenny's trembling back. Unsure of what to say, she prayed her gesture would convey the compassion she felt toward Jenny.

"I've been oot buyin' gifts—I thought she'd last 'til Christmas—I should be wi' her now—but if I gae tae her, she'll die—she's hangin' on 'til I come—I canna dae this," Jenny sobbed. "I canna dae this alone."

"What if we went with you, Jenny?" Kate said softly. She hoped Melissa would agree with this unusual course of action. She glanced up at her companion, who nodded her approval.

"I canna bear the thoughts of her dyin'! I'll ne'er see 'er again!" Jenny wailed.

"You will," Melissa soothed, sitting down on the bed. She wondered if Jenny had heard Kate's suggestion.

Jenny's sobs seemed to lessen somewhat. "How kin y'say it, how kin y'know?" she asked in a pleading tone.

"We know, Jenny. That's part of our message to the world. We know families can be together forever," Melissa softly answered.

Jenny slowly rolled over to gaze up at Melissa. "Y'really believe that?"

Melissa nodded. As Jenny struggled to sit up, Melissa gathered the grieving young woman into a warm embrace. "It'll be all right," Melissa tried to assure her. When Melissa released her, Kate took over, drawing Jenny into an intense hug. Clinging to Kate, Jenny cried for several minutes. Then, pulling away, she hurried into the small bathroom.

"Will it be all right if we take her to Edinburgh?" Kate asked in a hushed voice. "I don't think she should be alone right now." The concern she felt was reflected in her companion's eyes.

Melissa slowly nodded. "We're here to serve however we can. And you're right, Jenny shouldn't be alone right now, not like this." She considered the problem they now faced. Edinburgh was over sixty-one miles away. It would mean another long bus trip unless they could think of something else. "I'll need to clear this through our district leader, but I'm sure we can arrange something."

"You think Elder Frank will give us clearance for this?" Kate asked skeptically.

"Good point—he's still not very fond of us," Melissa sighed. "He's probably not in right now anyway. Maybe I could get hold of President Everson when we reach Edinburgh." She smiled sadly at Kate. "I think this is one of those times when we're better off to ask forgiveness later than permission now."

Nodding, Kate motioned to the door as Jenny reappeared.

"Are y'serious aboot gaein' wi' me?" Jenny timidly asked, indicating that she had heard Kate's offer. These two were strangers, but it had been comforting having them here. She didn't know who else to ask and felt certain she wasn't up to making this trip on her own. Her reservoir of strength was gone.

"Yes," Kate answered firmly.

"Then we'd better leave. I hope I haven't waited tae long." Brushing past Kate, Jenny reached for the coat she had thrown on the bed. "I'll pay yer way on the bus, it's the least I kin dae."

"I've got a better idea," Melissa replied, formulating a plan. "What if I give Bishop Monro a call?" she suggested.

"Bishop Monro?" Jenny asked, puzzled. "A Catholic bishop?"

Melissa shook her head. "An LDS bishop."

"Ane of yers?" Jenny worriedly asked.

"Yes," Melissa answered. "If he can't drive us there, I'm sure he'll find someone who can."

"He would dae this for me, someone he doesna even know?"

Kate nodded.

"Why?"

"It's how LDS people are. We try to help others whenever we can," Kate replied.

Jenny gazed at Kate. "LDS—y'said that b'fore. Whit does it mean?"

"Our full name is The Church of Jesus Christ of Latter-day Saints," Melissa explained. "LDS for short."

"I thought y'were called Mormons?"

"It's a nickname. It comes from the Book of Mormon."

From the look on Jenny's face, Melissa could see whatever she had heard about that book wasn't very complimentary. She wondered if Jenny distrusted their motives, thinking that their efforts on her behalf were only a way for the missionaries to try to convert her. Certain that she was being prompted to say what came to mind, Melissa caught Jenny's worried gaze.

"Jenny, before we leave, I want you to know somethin'. We are missionaries and we are here to teach people about the gospel of Jesus Christ, but only if they want to hear it. We don't force ourselves on anyone. I think it's important that y'all know we're not helpin' you because we think you'll join our church."

Stunned, Jenny stared at Melissa. Had this girl read her mind?

"I hope y'all can believe that," Melissa continued. "We want to help you because we care. Our concern for you is genuine and we won't ever expect you to do anything in return." Jenny started to cry again and Melissa held her tightly, sealing her promise with a hug. "We're friends now, Jenny. Y'all remember that."

When Jenny had regained her composure, Melissa asked to use the phone.

"If I had ane, y'could use it. M'landlady has ane," Jenny said, wiping at her eyes with some tissue Kate had handed her.

When Jenny was ready, Melissa and Kate followed her out of the small flat.

CHAPTER 24

Bishop Rupert Monro couldn't leave work, but his wife, Maura, was available. It didn't take long for Maura to find Jenny's apartment building. She rang the buzzer and patiently waited for the three young women to walk down. Smiling warmly at them, she led them to her small grey car and opened the trunk. Kate and Melissa quickly loaded the Christmas gifts Jenny had purchased earlier. Gifts they had helped wrap while waiting for Maura.

"There now, that should do it," Maura said with a cheerful Scottish lilt although her accent wasn't as pronounced as Jenny's. "Why don't you girls hurry into the car out of this cold?" She quickly moved to the driver's side and slid behind the wheel.

"I thank y' for this," Jenny said as she shyly slipped into the car. She had elected to sit in the back with Kate, leaving Melissa to sit up front with Maura.

"You're welcome," Maura said. "Before we leave, could I ask one of you girls to offer a prayer for us?"

Melissa smiled at Maura, then at Kate. "I'll say it, if that's all right."

Kate nodded before folding her arms and closing her eyes.

Jenny noticed that Maura and Melissa did the same thing. Feeling awkward, she closed her own eyes.

"Dear Father in Heaven, we are so grateful for the many blessings we enjoy. For the opportunity to serve in this beautiful land. We ask now for a special blessing to be upon Jenny and her family at this time of sorrow. Grant them comfort and peace and let them feel the great love that thou hast for them. We also ask that we might travel in safety this day."

As Melissa closed the prayer, tears streamed down Jenny's face. She opened her eyes, avoiding Kate's worried gaze. Kate didn't press, but instead reached into her pocket for a handful of tissue which she quietly offered to Jenny.

"Thank you, Sister Larsen. I always feel better aboot travelin' after a prayer," Maura said brightly. She too had noticed Jenny's tears and decided it would be best not to comment. Her husband had explained the situation, instructing her to use extreme caution. Anything that would make Jenny feel uncomfortable was to be avoided. She turned on the radio and soon the car was filled with Christmas music. This brought more tears from Jenny who cried against Kate's shoulder for several minutes. Silently chiding herself, Maura shut off the radio.

"I've never shed sae many tears," Jenny said, embarrassed as she accepted another handful of tissue, this time from Melissa. "I canna get m'self under control."

"There's no shame in cryin'," Melissa softly replied. "It's worse if you don't."

Jenny slowly nodded. "I dinna ken how tae thank ye. I couldna have done this alone."

"We're glad to do it," Maura replied. The mother in her wanted to stop the car and gather Jenny in a fierce embrace. Instead, she drove on, her heart aching for the young woman in the back seat of her car.

* * *

The rest of the trip Maura directed the conversation. Sensing Jenny's unwillingness to talk, she asked Kate and Melissa about their families and the places they were from. Jenny sat in a daze, stray tears wandering down her face periodically. Eventually they reached Edinburgh. As Maura drove through Scotland's capitol, Kate was again impressed by the majesty of the city. As they traveled along Princes Street, Edinburgh's main thoroughfare, Kate spotted the memorial honoring the famous Scottish novelist, Sir Walter Scott. Kate remembered reading one of Scott's novels, *Rob Roy*, in a college literature class she had taken at BYU. She sighed. There were times when she couldn't believe she was in Scotland—times when it didn't seem possible that she was actually riding through historic cities like Edinburgh.

"Is this the biggest city in Scotland?" Kate asked.

"No," Maura replied. "It's the second biggest. Glasgow is larger."

"I love how they've mixed the old with the new," Melissa commented, glancing out of the window on her side of the car.

"It's actually split up into two districts that we call Old Town and New Town." Maura pointed out the window toward the section of Old Town. "Y'can't see it now because of the snow, but in the spring and summer months, the two sections are separated by Princes Street Gardens where beautiful flowers line the bed of a drained loch."

"It is gorgeous," Melissa agreed. "We'll have to show you next spring," she said to Kate.

"I'd love it. I'd also like to check out some of those older buildings," Kate said excitedly. The historian in her could hardly wait.

"You should start with Edinburgh Castle," Maura suggested. "It's older than the city of Edinburgh."

"It looks like it grew right out of the rock," Melissa commented.

"Aye, it does appear that way. You c'n see why it offered such protection during the Scottish wars for independence," Maura supplied.

"When did Edinburgh become a city?" Kate asked.

"Let's see now. If I remember right, Edinburgh was granted a city charter in the 1300s by King Bruce," Maura answered, pleased by Kate's interest.

"King Bruce? Isn't he the one who betrayed Sir William Wallace?" Kate asked.

"You mean Braveheart?" Melissa added.

Maura smiled. "You saw the movie?"

Melissa shook her head. "I wanted to but I made a commitment when I was sixteen not to see R-rated movies."

Maura smiled sheepishly. "Here it was a matter of Scottish pride. We wanted to see if they got the story right."

"And did they?" Kate asked, who hadn't seen the movie either.

"In places. You know how movies are—they add a bit of glamour here, a touch of romance there. And, in the interest of time, some things are condensed or run together."

"Did they really kill his wife?" Melissa asked.

Maura smiled, well aware of the controversy that existed on that question. "There's one account that claims Wallace was married and his young bride was killed for helpin' him escape the garrison of soldiers who had picked a fight with him. According to this account, her death led Sir Wallace on a path of retribution against England that secured him an honored place in Scottish history forever."

"You hinted there were other versions?" Kate prompted.

"Yes. Another account claims Wallace never married. Supposedly he fell in love with an eighteen-year-old heiress named Marion Braidfute. In this version, Marion gave birth to William's daughter and was murdered by the English shortly afterward although many historians dispute there is evidence that Wallace had any offspring. It was Marion's death that was said to have spurred Sir Wallace into taking action against England."

"Marion, huh?" Kate said thoughtfully. "Maid Marion?"

Maura laughed. "You're no'the first to put that one together. According to one theory, the legend of Robin Hood came from the escapades of Sir Wallace, who was a giant of a man. He had a friend named Edward Little and a brother named John. Some think those three things were combined to come up with—"

"Little John!" Kate exclaimed.

"Aye. And there was a Benedictine monk who left his monastery to join up with Sir Wallace who lived for a time as a fugitive in the forest."

"Friar Tuck," Melissa said with a smile.

"Perhaps." Maura smiled at the enthusiasm of the sister missionaries. "Sir Wallace and his band of men wreaked mischief and mayhem on anyone or anything that bore the English insignia. It is said that one day Sir Wallace was catching fish for an elderly uncle who was unable to take care of himself. The last five soldiers of an English garrison that was passing through stopped and tried to take the fish from Wallace. When Wallace asked if he could at least keep half of what he had caught, one of the soldiers became angry at his insolence and charged at him with a drawn sword."

"That doesn't sound very fair," Melissa commented.

"Aye. Wallace had nothin' but a fishing pole to defend himself.

He hit the soldier with the pole and was able to take his sword. And here's something else you might find interesting. It's a phrase Wallace learned from his uncle who was a wealthy priest. 'My sonne I say freedom is best, then never yield to thrall's arrest.' It is said that this theme influenced Wallace more than any other."

"What's a thrall?" Melissa questioned.

"A thrall is one in bondage—a slave," Maura explained. As Kate and Melissa reflected on this, Maura continued. "You asked if Robert Bruce betrayed Sir Wallace. He did side with England at the time Wallace was captured. It's something he later regretted. After the death of Sir Wallace, he fought against England and went on to become one of the greatest kings Scotland has ever known."

"Your people have quite a history," Melissa commented.

"As do yours," Maura responded. "I often think of the Mormon pioneers and all they suffered in their struggle to freely practice their religion. As with Wallace, they weren't willing to become thralls in a society that neither respected nor understood the importance of their spiritual quest."

"There's the infirmary," Jenny interrupted, pointing to the hospital. Maura's comparison of the Mormon pioneers to Sir William Wallace disturbed her. Surely the Mormon pioneers hadn't suffered as much as the Scottish people of Wallace's time. She would ask Kate and Melissa about it later.

Kate glanced at the pale young woman. For a while, she had forgotten their purpose in coming. Looking at Jenny's tearstained face, Kate imagined how she would feel if she were to lose her mother. Silently pleading for guidance, she vowed to help Jenny any way that she could.

* * *

Jenny introduced Kate, Melissa, and Maura to her father as friends, and nothing was said about Kate and Melissa's purpose in Scotland. Fraser MacTavish was so overcome with grief that he didn't seem to notice the American accents. After greeting his daughter, he hovered near his wife's side.

The three women were then introduced to Jenny's older

brother, Alec, his wife, and two small children—a seven-year-old boy, and a three-year-old girl. Alec MacTavish was a younger version of his father; both with medium builds, sandy hair, and deep blue eyes. Expressive eyes that revealed the depth of their pain as they contemplated the loss of their wife and mother.

After making all of the introductions, Jenny went into her mother's room, taking with her the presents she had brought, gifts that now seemed out of place. Setting them in a chair, she approached her mother. Janet MacTavish had lost so much weight in recent months that she appeared fragile and small as she gripped the metal railing of the hospital bed for support.

Janet beckoned her daughter to open the gifts, and Jenny reluctantly unwrapped the presents she had brought with her. A blue robe. A pair of new slippers. Other items her mother would never get the chance to use. Opening the last box, Jenny held out the gift she had had her eye on for weeks, knowing it would appeal to her mother.

"Aye, it's lovely, dear," Janet said softly, gazing at the musical globe that contained a small village, covered with sparkling snow. "Wind it f'r me."

Blinking rapidly, Jenny obediently wound the key, setting the beautiful globe on the table near her mother's bed. A delicate melody filled the room.

"It's beautiful, Jen," Janet rasped. "Thank ye, it reminds me o'hame." She beckoned her daughter to come to her. Jenny slid a chair next to the bed and released the metal railing. Sitting down, she leaned forward to rest her head near her mother's heart.

Stepping out into the hall after her mother lost consciousness, Jenny's resolve to be strong disintegrated into tears. Her brother embraced her, whispering words of comfort that only she could hear.

Maura motioned to the sister missionaries. "How long do you want to stay?" she asked quietly.

Melissa glanced at Kate. She knew what her heart was telling her, but she didn't want to inconvenience the bishop's wife.

"If you need to leave . . ." Melissa began.

"No. Rupert mentioned that you two were concerned aboot what the mission president would think of this, and I thought it would help if I talked to him. You two girls are needed here."

"You don't think we're in the way?" Melissa asked.

Maura shook her head. "I think it's important for you two to stay—at least until we see what develops with Jenny's mother." She and the sister missionaries had offered to arrange for a priesthood blessing for Janet, but Jenny had declined, fearing what her father and brother would think.

"I'm not sure what we're supposed to do," Melissa whispered, "maybe it's the moral support she needs right now."

Maura nodded. "You never know where acts of service will lead," she said before she went on her way.

* * *

"She's gone," Jenny wailed, moving out of her mother's room. "I canna bear it." Alec hurried into the room where they had been keeping a steady vigil for several hours.

Melissa quickly gathered Jenny into a close embrace. "I'm so sorry, Jenny," she whispered. When Jenny finally pulled away, Kate took over, drawing Jenny into her arms and holding her.

"We're here for you," Kate murmured softly. Jenny clung to her, sobbing.

Maura glanced at President Everson. He had decided to come check out the situation for himself.

"This is irregular," he had said as they had driven to the hospital. "But if these sister missionaries felt prompted to help this girl, there must be reasons we don't know about. As you already said, their service today could influence this young lady toward the Church. You never know. I'll call their district leader later and fill him in on what's taking place."

Now, as President Everson watched, he could see that Jenny was drawing on the supportive love she felt from the sister missionaries. He sensed an invisible bond between the three young women, but was puzzled by it.

"Uncle Jamie," Jenny suddenly cried out, running into the arms of a tall, broad-shouldered man who had just arrived.

"Steady lass. Easy girl. Is it bad as a' that?"

Jenny nodded, fresh tears making an appearance. Alec and Fraser MacTavish joined them, breaking the news to Jamie that his sister was gone.

"It canna be," he groaned. "I hurried as fast as a man kin! I left Campbeltown as soon as you called tae tell me how ill she'd become. I flew from the Machrihanish Airport to Glasgow, then here to Edinburgh."

Kate's eyes widened. This man was from Campbeltown, the town where her ancestors had lived years ago? She made herself a mental note to somehow learn if he knew anything about the MacOwen family. Maybe she could finally discover the whereabouts of that branch of the family tree.

CHAPTER 25

Kate and Melissa stood together with Maura Monro near the group of family and friends who had come to the cemetery. Their hearts ached for Jenny and her family as they saw the sorrow in their somber faces. It was frustrating, knowing they could have eased their pain somewhat by teaching them the plan of salvation. The gospel explained so much about the purpose of life and death. The knowledge that death wasn't the end was a precious gift, one that all three women longed to share with this grieving family. But, under the circumstances, they remained silent, praying fervently for the Comforter to intercede, to provide inner peace.

After the brief graveside ceremony, Kate, Melissa, and Maura waited to speak to Jenny. They knew the young woman would need a great deal of loving support in the days ahead and were determined to provide that whenever possible. To their surprise, Jenny broke away from the crowd to find them, dragging her favorite uncle with her.

"Uncle Jamie, I'd like y'tae meet some wonderful ladies who helped me sae much the day we lost Mother," Jenny said, leading her uncle to where Kate, Melissa, and Maura were standing. "They arranged a ride for m'tae gae to Edinburgh—I spent precious time wi' Mother because of them," she tearfully explained. "Kate, Melissa, Maura, this is m'uncle, Jamie MacOwen."

If Melissa hadn't been there to stop her, Kate would've sunk to her knees in the snow-covered ground. Grabbing her from behind, Melissa and Maura steadied Kate.

"Whit's wrang?" Jenny asked, concerned by how pale Kate had become.

Melissa shook her head. "I'm not sure. Kate, what is it? Are you sick?"

Kate stared at Jenny, then at Jamie. "You're a MacOwen?" she weakly asked.

"Aye," Jamie replied, puzzled by Kate's reaction.

Still shaken, Kate continued to stare. "Have you ever heard of Dougal or John MacOwen of Campbeltown?"

Melissa met Maura's inquisitive gaze. It was all starting to make sense. "Kate, aren't those your ancestors from Scotland?" she asked.

Kate slowly nodded.

"Dougal MacOwen was m'second great-grandfather," Jamie said, staring at Kate. "Dae y'mean to tell me y're a MacOwen, too?"

"No, I mean, yes. I'm not explaining this very well. I'm sorry— this is such a shock," Kate stammered. "I'm not sure I can explain."

"Take yer time, lass," Jamie said, placing a protective arm around Jenny's shoulders. He had heard that these Mormon women had befriended his niece and wasn't sure he liked that idea. Especially now that one of them was claiming to be a relative.

"Dougal MacOwen was my third great-grandfather," Kate began.

Seeing the truth in her face, Jamie broke in excitedly. "Y're from the American MacOwens," he said. "Dougal John, Dougal's grandson, is m'direct ancestor."

"My mother is a descendant of Helen, Dougal John's youngest sister," Kate said tearfully.

Jamie shook his head. "I canna believe this."

"Neither kin I," Jenny exclaimed. "We're cousins, Kate," she said, drawing Kate into a warm embrace. "God led y'tae us."

* * *

Three weeks later, Melissa and Kate found themselves in the Dumbarton church house in the presence of the mission president. Word that President Everson wanted to meet with them had caught up to them, compliments of Elder Frank.

"You two are in for it now," the district leader had said gleefully. "You just think you're above mission rules. He'll straighten you out."

Elder Frank was still smarting over the fact that President Everson had been supportive of their unplanned trip to Edinburgh in December.

Now, as they nervously sat in the bishop's office, Melissa and Kate wondered what they were in for. A lecture—a transfer? The thought of separation filled them with dread.

President Everson smiled at the sister missionaries. "Let me begin by congratulating you two on your success in Dumbarton."

Melissa focused on the floor. It was a transfer, she could feel it.

"You've been responsible for two baptisms and it looks like a third might be in the future," he said, consulting a notebook on the desk.

"Jenny has been receptive to the discussions we've had so far," Kate ventured. They had been meeting with Jenny since Christmas. While Kate felt it was due in part to Jenny's desire to become better acquainted with her American cousin, it had led to a series of questions about the LDS church.

"I'll come right to the point. It's time for a change—"

No! Melissa silently protested.

Kate gazed dismally at the mission president. Didn't he realize how much she and Melissa could accomplish? How much they had done in the three months they had spent together?

". . . and if you'll pray about it, you'll know it's the Lord's will."

Melissa couldn't bring herself to look at Kate.

"It'll be a challenge, but I know you're up to it."

Staring at her hands, Kate wondered if this was hitting Melissa as hard. She had always known this day would come, but she was completely unprepared. Melissa had been more than a companion—she had been a sister, a friend. And now they were being asked to go their separate ways. Reminding herself that there were other priorities, other reasons for continuing her mission, Kate forced a strained smile.

"I hate to break up a successful team—"

Melissa flinched. She was sure she'd learn to love another companion, but no one could replace Kate as a friend. She was certain theirs was an eternal friendship. She might never meet Kate again in this world, but there was always the next.

"Which is why you two will serve together as companions in the peninsula of Kintyre."

At first, it didn't register. Then, as his words began to sink in, Kate and Melissa stared at President Everson in stunned surprise.

"As I said, I know this is the Lord's will. A strong witness was borne to me during prayerful consideration. Much good will come from this transfer. We've already made arrangements for you to travel by bus from Glasgow to Campbeltown."

Kate's eyes grew wider. "Campbeltown?"

"Yes. It's on the very end of the peninsula."

"When do we leave?" Melissa stammered.

"Monday."

"That only gives us two days," Kate protested.

"I didn't think you girls had that much to pack," President Everson teased.

"No, it's not that—you can't know what this means to me, to keep Melissa as a companion and be able to go to the town my ancestors are from—but what about Jenny MacTavish?" Kate worriedly asked.

"I'm sure the elders can manage," President Everson said.

Kate shuddered, imagining Jenny's reaction to Elder Frank. In her opinion, he was an egotistical snob. She now thought quite highly of Elder Peterson, but wasn't sure his warm-hearted approach could override his companion's obnoxious personality.

"Here's the information you'll need concerning this new assignment," the mission president continued.

Sighing, Kate sat back in her chair.

* * *

"Y're really leavin'?" Jenny asked, glancing from Melissa to Kate.

Kate slowly nodded.

"But, why? Dae ye no like it here?" Jenny asked, dismayed by this information. Having Kate and Melissa in her life had been a breath of fresh air. They had freely offered comforting love, opening their hearts before even knowing of the special bond that existed between herself and Kate. They had answered the numerous questions that had arisen since her mother's death, giving her hope during a time in her life when all seemed bleak. Most important, they had been her friends—a rare and precious commodity.

"It's not that, Jenny," Kate tried to explain. "We love Dumbarton, but we know we're supposed to be in Campbeltown now."

"How dae y'know? Let me guess, y'prayed aboot it," Jenny snapped, suddenly angry. How could they leave her like this? "I wish prayer worked f'r me. I n'ver seem to get anywhere wi' it."

"It can work for you," Melissa replied. Concerned by the defiant look on Jenny's face, she searched for the right words to explain.

"I'm no' sae sure. I've been prayin' like y'said. It still hurts that m'mother's gone. I still dinna ken the Book of Mormon's true."

"It takes time," Kate answered. "It took me months to gain a testimony."

Jenny stood, glaring at the sister missionaries. "How kin they send y'away—we're family!" she exclaimed, getting back to the heart of the matter.

Rising, Kate stood in front of her cousin. "Jenny—we won't be that far away. Maybe you could come down for a visit some time," she tried to soothe. "Uncle Jamie would like that."

"It's no' the same," Jenny said, moving to stare out of the small window in her living room. She was the only member of her family who lived in Dumbarton. With Kate and Melissa around, she hadn't felt so alone.

Kate gazed at Melissa. She had known this would be difficult. If only they had had more time with Jenny. As it was, they were leaving her when she was still so vulnerable, still full of pain from losing her mother.

"I've grown sae fond of the two of ye," Jenny said softly to the window. She didn't trust herself to face Kate or Melissa.

"Jenny, you know we care about you," Kate replied, crossing the room to stand next to her cousin. "As you said, we're family. This isn't goodbye forever."

"Naw, that's right. If I join y'r Church, I'll see y'again in heaven," Jenny said angrily.

"Jenny—"

"M'faither said this church would bring me nothin' but pain. He was right!" Jenny exclaimed.

Kate shook her head. She knew Jenny didn't mean that. She had seen the excitement in her eyes as they had taught the discussions.

Spirit had spoken to spirit. "Jenny, we've shown you how you can be happy for eternity. It's up to you to accept what I know you've felt— you know there's something special about our church. Our ancestors sacrificed so much to be members. I've told you what I learned a few years ago from Meg MacOwen's journal. As soon as Mom sends me copies of it, I'll send one to you. You can read for yourself what the gospel meant to our second great-grandmother."

Jenny continued to stare out the window. She had never had sisters before; the nearest thing had been her brother's wife, and the two of them had never been close. Kate and Melissa had filled that void and now they were deserting her. What did she care if the Church was true? It meant nothing without Kate and Melissa.

"You can learn the truth for yourself," Kate stubbornly repeated. "Keep reading the Book of Mormon and pray about it. This is something you'll have to do on your own. No one can do it for you. Not me, not Melissa, and not the elders who will come visit you if you want to finish the discussions." Kate gazed at her cousin, a lump forming in her throat. It had meant so much to know that she had been able to share the gospel with a family member. "Please, Jenny? We leave Monday. Let's not waste what little time we have arguing."

Jenny turned from the window, revealing her tears. Wordlessly, she reached for Kate.

Opening her arms, Kate held Jenny tight. She knew her cousin might hold a grudge for a while because of the transfer, but because of the time they had spent together, Jenny would never be the same. Eventually, she would start searching for answers again.

"I'll miss y'sae much," Jenny finally whispered, drawing back.

"I'll miss you, too," Kate replied, offering a watery smile.

Turning, Jenny went to Melissa. Tears flowed freely as the two young women embraced. As Kate tearfully watched, she knew this wasn't the end of their friendship. In a lot of ways, it was just the beginning.

CHAPTER 26

Feb. 12

Dear Mom, Dad, Ty, and Sabrina,

I can't thank you enough for the copies of Grandma Meg's journal. I sent off a copy to Jenny this afternoon. I hope she'll read it and come to understand why most of the MacOwens left Scotland for America. I think I mentioned to you in my last letter that we're all thought of as the black sheep of the family. I think that's part of Jenny's problem. I know she's felt the promptings of the Spirit, but it frightens her. She fears what her family will think—what they'll say. I'm seeing for myself how difficult it must've been for Grandma Meg and her family. I love Scotland and I love its people, but they can be stubborn when it comes to religion.

I'm saving a copy of Grandma Meg's journal to give to Uncle Jamie—as he's asked me to call him. Melissa and I will be going out to the family estate next prep day. I don't think Uncle Jamie's wife, Francis, cares too much for us, but Uncle Jamie has been very receptive. Jenny has always been one of his favorites, and he appreciated all that we did for her when her mother died.

I wish I'd had the chance to know Jenny's mother. The way everyone describes her, it sounds like Aunt Janet was a lot like Grandma Meg. Strong and spirited, but gentle and kind as well.

How is everything at home? Bozeman seems so far away. It's a good thing I'm too busy to think about it much—I miss you guys. I can't believe I've already been out for four months. Fourteen more to go. If they go by as fast, I'll be home before you know it.

We're not making much progress in Campbeltown yet. We meet with the small branch here each Sunday. Melissa and I are often called upon to teach Sunday School or Relief Society. We've already spoken twice in sacrament meeting. Maybe that's part of why we're here, to strengthen the existing Saints. I know what the other reason is. Although Uncle Jamie hasn't agreed to hear the discussions yet, he's interested in our beliefs. He's teaching us how to ride horses and we try to answer his questions. His sister's death has softened his heart and there is so much he desires to know. We can help him, but it's a matter of convincing him of that.

Well, I'd better close. Take care of each other and always remember how much I love each one of you.

Love always,
Kate

P.S. Your cookies were wonderful, Mom. Melissa wants the recipe.

Sue blinked rapidly.

"Sounds like she's doing great," Greg commented.

"She is. I still can't get over how she managed to meet up with our relatives." Sue carefully folded the letter she knew she would read at least a dozen more times before the day was over.

"I guess we know now why she was so intent on serving a mission."

Sue gazed at her husband. "I was afraid she was running from Mike."

"That thought crossed my mind, too," Greg admitted. "But she did have her heart set on a mission before he returned."

"She did." Sue's chin quivered. "I'm so proud of her," she said softly. "She'll probably never know how proud."

"She knows," Greg assured her. "And if she doesn't, you can make it clear to her when she comes home."

* * *

March 15

Dear Aunt Paige, Uncle Stan, & family,

Here it is at last, a letter from me. I'm sorry about not being a better letter writer. In the beginning, my goal was to send off letters to all *of you once a week. I manage to send one off to Mom and Dad on a weekly basis—the rest of you I try to catch up with when I can. Please don't let that stop you from writing to me. I love your letters.*

In your last letter, you asked what Dougal MacOwen's estate is like these days. You'll recall that when Dougal was alive, he was one of the wealthiest men around. That part has changed. Our family has seen some hard times. Bad investments, that sort of thing. Uncle Jamie tried to explain it to me. They're not as wealthy as Dougal was, but things are improving. Uncle Jamie has managed to build up the stables and does well with his horses.

The old rock house is still intact. Jamie's wife, Francis, doesn't care for Melissa or me, so we have yet to see the inside of the house, but the outside is beautiful. It looks like a postcard. The grey rock glistens when the sun shines and green moss grows along one side. I'll have to send you a picture.

Uncle Jamie's love for horses is contagious. He allows Melissa and me to go riding with him every prep day that we can manage to make it out to the MacOwen estate.

Uncle Jamie lets me ride a small black mare named Spitfire. He thinks she and I have a lot in common—the big tease. He reminds me a lot of Uncle Stan. He claims he's not interested in joining the Church, but he loved getting a copy of Grandma Meg's journal. You never know, maybe we've planted a tiny seed.

Uncle Jamie has only one child, a son who's twenty three. Davie, as he is called, is away at school at the University of Glasgow. I haven't met him yet. He didn't come to Aunt Janet's funeral—he was sick with the flu then. There's talk that Davie may come home in May. I'm excited to meet him.

I haven't heard from Jenny since I sent her the copy of Grandma Meg's journal. I'm worried about her. I'll send her another letter today, but there's no guarantee she'll answer. Please remember her in your prayers.

I enjoyed hearing Tami's reaction to the resemblance between herself and Jenny. Assure her it's a compliment. Tell everyone "Hello" for me.

Much love,
Kate

April 4

Dear Jan,

    Thanks so much for keeping in touch—despite my poor ability to send off letters. Now I understand why I ended up with so many short notes from Randy.

    That reminds me, I'm tickled everything went well with Laurie and the new baby. Tamra Jan is a cute name. I'll bet she's a doll.

    As for how things are going, this is a difficult area. No one wants to hear about the gospel, including my uncle Jamie. We get along great as long as I don't mention anything about the Church. So, I guess for now, we'll keep things light between us. I feel it's important to establish good family ties. Maybe the rest will come later.

    There's still no word from my cousin Jenny. I don't know what to think. I'll keep sending letters to her, but aside from that and prayer, I'm not sure what else to do. I guess I'll leave it in the Lord's hands.

    I know this is going to be short, and again, I apologize. Thanks again for keeping in touch. Your letters mean a lot.

                             Love,
                             Kate

May 20

Dear Mike,

    *So, you want to be Smokey the Bear's friend when you grow up? Kidding. Actually, I think you'll love working as a **Forest Technician**, as you called it. How many years of biology will it take?*

    Things are still pretty slow here in Scotland. I love the chance I've been given to get acquainted with my Scottish relatives. I finally got to meet my cousin, Davie MacOwen. What a hunk! (Don't worry, we're related, remember?) Thick black hair, green eyes, and smile that never ends. He's the only member of the family who seems interested in the Church. Melissa and I have already taught him the first discussion. I think his mother hates us. Uncle Jamie didn't seem too thrilled, but he decided to listen in. I'll keep you posted on how it all turns out.

    It's great, teaching the discussions in the house my ancestors lived in. What a beautiful place. I wish we could see the entire thing, but until

Aunt Francis decides we're not intruders, that will have to wait for another time.

Well, I hate to run, but I have about a million things to do today. Laundry, cleaning up the apartment, shopping for unnecessary items like food—things like that. Sometimes having one day a week to catch up on all of this stuff doesn't work so well, especially when I spend most of prep day visiting with relatives who are still speaking to me. (Aunt Francis, Uncle Jamie's wife, never has spoken to us, actually.)

Love ya,
Sister Kate Erickson

As Kate wrote, Melissa walked across the small living room of their apartment and into the tiny kitchen. Stepping behind Kate, who was seated at the table, Melissa peered over her companion's shoulder. "Love ya, huh?" she questioned.

"This is a private letter," Kate informed her.

"When your private letter interferes with my schedule, I feel I have every right to look it over," Melissa teased.

"I'm finished."

"Which brings me back to how you ended it. *Love ya?*"

Rising, Kate quickly sealed the letter inside of an envelope. "It's how I close all my letters."

"Uh-huh. I noticed it's how Mike closes his letters, too."

"Don't we have some laundry to take care of?" Kate hinted, moving out of the kitchen.

"Killjoy," Melissa accused, following Kate into the living room.

Ignoring Melissa, Kate walked into the bedroom, grabbed the duffle bag of dirty clothes, and returned to the living room. "Let's go. I'm ready. I'll mail these letters on the way."

Melissa glanced at the duffle bag. Doing laundry wasn't what she had had in mind for the day. "Actually, I was thinking more along the lines of going riding with Uncle Jamie."

Kate grinned at her companion. "Don't you mean, *Cousin Davie?*"

Melissa blushed.

"I thought so. I'll grab my jacket and we'll go." Kate eased past her companion, but not before receiving a pinch from Melissa.

"Ow! What's that for?"

"If you have to ask, you're slower than I think," Melissa drawled.

As Kate disappeared into the bedroom, Melissa moved to the living room window and stared out into the street below. Shivering, she forced herself to think of something else besides Davie MacOwen.

CHAPTER 27

Kate stared at Melissa. "A transfer?"

Melissa slowly nodded. "Kate, we've been together longer than most companions—it's been seven months. Three more and I go home."

"I thought we'd be together until then," Kate said, sinking down into a wooden chair in their living room.

"It'll be better this way," Melissa began, sitting on the lumpy couch.

"How could it be better?"

Melissa glanced down at her hands. This was going to be a tough one to explain.

"Have I upset you?"

"Kate, I didn't request the transfer. But President Everson is definitely in tune. This *is* an inspired change."

"How can you say that?"

Melissa remained silent. She didn't know how to explain what had become an unbearable situation.

"Are you sure I haven't done something—I mean, I know I snore—a little. Heidi used to complain. Sometimes I'm pretty stubborn—" Kate stammered, aware that Melissa was hiding something. Whatever it was, it had been bothering Melissa for days.

"Kate, it isn't anythin' you've done," Melissa said, close to tears. Shutting her eyes, she wished Kate would back off, but knew her companion too well to believe that she would.

"Then what?"

Opening her eyes, Melissa gazed sadly at Kate. "It's just meant to be. That's not much of an answer, but if you pray about it, you'll know it's right." Forcing a smile, she tried to shrug off the pain in her heart. "Look on the bright side, you'll probably get a companion who's easier to get along with than me."

"I doubt that," Kate stiffly replied. News of the transfer hurt, but it hurt more knowing Melissa wasn't being totally honest with her. "You're not going to tell me what's really going on, are you?" she added, glaring at the other young woman.

"I can't," Melissa stammered, rising to stare out the window. She couldn't take much more of the hurt look on Kate's face.

"Why not?"

"Sometimes you ask too many questions," Melissa replied, keeping her back to Kate.

"And sometimes you don't give me enough credit. If it isn't me, then it has to be Davie."

Melissa whirled around to stare at Kate.

"I haven't said anything, but I know how you two feel about each other," Kate murmured. She had observed the way Davie had been looking at Melissa lately, and had been very aware of the attraction Melissa felt for Davie. Even Uncle Jamie had commented on it. Fortunately, Aunt Francis had been too concerned over Davie's interest in the LDS Church to notice.

"Kate . . . I . . . we haven't—" Melissa stammered, flustered with embarrassment.

"I know. I've been with you twenty-four hours a day, remember?" Kate gently reminded her. "You haven't done anything wrong."

"I didn't mean to feel anythin' for Davie," Melissa said miserably as she moved to sit back on the couch. "Here I am, a representative of the Church, and I've fallen in love with a contact."

Smiling her support, Kate sat next to her. "I think you two would make a wonderful couple," she commented.

"I'm not supposed to be thinkin' of things like that. We're missionaries, remember?"

Kate searched Melissa's face. "You are for three more months— how about after that?" If Melissa loved Davie as much as she suspected, this wasn't going to go away overnight.

Lowering her eyes, Melissa stared at the gold-colored sofa they were sitting on. It was as uncomfortable as this conversation they were having. "After that I return home to Tennessee. I'll never see him again. So, like I said, this transfer is the best possible answer."

"But Davie's so close to baptism," Kate protested. She didn't want to see the same thing happen with him that had happened with Jenny.

Melissa gazed intently at Kate. "Don't you see, that's why it's better this way. I don't want him joinin' the Church because of me. He needs to do it for himself if that's what he wants."

Kate reluctantly nodded, realizing Melissa was right.

Rising, Melissa walked into the kitchen and began organizing the dishes that needed to be washed. She filled their sink with soapy water, then stepped out of the way as Kate filled the large bowl they used for rinsing with clear water. In silence, they worked together. It didn't take long to tidy up the kitchen. Feeling slightly better, Melissa smiled at Kate. "Three months in Glasgow will be fun. It'll give me a chance to see more of Scotland before I go home." She sighed. "They haven't given me long to pack. I'd better get started."

"Do you need any help?"

Melissa shook her head, moving into the bedroom.

Sensing her wish to be alone, Kate began straightening the living room and wondered how she would break the news to Davie.

* * *

The day of departure came too soon for both girls. A member of the Church from Glasgow had driven Kate's new companion down to Campbeltown and was now waiting to take Melissa back. As they walked toward the car, Kate shivered in the chilling rain, convinced it was the proper setting for this event.

"Figures, doesn't it, that I'd meet Mr. Right at the wrong time?" Melissa said ruefully as she hugged Kate goodbye.

Kate returned Melissa's embrace. "Don't forget either one of us."

Melissa pulled back to look at Kate reproachfully. "How could I ever do that?"

"Melissa—Sister Larsen," a deep Scottish brogue interrupted. Melissa whirled around to stare at Davie MacOwen. In his hand was a small bouquet of purple heather.

"What are you doin' here?" Melissa asked, reluctantly taking the flowers.

"Comin' to bid ye farewell," he sheepishly replied.

Melissa gave Kate a dirty look. "You told him I was leavin' today, didn't you?"

Kate shrugged. "I didn't see anything wrong with you two exchanging addresses."

"Aren't y'glad tae see me?" Davie asked, as Kate moved a short, safe distance away.

"Oh, Davie, you know I am. It just makes this so much harder."

"Did Kate tell y' I'm thinkin' of goin' to America?"

"You are?" Melissa said, stunned.

Davie nodded. "My father's none tae happy aboot it, but I'd like to visit m'ancestors' graves. I'd like tae see f'r m'self why America called tae them. I might even decide tae study at the University of Brigham Young, if they'll have me."

Smiling at the way Davie had turned BYU's name around, Melissa felt lighter inside than she had in days. "Seriously?"

Davie solemnly nodded. "I've ne'er been mair serious aboot anythin' in m'life."

Tears welled up in Melissa's eyes. "I've been thinkin' about checkin' out BYU myself. Kate's made it sound real attractive."

"Sae I might see you there then?" Davie hopefully asked.

"You might," Melissa encouraged. She glanced at Kate, hoping her former companion knew how much this meant.

"Could I look y'up sometime?"

Melissa slowly nodded.

"You have m'address?"

"Yes. Kate can give you mine. I'd better go now. We have a long way to travel today." She shook the hand Davie held out to her and quickly gave Kate another hug before climbing into the car.

Davie's eyes followed Melissa until both she and the car had disappeared from sight.

"It's okay, Davie," Kate said bravely. "I know we'll both see her again."

"I hope y'r right," Davie murmured. "I couldna bear it any other way."

Silently agreeing, Kate slowly turned to lead her new companion out of the rain.

* * *

Unlike Kate's former companion, Dori Nelson was tall, blonde, and on a mission for all the wrong reasons. Her attitude toward the people of Scotland revealed her complete lack of respect for them. Dori hated Scotland and she didn't care much for its people either. She hated the wind, the horizontal rain, and the food—which in her opinion was not only fattening but disgusting—and she had no interest in the historical landmarks that surrounded them. Kate could see that Dori wasn't eager to teach the gospel. It showed in the lack of enthusiasm every time Kate mentioned tracting, and it radiated from the hollow testimony Dori thought others wanted to hear. Dori had lasted one month with her last companion, and there were days when Kate wondered if she could last that long.

"You think because you're the senior companion you can boss me around!" Dori accused Kate.

"That's not true," Kate replied, her temper flaring. She held her breath until she felt she could continue the conversation without exploding.

"You always think I do the wrong thing," Dori whined.

Kate cringed. She could tolerate most things about Dori, but the whining grated on her nerves like fingernails on a chalkboard.

"Sister Nelson," Kate said carefully. "I don't want to fight with you. The only reason I mentioned that you might want to refrain from wearing that short red skirt is that it gives the wrong impression."

"You're so mean," Dori sobbed as she ran into the bedroom and slammed the door.

Kate clenched her teeth. It would be a very long night.

* * *

"So, you think Davie might eventually commit to baptism?" Elder Kris Lattimer asked Kate, trying to be heard above the crowd waiting at the bus stop. Kate shook her head at him, not understanding. He repeated the question.

Kate nodded her head. "Yes, I do," she replied, raising her voice to match Elder Lattimer's.

She felt a sense of relief turning Davie's instruction over to Elders Lattimer and Boyle, two humble young men who radiated the

Spirit of Christ. She knew if the Church was what Davie really wanted, these two young men could help him. The two elders were replacing the sisters in Campbeltown since Kate would be returning to Dumbarton and Dori had been transferred to the Isle of Lewis, located in the Western Isles of Scotland.

After enduring two months of Dori, this transfer had come as a welcome relief. Kate hated to leave Campbeltown before feeling a sense of closure with Jamie and Davie, but she knew in her heart it was time to move on. With Dori as a companion, her efforts as a missionary had been greatly hampered.

Although Kate had tried to help Dori understand that serving a mission was more than just a chance to spend time with the elders, in her opinion, she had failed miserably. Dori had resented every effort Kate had made in her behalf, and her sullen disposition had alienated the few contacts Kate had established with Melissa's help. Even Uncle Jamie had started keeping his distance. Instead of stopping by for a quick visit as he had done in the past, he had frequently given the excuse that he didn't have time. Invitations to the family estate had been limited after Dori had complained about the smell in the stables. This transfer had definitely come as an answer to prayer.

Dori was also excited about the change, although for different reasons. On the Isle of Lewis she would have access to a car instead of relying on buses, trains, or members of the Church for transportation. In her opinion that elevated her standing. Since news of the transfer had come, she had repeatedly mentioned that it was too bad Kate would be forced to rely on *common* transportation. Kate didn't care; she was grateful for anything that would put distance between herself and Dori.

Sighing with sadness and relief, Kate shared a final hug with Jamie and Davie; both promised to look her up before she returned to the states. She then boarded the bus, following the sister member who would serve as chaperon to Kate and Dori until they reached Glasgow.

Kate took a seat by a window, smiling as she recalled Davie's request to pass his hug on to Melissa if the occasion ever presented itself. Kate doubted it would as Melissa would be returning home in a month.

"Glasgow has a mall!" Melissa had excitedly written in one of her first letters. "It's called St. Enoch Center. I went there with my companion last prep day. There's also a McDonald's and a Pizza Hut. It makes me homesick for America."

Melissa had also written of the challenges: the indifferent attitudes of most she came in contact with and the small acts of violence. In one area, particularly, it was not uncommon for the Scottish people to throw bricks and stones at the missionaries. At times, the elders had even been threatened with knives.

When Kate had written a concerned letter suggesting that Melissa keep a low profile, Melissa had sent back a short note assuring her former companion that there was no need to fear; her life was in the Lord's hands. Reflecting on Melissa's reply, Kate knew it was true in her own life. Through numerous trials, Kate had felt a protecting love, a gentle guidance that had eventually led her to becoming a missionary. An emissary of Jesus Christ, she now had the opportunity to serve a people she loved in a land that would always have a hold on her heart. She knew that with the Lord's help, all things were possible, that there was no need to fear, to doubt, or to hesitate. She, like Melissa, would be watched over at all times. That knowledge made all the difference in the world. That promise made days like today bearable.

CHAPTER 28

When her companion had first handed her the letter from Mike, Kate had been thrilled. It had been weeks since she had heard anything from him. Sitting down in a chair to savor his letter, she hurriedly tore open the envelope. "Oh, no!" she cried out a few minutes later, crumpling in the chair.

"What is it?" her new companion asked timidly.

Looking up at her new companion, Kate tried to reply, but found she couldn't. She knew Mindi King wouldn't understand. Red-haired and slightly overweight, Mindi was terrified of men and would never comprehend the devastation Kate now felt. Closing her eyes, Kate willed herself not to cry.

"Bad news from home?"

"No," Kate said, gritting her teeth. "But I need some time alone." As she moved into the bedroom, she added, "It's nothing personal, Sister King. I just need to be by myself for a while."

Mindi stared as Kate quietly closed the door.

* * *

"Kate, whit's wrong? Why are y'sae pale?" Jenny asked, inviting the sister missionaries into her flat.

Kate shook her head. "Nothing, I'm fine," she said.

Jenny's eyes narrowed. She knew Kate well enough to know something wasn't right. "I've told y'sae much aboot m'own troubles, dinna y'think y'c'd tell me y'rs?"

But Kate insisted it was nothing. "I'm probably just getting a cold," she said as she took a seat on the couch.

Jenny watched with amusement as Mindi shyly positioned herself to hide behind Kate. Mindi was the most timid thing Jenny had ever seen. "She'll no' last a week," she had assured her cousin when she had first laid eyes on Kate's new companion.

"She'll learn," Kate had replied. But Jenny had her doubts. As Kate began talking about the priesthood, it was obvious that Mindi was perfectly content to let Kate do all the talking. Glancing at Kate again, Jenny was struck by the feeling that all was not well in Kate's life. Deciding to keep an eye on her American cousin, Jenny willingly agreed to meet frequently with the sister missionaries.

* * *

"Excuse the expression, but y'all look like something the cat dragged in," Melissa exclaimed as she gave Kate an intense hug. "What's wrong with you?"

After keeping everything inside for the last week, Kate wasn't sure how to begin. She had thought she would be able to work through it alone; she hadn't planned on running into Melissa at a special missionary conference.

"I'm fine," Kate mumbled as Melissa squeezed tighter.

"This is me, remember," Melissa reminded her, pulling back to give Kate a no-nonsense look.

"Melissa—I can't. Not here. This is a missionary conference, remember?" Kate replied, glancing around at the beautiful grounds where missionaries from all over Scotland had gathered. Because of the pleasant weather, they were meeting outside near some castle ruins outside of Dumbarton.

"Under normal circumstances, I'd agree with you, but something is very wrong, I can tell. Let's slip away for a bit."

"What about our companions?"

Melissa glanced around. Everyone was crowding together to get a closer look at the guest speaker who was rumored to be from England. "I doubt they'll even miss us. C'mon, we need to talk."

Numbly Kate allowed Melissa to lead her away from the crowd of missionaries gathered on the bright green lawn surrounding what was left of the castle. Finding a low, moss-covered rock wall, Melissa eased herself into a sitting position and motioned for Kate to join her. Kate stared at the wall, then turned her back to Melissa, wrapping her arms around herself.

"Kate, what is it? Did somethin' happen at home?"

Kate slowly nodded.

"Your parents?"

"No," Kate managed to say.

"Not your brother or sister?" Melissa asked, rising.

"No," came the muffled reply.

Melissa reached for Kate and gently turned her around.

Seeing Kate's tears, Melissa shook her head. "That's what I thought." Melissa pulled Kate into another hug. "A few tears never hurt anyone, Kate Erickson," she softly chided. "Now you just cry until you get it out of your system, and then we'll talk."

* * *

Dumbfounded by Kate's news, Melissa stared at her. "I can't believe this has happened to you again!"

"Tell me about it," Kate replied, sniffling. "But this time, at least, there's a difference—there were no promises between us," she said, remembering her last conversation with Mike. He had hinted then that he might not be waiting around after her mission.

"Maybe not, but the way you lit up every time you talked about him, I thought for sure you two would make a go of it."

Kate stared off in the distance for several moments, then closing her eyes, she tried to shut out the pain. Mike had found someone else—just as her mother had warned.

"Now what?"

Her shoulders sagging, Kate glanced at Melissa. "I'm not sure. He's getting married eight months before I head home, and there's not a thing I can do about it."

"Dang men anyway!" Melissa exclaimed, giving Kate an indignant look. "We both have been put through too much because of them! I almost wish our church had a convent we could go to when these things happen. I swear I'd be right there beatin' at the door!"

Full of empathy for what Melissa had been going through, Kate nodded. "That reminds me, you may not want to hear this, but Davie sends his love."

Melissa looked startled for a moment, then shrugged. "Oh, that helps a lot," she said sarcastically. "I go home next week, remember?" Her eyes grew soft at the thought of all she would be leaving behind. "Kate, it won't make you feel better, but I do know exactly how you're feelin'. I'm in love with a man I'll probably never see again. Some days my heart feels like a wringer-washer, the kind my grandmother used to have." Looking down beside her, she ran a hand over one of the large, smooth stones that made up the wall they were sitting on.

Kate sighed. At least Melissa had a slim hope. Davie was determined to go to the states as soon as he could. "Davie is committed to be baptized," she said. "I received a letter from him last week."

"He's gettin' baptized? That's terrific," Melissa exclaimed, cheered by the news. "What does Aunt Francis think of it?"

"She's furious. But Davie's an adult. He made his decision without you or me there to influence him," Kate replied, giving Melissa a meaningful look. "He bore his testimony to me in his letter. I get goose bumps every time I read it."

"Well, I'm glad something good came out of that." Melissa was silent a moment. "How's Jenny doin'?" she said, changing the subject.

Kate shrugged. "We're going through the discussions again, but I don't know if she's ready to commit. She didn't care for the elders at all and finally asked them to quit coming around. That's why I didn't hear from her when I was in Campbeltown. She thought I would be disappointed. It took some doing to convince her that no matter what, we're family." Smoothing her dress down, she finally took a seat beside Melissa.

The two young women sat in silence for several minutes, thinking of the young men who were responsible for their current state of depression. "Kate, tell me something," Melissa mused, "are you sorry you decided to serve a mission?"

Kate bit her bottom lip, imagining Mike married to the cute freshman girl he had met at Ricks. Ivy Todd from California. Pushing that unwelcome image from her mind, Kate saw instead the people she had met while serving in Scotland. People like Emily Stewart, her first baptism. She pictured Jenny, Uncle Jamie, Davie, and the people from the wards and branches whom she had met. The small children who had loved her, the lonely widows who had appreciated her thoughtfulness. The men who had given her such a bad time. Some, good-naturedly, others with ill intent. As she reflected on her different companions, she turned to look at Melissa. Here was an eternal friend—someone she would've never met at home.

"So, what do you think?" Melissa pressed. "Was the cost too high?"

Kate shook her head. "I know this is where I'm supposed to be right now. If that means losing Mike . . ." She couldn't finish the sentence. Melissa put an arm around her shoulders.

"They never warn you about the Dear Jane letters in the MTC," she quipped. "All you ever hear about are the Dear Johns. Kind of a double standard if you ask me," Melissa sighed. "Sometimes mission life requires sacrifice," she added, thinking of Davie. There were no guarantees that things would work out between them. It didn't keep her from gazing each night at the dried purple flowers she kept in a journal. "I tend to think we're blessed because of it. Like with my grandpa. After his stroke, they didn't think he'd live to see me serve a mission." She grinned. "Guess who'll be there to greet me when I come home."

"Your grandpa?"

Melissa nodded.

"That's great."

"It is," Melissa agreed. "Let's make a deal—no matter what happens, we'll concentrate on the positive things in our lives, okay?"

"I'll try," Kate responded.

"And, I hate to say it, but before our companions have the fantods, we'd better return to the conference. It looks like the speaker has finished."

Kate glanced up toward the castle ruins. She imagined the panicked look on Mindi's face and knew Melissa was right. Mindi would be lost without her, just as she would have been lost without Melissa. Grateful for Melissa's friendship, Kate realized that it had happened again. Every time things started going wrong, someone was always there to help her, giving her the encouragement she needed for the next round with life.

"I probably won't get a chance to see you again before I leave," Melissa said as they wandered back toward the group of missionaries. "I'm glad we were able to work in another chat."

"Me, too," Kate agreed. Purposely keeping things light, the two young women teased each other until they reached the outskirts of the group that had gathered. Parting with a final hug, they walked in opposite directions, never looking back.

CHAPTER 29

With Kate's encouragement, Mindi began leading some of the discussions. Tracting with the self-conscious young woman had proved to be a challenge, but one that Kate threw herself into with renewed effort after the missionary conference. As Kate focused on the gospel and her purpose for being in Scotland, the inner pain softened, becoming a bearable twinge.

By the time another transfer came along, Mindi had transformed into a confident missionary, eager to teach anyone who would listen. President Everson praised Kate for her part in Mindi's growth. Embarrassed, Kate insisted that she had done little to help her companion.

"I know differently," President Everson assured Kate. He gazed at the smiling, beautiful young woman. The pain that had been so evident weeks before had faded. The weight loss Kate had experienced had concerned him, but he attributed it to the heartache she had suffered. The Kate he was looking at now was stronger, less vulnerable.

The mission president returned Kate's smile. He and his wife were escorting Kate to Edinburgh to meet her new companion. Fresh out of the MTC, Savanna Glenn needed someone like Kate to lovingly guide her through those first harrowing weeks that often went with mission life. Ready for the challenge, Kate determined to make the best of this new companionship. She had learned that when the Spirit was invited into any partnership, wonderful things could happen.

* * *

October 25

Dear Mom, Dad, and sibs,

    As you can see, I've been transferred again. This time, I'm in Edinburgh. There's so much to see, so little time. I'm planning on checking out a few things though, like Edinburgh Castle as soon as I'm able.

    My new companion is from Utah. Cedar City, to be exact. Her name is Savanna Glenn. She's about my height and has long, brown hair. Her twin brother came home from his mission in time for her to leave. She's the oldest in her family (her brother, Larry, was born immediately after she arrived so she considers herself to be the oldest) so we have a lot in common. She's a little scared, but I think we all are at first. Don't worry, I'll break her in right.

    I received a letter from Jenny yesterday. She's still dragging her feet about the Church. She doesn't want to do anything to upset her father. But, she had a dream about her mother a few nights ago that might change things. In this dream, Aunt Janet told her that I held the special key that would unlock the door that separated them. Jenny wants to know if her dream means anything. She's coming to see me on my next prep day. Prayers on our behalf would be appreciated. I'll need all the help I can get, and so will Jenny.

    Speaking of prayer, you can quit worrying over me when it comes to Mike. I won't say that it doesn't hurt anymore, but I can live with his decision.

Sue looked up from the letter in her hands.

Greg smiled encouragingly. "See, honey, she'll be fine."

"I don't know, Greg. I'm still worried," Sue replied, looking down at the paragraph she had just read.

"I think you always will be," Greg teased.

Setting the letter on the counter, Sue motioned to the fridge. Puzzled, Greg glanced at Sue, then at the fridge. "We didn't even get an invitation to Mike's reception. Neither did Kate."

Greg glanced at the wedding invitation that was hanging on the fridge. His niece had found herself a young man at Boise State University and despite her parents' protests, now planned to marry the nonmember boy she had fallen in love with. "Sue, we've been over this before. Kate knew she was taking a chance when she left on her mission. Am I surprised Mike found someone else? No, and you shouldn't be either."

"But we weren't even invited—"

"To Mike's reception?" Greg said, cutting her off. "I heard it was going to be in California. Would you really want to go to that?"

Sue shook her head. Moving to the sink, she poured herself a glass of water. "Don't they usually have an open house for the groom? That would be here in Bozeman."

Greg sighed. This had been an uphill battle. Sue had been so certain that Mike and Kate would end up together. He wondered if he should remind his wife of the plans Jan Miles had had for Kate and Randy. Deciding it wasn't in his best interest, he refrained. "Not always. If you have any questions, call and talk to Mike's mother."

"I can't do that!" Sue exclaimed. "It'd be too humiliating!"

"Then quit worrying about it. If Kate can handle it, we can."

Sue frowned at her husband. "That's what has me worried. Is Kate handling it?"

"As well as can be expected." He picked up Kate's letter and handed it to his wife. "Now, here, read the rest of the letter. What else does she have to say?" he said, hoping to get her mind on other things.

* * *

December 12

Merry Christmas Mahoney Clan,

Hope all is going well for everyone in your family. Aunt Paige, congrats (or sympathy if you prefer) on your new calling. Out of the frying pan, into the fire. From Relief Society president to nursery leader. I'm sure you'll love it. As for you, Uncle Stan, continued success with your calling as a counselor in the bishopric. (By the way, is it your fault Aunt Paige pulled nursery duty?)

Myself, I'm still in senior comp mode. Savanna, my new companion, is shaping up nicely. I've only had to come down on her twice—she seems to think that we should spend most of our time sightseeing. I'll admit, there's a lot to see here in Edinburgh, but there's also a lot of people who need our message.

I guess you've heard by now that Mike Jeffries is an old married man. I'd appreciate it if you guys could convince my mother that my life isn't over. It felt like it at first, but I'm moving on and I wish Mom would, too. I think she's taking Mike's marriage harder than I am.

I can't believe I'll be coming home in June. Six months! A lot can happen in that time. Did I mention that Jenny finally joined the Church? I couldn't remember if I sent you guys a note in November. That dream she had about her mother was the clincher. After we talked about it, she felt certain that Aunt Janet was trying to tell her something. When I mentioned to Jenny that her mother's temple work could be done, that our church believes in vicarious work for the dead, she was ecstatic. I know I've mentioned that to her before, but I guess she wasn't ready to accept what it meant. Knowing she can be eternally linked to her mother and to other family members has made all the difference in the world. I received special permission from President Everson to attend Jenny's baptism. Davie and Uncle Jamie were there, too. I might have been imagining things, but I could've sworn Uncle Jamie shed a few tears that day.

Well, take care. Tell everyone hello and feel free to send a poor starving missionary anything that's edible. (That was a subtle hint, in case you missed it.)

Love ya,
Kate

March 16

Dear Melissa,

I was sorry to hear of your grandfather's death. I know how close you two were. How fortunate we are to know what this life is all about, to know that we can all be together again someday. It's still difficult to lose loved ones, but the gospel makes it bearable. It's my prayer that the Comforter will stay with you and your family until the pain of your loss softens.

I thought you might like to know that Davie MacOwen is still planning on coming to America. He wants to leave Scotland the same time I do, in June. If you're interested, I'll let you know which flight and where we'll be landing.

Things are moving slowly. The last baptism I attended was Jenny's. People aren't very receptive at the moment, but we're not giving up. Aside from that, things are going smoothly.
Take care of yourself and know my thoughts are with you.

Love always,
Kate

* * *

President Everson smiled at the young woman sitting in front of his desk. "So, Sister Erickson, what are your thoughts on your final day in Scotland?"

Fighting tears, Kate gripped her scripture bag. The mission president had asked her to bring it for this last interview. "I'm excited to go home . . . to see everyone again . . . but it's tough saying goodbye to everyone here."

Nodding sympathetically, President Everson pulled out a box of tissue and set it close to Kate. "That's why I always see to it I have a box of this around," he said brightly. "I'll let you in on a secret— sometimes the elders need it more than the sister missionaries."

Kate laughed. She loved his sense of humor. It was another thing she would miss.

"What are your plans?"

"I guess you know that my cousin, Davie MacOwen, will be flying out with me?" Kate asked, sitting back in the padded chair.

"I had heard that. I think it's wonderful." He gazed thoughtfully at Kate. "You realize you were instrumental in bringing this side of your family into the Church?"

Nodding, Kate reached for a handful of tissue. "I wish Jenny was coming with Davie and me," she said, wiping at her eyes. "We'd have a blast together at BYU."

"You and Jenny are very close," President Everson observed. "It'll be difficult for her, being the only member in her immediate family. I hope you'll keep in touch with her—letters, phone calls, anything to let her know how much you care. If she's anything like you, she'll soon convert the rest of the family. You certainly are an inspiring young lady, Sister Erickson."

Kate blushed, embarrassed by his praise.

"It's true—you've been a wonderful missionary. You've never given me cause for concern . . ." he paused. "Except for a few weeks when you went on a starvation diet," he said, alluding to her heartache over Mike's engagement.

Kate blushed again. "I didn't have much of an appetite then," she admitted.

President Everson nodded, remembering her distress. He had been relieved to hear Melissa Larsen's report that Kate would be all right. Before going home, Melissa had confessed to him about sneaking off for an emotional visit with her former companion. "I'm glad you and Sister Larsen became such close friends. You were good for each other," he commented now, glancing at Kate. "And I'm pleased this relationship will continue," he said, referring to their plans to room together at BYU, "and maybe even blossom into another family tie," he added, a twinkle in his eye. He had been well aware of the feelings Melissa and Davie had developed for each other. "Does your cousin realize what a fine young woman Sister Larsen is?"

Kate nodded.

"As for you, know that you will be blessed for serving the Lord, for spending eighteen months of your life in the mission field." He gazed steadily at Kate. She looked very becoming in the dark grey suit she had selected to wear. She had always taken great pains with her appearance, and today was no exception. Adding to the attraction was her glowing countenance.

"Your Father in Heaven has something or someone very special in mind for you," her mission president continued. "I sense that quite strongly," he stressed, his words sending a shiver down Kate's spine. "Stay in tune so you'll be receptive to the Spirit when it prompts you, and you will accomplish a lot of great things in your life." Reaching for his quad, he opened it up to the Book of Mormon. After putting on his reading glasses, he thumbed through several pages, pausing in the book of Alma.

"I came across this earlier this morning and thought of you. If you'd like to follow along, I'm in chapter forty-nine." He patiently waited for Kate to find the right chapter. "Take a look at verse 8. I'll skip around a bit—don't let me lose you." Clearing his throat, he began to read: "'But behold, to their uttermost astonishment, they were prepared . . .'" he glanced up at Kate. "This is talking about you, young lady. You are prepared. It may come as a surprise, but you are now prepared to handle whatever life has in store for you." He smiled, then returned his gaze to the scriptures in front of him. "Jump to verse 13. 'For they knew not that Moroni had fortified, or had built forts of security . . . with a firm determination.'" He looked again at Kate. "Whether you realize it or not, this entire mission has been preparing you for the life that is ahead of you. You have been fortified by the Lord, and now you have a new, firmer determination to continue serving him any way that you can. Am I right?"

Kate slowly nodded, underlining the words that had been read to her.

"Now, skip to verse fourteen. 'But behold, to their astonishment, the city of Noah, which had hitherto been a weak place, had now . . . become strong . . .'" Removing his reading glasses, President Everson gazed intently at Kate. "How could we apply that scripture to you?"

Rereading what she had highlighted, Kate gave it serious thought. "Do you mean that where I was weak, I've been made strong?" she finally asked.

President Everson nodded. "Yes, exactly. You've changed, Kate. Don't get me wrong. You were a strong young woman to begin with, but I see a new growth in you that wasn't there before. You are a leader. You have learned to listen, to labor, and to love—the three L's that I talk about from time to time. You have learned patience, understanding, and empathy for those around you. In essence, you are becoming a true disciple of Christ." Rising, he reached to shake her hand. "I commend you, Sister Erickson, for a job well done. You have truly been an instrument in the Lord's hands."

Her eyes glistening, Kate shook his hand. Her heart was filled with gratitude for the past eighteen months of her life.

* * *

Settling back in his cushioned seat, Davie glanced out the small round window. Seeing nothing but clouds, he turned to look at Kate. "Are y' nervous?"

Kate glanced at her cousin. "Are you?" she asked. He had been fidgety for the past hour, and she was glad their flight was nearly over.

Davie shook his head.

"Yeah, right," Kate teased.

"A'right, y'win. I'm a wreck here. How soon dae we land?"

Kate glanced at her watch. "In about thirty minutes. Prepare for a series of intense hugs."

"Thanks f'r the warnin'—it's ane hug in particular that I'm leery of."

"Melissa's?"

Davie blushed.

"C'mon. You two have waited for this for a long time. Relax—enjoy it," she said, grinning.

"Relax? I'm fair tremblin'. Look at m'hand shake."

Kate laughed, knowing Davie was intentionally causing his hand to shake. "Look, I've been through this kind of thing before. Don't rush it. Be yourself. Let nature take its course. You two will be going to school together this fall. See where it takes you."

"And you?"

"I'll be in Provo, too. Melissa and I are planning on being roommates, remember? That's part of the reason she's meeting us in Salt Lake today. She flew in to check out Brigham Young University and to find us an apartment to share."

"That arrangement won't last long if I have anythin' tae say aboot it!" Davie threatened, his green eyes shining with excitement.

"You shy thing, you," Kate teased. "You're already staking your claim?" She grinned when he blushed again. "Now, sit back and behave. Watch the movie if you want," she suggested, knowing he'd never be able to concentrate.

Nearly forty minutes later, the two cousins entered a reception area of the Salt Lake airport. As expected, squeals, hugs and tears flourished.

"Oh, Kate," Sue exclaimed, clinging to her daughter. "I can't believe you're finally here."

"I can, now," Kate teased as her mother's grip tightened. Sue finally pulled back to let Greg take over. Then Kate found herself being mauled by her eighteen-year-old brother, Tyler, who had grown at least a foot in her absence. "Ty, I can't breathe," she wheezed. "Ty!"

"Let 'er go, Tyler," eleven-year-old Sabrina demanded.

Kate stared at her younger sister who had also grown a foot taller. She noted the nylons and light makeup. Had she really been gone that long? "Breeny?" she asked, reaching for a hug.

"I haven't been Breeny for a very long time," Sabrina informed her sister. Kate believed her.

While Kate was occupied with greeting family members, a petite young woman held back. Melissa watched with amusement as Kate introduced Davie to the family. Sue was the first to embrace the young Scotsman.

"Welcome to America." Paige stepped forward next, at the same time nudging Stan forward. "Davie, this is your cousin, Stan."

Melissa smiled as the two cousins struggled through an awkward handshake. "Those two need to go fishin' together," she quietly murmured to herself. "That would cut through the ice." Then, it was her turn. Kate spotted her first.

"Melissa?!"

The two former companions shared a lengthy, emotional hug. Then, with a mischievous gleam in her eye, Kate led Melissa to Davie. "See, I delivered him just like I promised."

It was difficult to tell who blushed more, Melissa or Davie.

"Thanks, Kate," Melissa said drolly.

"And that goes double f'r me," Davie added, indignantly.

Kate grinned and urged everyone to give the young couple some space. Glancing over her shoulder, she was tickled to see them embrace. In her opinion, this was a moment long overdue.

CHAPTER 30

Kate's first days at home seemed strange to her. It was great to be back in Bozeman, but she felt a little lost. Driving around the town, she remembered Mike's reaction the afternoon he had shown her what had changed in his absence.

Thoughts of Mike were still troubling. Doing her best to block him out, she focused on making the most out of this limited time with her family. Uncle Stan had offered her a job for the summer in Salt Lake, and she decided to take it, knowing the money would come in handy when she returned to BYU in the fall.

On her final Sunday in Bozeman, as Kate sat next to her mother during sacrament meeting, she was pleasantly surprised to see Keith Taylor walk in. She hadn't heard from him in ages, losing track of him after he had left to serve a mission. Their eyes linked briefly and Keith grinned, happily pointing to the tall, short-haired young woman who had come in behind him. Immediately figuring out the connection between the two, Kate nodded, eager to talk to him after church.

After the closing prayer, Kate made her way back to where Keith was waiting. Without hesitation, Keith reached for a hug.

"Man, is it good to see you!" he said, pulling back to grin at her. "How was the mission?"

"Great," Kate replied, glancing at the young woman who had moved to Keith's side.

"I'm glad. We'll have to swap stories sometime." He paused, slipping his arm around the shoulders of the woman beside him. "Kate Erickson, I'd like you to meet my wife of six months, Amanda Haws Taylor."

Kate smiled warmly at Amanda, thrilled that Keith had finally found someone. They exchanged pleasantries for a while, then as Kate prepared to leave, Keith hit her with a question she wasn't prepared for.

"So, have you seen Mike yet?"

Trying to mask the pain that question triggered, Kate shook her head.

"What's wrong with that guy? I figured he'd—"

"Keith, Mike got married last October. Didn't he let you know?"

Keith shook his head. "Mike's not married. He was my best man six months ago and he was still single then."

Kate gaped at him. She felt a crushing pressure in her chest. Mike wasn't married?

"You'd better sit down," Keith said, alarmed by the look on her face.

A few minutes later, after Amanda had brought her a glass of water, Kate felt like she could breathe again. "So Mike isn't married?" she asked.

"No, he isn't," Keith replied. "He was engaged to a girl from California, but things didn't work out between them." He frowned. "I can't believe he didn't tell you."

Neither could Kate. Assuring Keith and Amanda that she was fine, she quickly left. She needed some time to absorb what she had just learned.

* * *

Later that afternoon, Kate called to see if Jennifer Jeffries was home. When Jennifer came to the phone, Kate invited her to go for a ride, certain Mike's younger sister could shed some light on this situation.

Several minutes later Kate pulled up into the Jeffries' driveway in the small red Neon she had recently purchased from her aunt Paige. When Jennifer bounced out of the house, Kate was startled to see how much the younger girl had changed. The eighteen-year-old had cut her hair quite short, which made her seem older and more sophisticated.

Curious about Kate's request, Jennifer climbed into the car. She hadn't talked to her brother's former girlfriend since she had left on her mission eighteen months before. The two girls exchanged a simple greeting, then listened to the car radio as Kate drove away from the house.

"Jennifer, I know this must seem strange," Kate finally said. "I was talking to Keith Taylor earlier today—he told me Mike didn't get married." She glanced at Mike's sister for confirmation.

"Mike didn't let you know?" Jennifer asked, startled. "That jerk! No wonder you seem so upset."

Upset was a mild description of how Kate felt. Taking a deep breath, she pumped Jennifer for details.

". . . Ivy was a snob. Their relationship boiled down to two things: she liked Mike because he's good-looking and because she thought he was going to be a doctor."

Kate stared at Jennifer. "How did she get that impression?"

"Mike told her he was studying biology. As air-headed as she is, Ivy assumed that meant he was going into medicine." Jennifer grinned. "You should've seen the look on her face when Mike finally told her he wanted to work for the Forest Service."

Jennifer told Kate how relieved they had all been when the couple had gone their separate ways. "When Ivy gave Mike back his ring, he was devastated," Jennifer said. "I think it was a pride thing. He'd never been rejected before."

Kate gripped the steering wheel, her mind still whirling with everything Jennifer had described.

"I know he's never stopped loving you, Kate."

Hitting the brakes, Kate stared at Jennifer. An annoyed driver behind them hit his horn in protest. Easing her car forward, Kate pulled into a nearby parking lot to finish this conversation.

* * *

Two days later, Kate and Jennifer made a trip to Afton, Wyoming, the small town where Mike was working for the summer. According to Jennifer, her aunt had arranged for him to work with the Forest Service in that area.

Leaving at five a.m. to begin the lengthy journey, they had both been filled with the spirit of adventure. Now that they were well on their way, Kate wondered if this was a good thing. It had been

Jennifer's idea to come. When she found out that Kate would be heading to Salt Lake this week, she had insisted on this detour, inviting herself along.

"I have a personal stake in this," Jennifer had added. "I know Mike won't be happy until he sees you." Kate had gazed warmly at the younger girl. Whether or not they were destined to become sisters, it was nice to know that Jennifer would always be a friend.

Their plan was relatively simple. They would tell Mike that Kate had brought Jennifer down to visit him as she passed through on her way to Salt Lake City. That way, Mike wouldn't feel any pressure. Kate had stressed that point to Jennifer. She didn't want to back Mike into a corner—not that he didn't deserve it. Still hurt that he had neglected her feelings in this matter, she had several pointed questions she wanted to ask. But, she had to admit, the knowledge that he was single had given her an inner lift. Even her mother had started humming around the house after Kate had shared everything she had learned from Jennifer and Keith. Kate had insisted that nothing was certain as far as she and Mike were concerned, but Sue had just smiled, giving her daughter a knowing look.

Driving toward the park entrance in West Yellowstone, Kate remembered her last trip through the park. It had been the summer after her junior year in high school. Her parents had forced her to accompany them on a family vacation, and it had changed her life forever. It was in Jackson that Kate had first met Randy. Kate remembered only too well the argument with her mother that had later led to the accident in Salt Lake City, the coma, and the dream she had had while in the coma. Some time later she had found Aunt Molly's journal, which had confirmed the experiences she had witnessed in her dream.

As she related all this to Jennifer, Kate realized again how that series of events had changed her life. The pain and soul-searching had led her to where she was now. As her mission president had pointed out, she had been fortified and prepared. And now, facing an unknown phase of her life, she felt a certain amount of excitement. What was it her Father in Heaven had in store for her? Would Mike be part of it? Shaking her head, she decided to take her own advice and let nature take its course.

Making good time, they stopped for lunch in Jackson. Kate suggested pizza and they slipped into an establishment called Mountain High Pizza Pie. The pizza was as good as Kate had remembered. Then, after they had a chance to stretch their legs, it was back on the road. As Kate maneuvered the Neon around several hairpin curves in Snake River Canyon, she was grateful the car still handled as well as it had before her mission. Occasionally they caught a glimpse of the Snake River as it wound around below them in a startling shade of green.

As they drove through Alpine, Wyoming, Kate was astonished at the growth the area had seen in her absence. New businesses were everywhere. "It's becoming another Jackson," she murmured to Jennifer, noticing that most of the new businesses catered to tourists.

At last they reached their destination, Afton, Wyoming. Slowing down to the city speed limit, she spotted the new Forest Service Building off to her right, and a thrill of excitement shot through her. She pulled in next to the log building and shut off the engine, but continued to grip the steering wheel.

"Scared?" Jennifer asked.

Kate nodded. What if this didn't turn out like everyone was hoping? What then? What if this wasn't what she really wanted?

"C'mon. Like my dad always says, 'Nothin' ventured, nothin' gained,'" Jennifer encouraged, jumping out of the car.

Slowly, Kate followed her example. As they walked toward the building, Kate paused to offer a silent prayer for guidance. Impatiently Jennifer walked back and dragged her forward. As they entered the log building, the only person in sight was a woman busily typing away at a computer.

"Be with you in a minute," the woman said as she continued to bang away at the keyboard, her hair bouncing as she typed. The name plaque on her desk read, "Bessie Sanders."

Kate glanced around, pretending to admire a couple of photographs of the area.

"Real good work," Bessie finally commented, standing up at last. Leaning over the counter, she nodded appreciatively. "Best I've seen in a long time."

"They're nice," Kate agreed, stepping to the side for Jennifer who was now craning her neck, trying to see.

"New guy took 'em," Bessie explained, grinning. "He's got a real talent there."

"New guy?" Kate asked, instantly thinking of Mike. Mike had always been good with a camera. Were these his pictures?

"Yeah. A greenhorn from Montana. His aunt works here. That's how he got a job for the summer. He claims he wants to do this sort of thing full-time when he's through with school."

"Mike?" Kate asked before she could stop herself.

"Matter of fact, that's his name." Bessie's hazel eyes narrowed as she glanced from Jennifer to Kate. They wouldn't be the first to come around here hoping for a glimpse of the handsome young man. She'd about had her fill of that. "You two friends of his?"

Not knowing how to reply, Kate slowly nodded.

"Actually, I'm his kid sister," Jennifer said brightly.

Bessie smiled, revealing a large gap between her front two teeth. Running a self-conscious hand through her wild hair, she introduced herself. "Name's Bessie Sanders," she said waiting for Kate and Jennifer to respond.

"I'm Jennifer . . . Jennifer Jeffries."

"And you are?" Bessie prompted, looking at Kate.

"Uh . . . Katherine," Kate answered, giving her full name, ignoring the disgusted look on Jennifer's face.

"Katherine," the woman repeated, turning it over in her mind. "I don't believe he's ever mentioned you before, but I'm sure there's a lot we don't know about Mike—yet."

Kate sensed Bessie was sizing her up. "Mike and I went to high school together in Bozeman. I was coming through on my way to Salt Lake—Jennifer needed a ride down—I thought I'd stop in to say hello."

"I'm sure Mike will be pleased," Bessie replied, wondering at the way Katherine was flushing. "He ain't here right now, he's out workin' on a new bridge. Spring runoff took out the old one."

"Oh. I see. Well, I'll catch him another time then," Kate replied, moving toward the door.

"Now, hold on, I'll see if I can reach him on the radio," Bessie insisted, moving back to her crowded desk.

"No, it's okay, he's probably busy . . ." Kate stammered, anxious to leave.

"You're not leaving until you talk to Mike!" Jennifer insisted, grabbing Kate's arm. Just then a tan-colored truck pulled in next to the office window. Staring out the window, the two girls saw that the uniformed driver was Mike. Seated next to him was a slender, honey-blonde girl wearing a similar uniform. They watched in horror as Mike stepped down out of the truck and reached to help the young woman out on his side. When the young woman in question drew Mike close for a kiss, Jennifer released Kate's arm and sank into a plastic chair. "You idiot," Jennifer muttered under her breath, mentally cursing her brother.

Bessie had missed the romantic moment in the parking lot. Glancing up from her radio, she grinned as she spotted Mike through the window. "Well, there he is now, Mr. Wonderful himself!"

Feeling claustrophobic, Kate reached for the door. Before she could touch the handle, it swung open and she stumbled into Mike's arms.

"Nice catch," Bessie announced, winking at Mike.

Shaking his head at Bessie, Mike helped the young woman regain her balance. When she turned to face him, he stared in stunned surprise. "Kate?"

"Hi . . . Mike," Kate stuttered. She tried not to stare at Mike's attractive companion, focusing instead on Mike. Mike, whose shoulders and arms bulged with new muscles. Whose face was so tan. Her eyes strayed to the deep brown eyes that were staring at her intently.

"Kate?" Bessie asked, staring at Kate. "This is the Kate we've all heard about for weeks?" She lifted an eyebrow. "I thought you said your name was Katherine?"

"It's her full name, Katherine Colleen Erickson," Mike explained, escorting Kate back to the wooden counter. "I can't believe you're here!" he exclaimed. Then, seeing Jennifer, he grinned. Stepping around Kate, he grabbed his sister, whirling her around the room.

"Put me down, you big jerk," Jennifer exclaimed, smacking him on the shoulder.

Startled by her anger, Mike obediently set her down. Neither of them had noticed that Kate had quietly slipped out of the building.

"And who is this?" another angry female demanded.

Mike turned to glance at his co-worker, Kerrie Toland. He was still upset over the kiss she had forced on him a few minutes ago. It was bad enough she had elected to nearly sit on his lap on the way back from Cottonwood Lake, but that kiss had been out of line, catching him by surprise. He glanced around, suddenly realizing that Kate was missing. "Where did Kate go?" he asked.

"She's probably on her way to Salt Lake!" Jennifer exclaimed.

"What?"

"Who is Kate?" Kerrie asked, glaring at Jennifer.

"None of your business," Jennifer assured her. "This is my fault," she muttered, moving to the window to watch as Kate pulled out of the parking lot. "I talked Kate into coming. She didn't want to. But, silly me, I figured you had a brain in your head." She whirled around to glare at her brother. "I thought I was doing you both a favor. Instead, I dragged Kate down here to see you smoochin' it up with this blonde fluff!"

Bessie's eyes widened as she grasped the situation. Secretly tickled over Jennifer's spunk, she enjoyed the outraged look on Kerrie's face. As the daughter of the boss, Kerrie always got away with too much. This time it looked like Kerrie had met her match.

"I am not a blonde fluff!" Kerrie insisted, grabbing Mike's arm. "Tell this annoying little twit to get on her broom and fly out of here," she said, pointing to Jennifer.

"This annoying little twit is my sister," Mike said, the shock of what had just happened wearing off. Kate had come to see him. That could only mean one thing. He grinned at the thought. The grin changed to a frown when Jennifer hit him again.

"'Annoying little twit'?" she demanded.

"Oh, yeah," he said, pulling away from Kerrie. "Kerrie, I'm the only one in this office who can call my sister by that name."

"Your . . . sister?" Kerrie stammered, glancing at Jennifer who, childlike, stuck out her tongue. Kerrie turned away, stomping back to her father's office.

"Where was Kate heading?" Mike asked.

"Hello, are you listening this time?" Jennifer snapped. "She's on her way to Salt Lake City."

"Not for long she isn't," Mike countered. "Let's go," he said, dragging her out of the building. "I'm taking this truck for the rest of the day," he called over his shoulder.

"Yes, sir," Bessie said, grinning. She watched as Mike helped his sister into the truck, then climbed into the driver's side and fired up the engine. As he roared out of the parking lot, Kerrie made an appearance.

"Where's my dad?" she demanded, her lower lip sticking out defiantly.

"Honey, I have no idea," Bessie informed her.

Kerrie glanced around. "Where's Mike?"

"He had an important matter to take care of."

"He was supposed to take me out for a sandwich," she said, stamping her foot.

Bessie loved bursting that particular bubble.

* * *

Still crying, Kate angrily climbed out of the car. Moving to the left front tire, she gave it a kick. This was par for the day. A flat tire. Wilting beside the car, she cried hard for several minutes. Then, deciding her tears weren't getting her anywhere, she gave herself a stern lecture. Mike wasn't worth crying over and neither was this. Her father had shown her how to fix a flat, and she felt confident she could handle the situation. Drying her eyes, she moved to the small trunk and unlocked it, groaning when she saw Jennifer's suitcase. She lifted it out and the two she had brought, then pulled up the carpeting from the floor of the trunk. As she gazed at the compact spare tire, it was tempting to cry again. She had never done this kind of thing before. Gritting her teeth, she rolled up the sleeves of the fancy new blouse she had worn and began loosening the center retainer bolt.

* * *

After Mike explained the truth about Kerrie, Jennifer quit fuming and urged him to hurry. "Maybe we can catch her," she said, encouraged by what she now knew. Mike still had strong feelings for Kate. Thrilled that she had been right all along, she was anxious to intercept Kate. Neither of them expected to find her as easily as they did. Spotting the red Neon first, Jennifer squealed at Mike, pointing to where Kate had pulled off the road. As Mike eased the truck behind the Neon, he was struck by the same sense of apprehension that had possessed Kate earlier. Rolling her eyes, Jennifer practically pushed him out of the truck. "What is with you two?" she muttered under her breath. Determined to give them a few minutes alone, she picked up a map off the seat and pretended to study it.

Sizing up the situation, Mike walked toward the front of the car where Kate was trying to adjust a small, portable jack. Unaware that she had smeared black grease across her nose, she glared defiantly at Mike. "What are you doing here?"

"Looking for you," he replied. "Need some help?" he asked, struck by how cute she looked right now. Guilt plagued him when he noticed her reddened eyes.

"No, I'm managing," she snapped. Just then, the car slipped off the jack. Fortunately, Kate and Mike were back far enough to avoid injury.

"I can see how you're managing," Mike said angrily. If Kate had climbed under the car, she would've been killed, he realized. "Let me finish this so you don't finish yourself off." He tried to move her out of the way, but she stubbornly held her ground.

"I can do this. Besides, don't you have a friend to keep happy?"

"Yes, I do," he replied, holding onto her arms. Again he tried to move her and again she wouldn't budge. "Look, you stubborn thing, let me help you!"

"Why?" she challenged, her eyes flashing.

Seeing the anger in her face, Mike suddenly remembered the last time he had seen Kate this upset. It had happened in high school their senior year. Rumors that had originated with Jennifer had spread throughout the school. Kate had reacted then as she was now, and Mike realized that her anger was a cover for the pain she didn't want to reveal. Relaxing his hold on her, he smiled. "Before we fix the tire, I think we'd better fix something else first."

Kate tried to avoid his steady gaze and found that she couldn't. Drawn to his pleading look, she finally nodded.

"According to my kid sister here, I have two things to apologize for. The first is my . . . how did she put it . . . lack of social grace? I'm sorry I didn't tell you about the breakup," he said, releasing her.

Kate gazed at him, trying to steady herself. Her heart had been pounding since his arrival. When he sat down near the car, she carefully sat across from him, waiting for him to continue.

Slowly, Mike revealed everything that Jennifer had already explained about his relationship with Ivy. "I really thought I was in love with that girl," he sighed. "I know now it was just a physical thing—for both of us. When I came to my senses and realized we had nothing in common, we were already engaged. Our breakup wasn't traumatic, but I was so humiliated—I'd already told everyone I was getting married."

"I think I know how that feels," Kate quietly reminded him.

"True—that's why I didn't contact you."

Kate gave him a puzzled look.

"I figured after what Randy had put you through, you'd never want to hear from me again." He gazed at his hands. "I've dated a few girls since then, but I'm not in a relationship right now." Seeing the inquisitive look on her face, he continued. "Kerrie Toland, the girl you saw back there at the office—"

Kate nodded. How could she forget?

"There's nothing between us. That's the second thing Jennifer said I should apologize for. The kiss you saw between Kerrie and me." He quickly explained what had happened, then smiled shyly at Kate. "There's only one girl in this world who has ever turned my heart to putty during a kiss and I'm looking at her now," he said hopefully. Leaning forward, his eyes invited her to respond.

Not quite ready for this, Kate hesitated. The angry pain that had consumed her was gone, but fears from the past still haunted her. Before she gave in to what she discerned could be between them, she would have to permanently lay those fears to rest.

Sensing her discomfort, Mike controlled himself and slowly stood up. "Now, would you be willing to let an old pro handle this tire for you?"

Nodding, Kate stepped to the side and watched Mike as he skillfully took care of one of her problems.

* * *

Jennifer and Mike teamed up and were eventually able to talk Kate into staying the night. Mike offered his apartment to the two girls while he gallantly made arrangements to spend the night at a friend's house. After he left, Kate made two phone calls, one to her aunt Paige who was half-expecting her to arrive later that night, and one to her mother to explain the situation.

"Sweetheart, that's fine," Sue assured her daughter. "I trust you. Spend some time with Mike. It's the only way you'll be able to decide if this is what you want."

Silently agreeing with her mother, Kate shared the plans Mike had already made for tomorrow.

CHAPTER 31

The next day was gorgeous. When Mike came by to pick up Kate for the picnic, he was quick to take credit for the perfect weather, claiming he had ordered it just for her. Jennifer had already made it clear that she had things to do that day. Mike and Kate both knew it was her way of giving them a chance to be alone. Mike had gratefully promised to make it up to Jennifer later.

Of the many beautiful places Mike had worked, he was convinced Cottonwood Lake was the most appealing—the perfect setting for this first date with Kate. Driving his truck through Afton, he turned off on a dirt road just outside of a tiny town called Smoot. The dirt road that led up the canyon was full of ruts and holes, so Mike drove slowly to avoid jostling Kate around in the truck. On the way up, he paused to point out the bridge he had finished yesterday. Later he stopped to show her a deer hiding in the bushes along the side of the road.

Finally they arrived at Cottonwood Lake. As Mike watched the delighted expression on Kate's face at the sight of the clear beauty of the crystal water, he realized that Kate had a lot in common with the lake. Like the lake, she was pure, fresh. A person could see into the beautiful depths of her heart, especially if he knew how to look.

When they had chosen a table near the lake, Mike hauled out the cooler he had stocked in town. Not much of a cook, he had packed sandwiches from the local Maverik, pop, and some chips. A box of doughnuts would serve as dessert. Kate had been too nervous to eat breakfast and Mike hadn't had time, so it didn't take them long to devour lunch. Then, after cleaning up the leftover garbage, they went for a walk around the small lake. As they walked, they spoke of future plans and learned that they were both heading to BYU in the fall to finish their degrees.

At the water's edge they took turns skipping rocks. Mike was chagrined to discover that Kate could skip them further and longer than he could. When she explained that she had had a good teacher, he demanded that she show him the technique she had learned from their branch president in Bozeman. Kate showed him how to select the perfect flat stone, then stood behind him, putting her arms around him to guide him through the proper steps. A willing student, Mike soon picked up the knack. Turning in her arms, he put his own around her and unable to resist, tenderly kissed her, reawakening the intense feelings they had harbored for so long.

* * *

The next day Kate headed to Salt Lake where her uncle Stan immediately put her to work. Day after day as she stared at a computer screen, Kate discovered how difficult it was to concentrate; thoughts of Mike tormented her. She wondered how Melissa had done it in the mission field.

At home with her aunt and uncle, Kate moped around, hovering near the phone each night as she waited for Mike's call. When it came, she was ecstatic, and when it was over, she slipped into despondency. Paige was almost as relieved as her niece when Mike finally came down to see her a week later.

"So what do you think?" Sue asked Paige a few nights later. She had called to talk to her daughter and was happy to learn that Kate was out with Mike—again.

"I think you'd better air out that wedding dress you bought a while back," Paige replied. "This time it's the real thing."

Thrilled with the news, Sue decided to take her sister-in-law's advice.

* * *

Kate wasn't the only family member working for Stan that summer. Stan had also hired Davie MacOwen, who was able to enjoy different parts of Utah while working at various construction sites. He had been down in Provo when Kate first arrived, and in August, he returned to Salt Lake. Since he and Kate were living at Stan and Paige's house, Kate had started calling it "The Mahoney Inn." Paige took it all in stride, enjoying this chance to spend time with Kate and with Davie.

A few weeks later Paige had a new tenant to look after when Melissa Larsen arrived early for school, anxious to spend some time with Davie. Kate understood her friend's impatience—she could hardly wait for Mike's next visit.

Paige teased both girls about runaway hormones and threatened Davie with his very life if he even thought about venturing downstairs. That, she told him severely, was the girls' domain. She complained that chaperoning two love-struck couples was worse than nursery detail, but she loved every minute of it.

* * *

Late one afternoon as Paige tried to carry on an intelligent conversation with Kate, they overheard a loud whinny.

"What was that?" Kate asked, glancing at her aunt suspiciously.

"It wasn't me," Paige said dryly. Moving the living room drapes to the side, she glanced out the window and gaped as she took in the scene. Melissa smiled and waved to her, reassuring her that everything was under control. Paige noticed that Sandi and Ian were standing at the side of the driveway. Now six months pregnant, Sandi was radiant.

Just then, Melissa burst into the house with Davie, both of them laughing.

"Let me get m'camera," Davie managed to sputter as he hurried upstairs to his room.

"Kate, want to come with me for a minute," Melissa asked, winking at Paige.

"All right you guys, what's going on?" Kate asked as Davie hurried back downstairs, grinning widely. Paige and Melissa firmly escorted Kate from the house. In the driveway stood a large white horse whose rider was wearing what looked like a ton of tinfoil. When Kate saw the horse and its rider, her eyes widened in surprise.

"It's about time, fair maiden. Forsooth, I have major sweating of my brow and other parts of my anatomy," Mike said, grinning down at Kate. "Damsel, close thy mouth and give me thine hand. We're about to ride off into the sunset."

"But . . . how . . . what—"

"Kate, for once in your life, y'all don't need to ask questions," Melissa drawled, pushing Kate forward. "Your knight in shining armor has finally arrived. The least you can do is go with him." When she and Davie had helped boost Kate up to Mike, Davie took several pictures.

"M'faither willna believe this," Davie exclaimed.

"Neither will mine," Kate called down to them as Mike urged the horse out of the driveway. "Is this legal?" she asked as Mike guided the horse along the side of a busy street.

"I don't know, but it's fun," he called back to her. "We're not going far," he added, pointing to a nearby park. A few minutes later, he nudged the horse forward to a large tree. Awkwardly slipping down, he tied the horse to the tree before helping Kate down. Taking hold of her hand, he led her to a pleasant, shady spot. "That's better. No wonder they use this stuff to cook with. I'm dying in here."

"I hope not," Kate murmured.

"Could I get that in writing?"

Kate slapped at his arm playfully, knocking a good-sized portion of tinfoil loose.

"Hey, watch it, I want all of my armor in place for this moment."

"What moment?" Kate asked as Mike tried his best to get on one knee.

"Katherine Colleen Erickson, light of my life, dream of my heart, wouldst thou consent to marry this poor excuse for a man who loves you more than life itself?" Reaching inside his manufactured armor, he pulled out a velvet box. He opened it, revealing a beautiful diamond ring.

At first, Kate was speechless. "Oh, Mike . . ." she finally stammered, tears streaming down her face.

"Those *are* tears of joy, right?" Mike held his breath.

"Yes," she managed to reply.

"And your answer, fair maiden?" he asked, carefully rising to his feet.

Still struggling for composure, Kate nodded.

Mike excitedly responded as he was sure the knights of old had done in similar situations. He slid the ring on her finger and then kissed Kate soundly.

The End

ABOUT THE AUTHOR

Music, sports, community and church service, and lots of family time can't seem to keep Cheri from writing. Cheri also plays guitar and piano by ear, writes songs, enjoys cooking, and loves racquetball, baseball, and volleyball. She heads a local chapter of the American Diabetes Association and serves in a Young Women's presidency.

A former resident of Ashton, Idaho, Cheri Nel Jackson Crane and her husband, Kennon, live in Bennington, Idaho, with their three sons. Cheri is the author of two best-selling young adult novels, *Kate's Turn* and *Kate's Return*, as well as a third novel, *The Fine Print*. She promises her readers that this is not the last they'll see of Kate.